BY ROBERT MUCHAMORE

The Henderson's Boys series:

1. The Escape
2. Eagle Day
3. Secret Army
coming spring 2010

The CHERUB series:

1. The Recruit
2. Class A
3. Maximum Security
4. The Killing
5. Divine Madness
6. Man vs Beast
7. The Fall
8. Mad Dogs
9. The Sleepwalker
10. The General

Look out for CHERUB: Brigands M.C.,
coming late 2009

A Catalogue record for this book is available
from the British Library

ISBN-13: 978 0 340 95649 6

Typeset in Goudy by Avon DataSet Ltd,
Bidford-on-Avon, Warwickshire

Printed and bound in Great Britain by
CPI Bookmarque Ltd, Croydon, Surrey

The paper and board used in this paperback by
Hodder Children's Books are natural recyclable products
made from wood grown in sustainable forests.
The manufacturing processes conform to the
environmental regulations of the country of origin.

Hodder Children's Books
A division of Hachette Children's Books
338 Euston Road, London NW1 3BH
An Hachette UK company
www.hachette.co.uk

EAGLE DAY

Robert Muchamore

Hodder
Children's
Books

A division of Hachette Children's Books

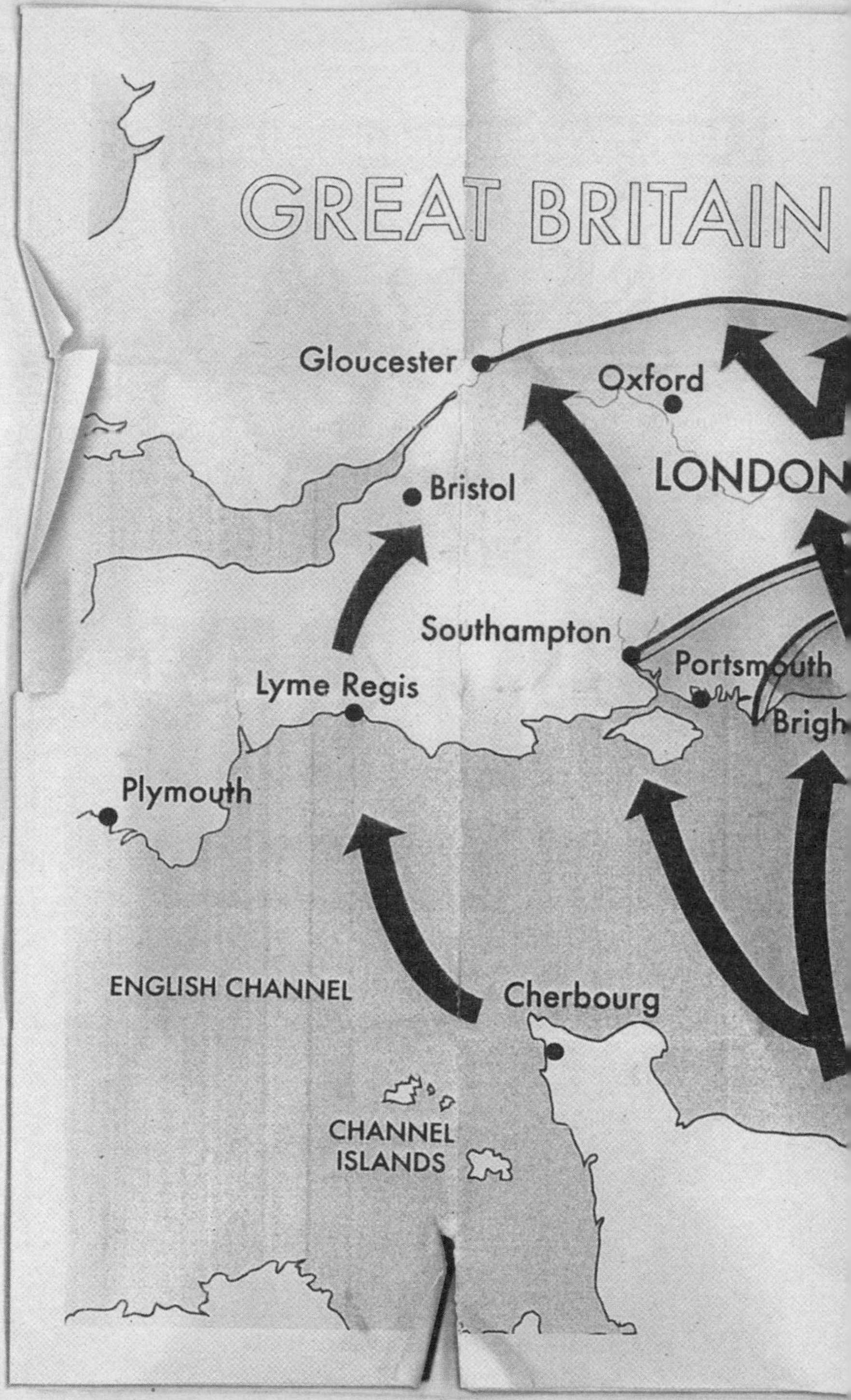
GREAT BRITAIN
Gloucester
Oxford
LONDON
Bristol
Southampton
Portsmouth
Brigh
Lyme Regis
Plymouth
ENGLISH CHANNEL
Cherbourg
CHANNEL
ISLANDS

THE PLANNED INVASION OF ENGLAND, 1940

Colchester

Gravesend

Ramsgate

Dover

Folkestone

Dunkirk

Calais

Boulogne

FRANCE

Dieppe

Le Havre

	RIVER
	SEA
→	PLANNED ATTACKS
	PLANNED BRIDGEHEAD
	FIRST OBJECTIVE
	SECOND OBJECTIVE

Part One

15 June 1940 – 16 June 1940

Bordeaux, France

Germany invaded France in May 1940. Within six weeks Paris had fallen and French troops were in full retreat. Millions of terrified civilians had fled south ahead of the invasion.

After withdrawing its beaten army at Dunkirk, France's ally, Britain, laid plans for a network of spies inside German-occupied Europe known as leave-behinds. But the swift German advance led to the capture of British intelligence headquarters in Amsterdam, and details of the entire spy network fell into enemy hands.

MI6 operatives in Belgium, Holland and France were either captured and executed or forced to flee. By the time the Germans took Paris on 14 June only one British spy continued operating in France, a thirty-three-year-old Royal Navy Commander attached to an obscure department known as the Espionage Research Unit. His name was Charles Henderson.

Henderson was tasked with stealing the blueprints for a revolutionary miniature radio transceiver. On the night of 15 June Henderson reached the port of Bordeaux, less than a hundred and fifty kilometres ahead of the German invaders. He had a leather case containing the prized blueprints, three young companions, and the Gestapo on his tail.

Henderson secured passage aboard the last steamer plying the route between Bordeaux and England, but twelve-year-old Marc Kilgour had no passport and French officials refused boarding. Henderson entrusted the blueprints to his other companions – eleven-year-old Paul Clarke and his thirteen-year-old sister, Rosie.

While the siblings boarded the SS Cardiff Bay, Henderson stayed behind with Marc, intending to get him a passport and take the next steamer to England.

CHAPTER ONE

It was eleven at night, but the port of Bordeaux crackled with life. Refugee kids slumped in humid alleyways, using their mothers' bellies for pillows. Drunken soldiers and marooned sailors scrapped, sang and peed against blacked-out streetlamps. Steamers lined up three abreast at the wharves, waiting for a coal train that showed no sign of arriving soon.

With roads clogged and no diesel for trucks, the dockside was choked with produce while people went hungry less than twenty kilometres away. Meat and veg surrendered to maggots, while recently arrived boats had nowhere to unload and ditched rotting cargo into the sea.

A man and a boy strode along the dock wall, alongside rusting bollards and oranges catching moonlight as they bobbed in the water between a pair of Indian cargo ships.

'Will the consulate be open this late?' Marc Kilgour asked.

Marc was twelve. He was well built, with a scruffy blond tangle down his brow and his shirt clutched over his nose to mask the sickly odour of rotting bananas. The pigskin bag over Marc's shoulder held everything he owned.

Charles Henderson walked beside him: six feet of wiry muscle and a face that would look better after a night's sleep and an encounter with a sharp blade. Disguised as peasants, the pair wore corduroy trousers and white shirts damp with sweat. A suitcase strained Henderson's right arm and the metal objects inside jangled as he grabbed Marc's collar and yanked him off course.

'Look where you're putting your feet!'

Marc looked back and saw that his oversized boot had been saved from a mound of human shit. With a hundred thousand refugees in town it was a common enough sight, but Marc's stomach still recoiled. A second later he kicked the outstretched leg of a young woman with dead eyes and bandaged toes.

'Pardon me,' Marc said, but she didn't even notice. The woman had drunk herself into a stupor and no one would bat an eye if she turned up dead at sunrise.

Since running away from his orphanage two weeks earlier, Marc had trained himself to block out the horrible things he saw all around: from mumbling old dears suffering heat stroke to escaped pigs lapping the blood around corpses at the roadside.

The port was under blackout, so Henderson didn't see Marc's sad eyes, but he sensed a shudder in the boy's breathing and pressed a hand against his back.

'What can we do, mate?' Henderson asked soothingly. 'There's millions of them . . . You have to look after number one.'

Marc found comfort in Henderson's hand, which made him think of the parents he'd never known.

'If I get to England, what happens?' Marc asked nervously. He wanted to add, *Can I live with you?* but choked on the words.

They turned away from the dockside, on to a street lined with warehouses. Clumps of refugees from the north sat under corrugated canopies designed to keep goods dry as they were loaded on to trucks. Despite the late hour a half-dozen boys played a rowdy game of football, using cabbages stolen from the wharves.

Henderson ignored Marc's tricky question, instead answering the one he'd asked two minutes earlier.

'The consulate will be closed, but we have nowhere to stay and the office is sure to be inundated by morning. We might be able to find our own way in . . .'

Henderson tailed off as a pair of German planes swept overhead. The lads playing cabbage football made machine-gun noises and hurled curses over the sea, until their parents yelled at them to cut the racket before it woke younger siblings.

'I'm French,' Marc noted seriously. 'I don't speak a word of English, so how can you get me a British passport?'

'We'll manage,' Henderson said confidently, as he stopped walking for a moment and switched his heavy case from one arm to the other. 'After all we've been through, you should trust me by now.'

The consulate was only a kilometre from the dockside, but Henderson insisted he knew better than the directions jotted down by an official at the passenger terminal. They traipsed muggy streets where the smell of sewage mixed with sea air, until a friendly-but-sozzled dockworker set them back on the right path.

'I wonder where Paul and Rosie are,' Marc said, as they broke into a cobbled square with a crumbling fountain at its centre.

'They'll be upriver, close to open sea by now,' Henderson reckoned, after a glance at his watch. 'There's U-boats[1] prowling and the captain will want to reach the English Channel before daylight.'

A courthouse spanned one side of the square, with a domed church opposite and a couple of gendarmes[2]

---

[1]U-boat – a German submarine.
[2]Gendarmes – French police officers.

standing watch, their main purpose apparently to stop refugees settling on the church steps. The British consulate stood in a neat terrace of offices, jewellers, pawnbrokers and banks.

One end of this row had suffered structural damage from a bomb meant for the docks. Even in moonlight you could see the dramatically warped façade above a jeweller's shop and broken roof slates swept to a tidy pile at the side.

With low-flying bombers and the German forces expected to reach Bordeaux within the week, the Union Jack flag had tactfully been removed from the consulate, but nothing could be done about the British lions woven into wrought-iron gates padlocked across the front door.

Several of His Majesty's subjects gathered on the front steps, with noticeably better clothing and luggage than the refugees scavenging food along the dockside, but Henderson was wary. The Gestapo[3] were still after him and they could easily have spies watching what remained of Bordeaux's British community.

Henderson would stand out amongst the other Brits in his peasant clothing and Marc spoke no English, so rather than join the queue and wait for nine a.m., he led Marc around the rear of the terrace and was pleased to find that it backed on to a sheltered alleyway. The

---

[3]Gestapo – German secret police.

bombing had fractured a water pipe beneath the cobbles and their boots swilled through several centimetres of water.

'Have you still got my torch?' Henderson whispered, when they reached the rear door of the consulate.

The batteries were weak and the beam faltered as Marc scanned the brickwork. After snatching his torch Henderson squatted down and aimed light through the letterbox.

'Nobody home,' he said, as the metal flap snapped shut. 'No sign of an alarm, no bars at the windows. If I give you a boost, do you reckon you can get yourself through the small window?'

Marc craned his head up as Henderson aimed the torch so that he could see.

'What about the two cops in the square?' Marc asked. 'They'll hear if the glass goes.'

Henderson shook his head. 'It's a sash window; you should be able to force it open with a lever.'

Henderson stepped back out of the puddle and found dry cobbles on which to lay and open his case. Marc noticed shadowy figures passing the end of the alleyway, then jolted at the distinctive click of Henderson loading his pistol.

Marc was delighted that a British agent was going to all this bother on his account. Henderson could have abandoned him at the passenger terminal and sailed aboard the *Cardiff Bay* with Paul and Rosie. But as well as a soft heart, Henderson had a ruthless streak and the gun made Marc uneasy.

In the three days since Marc first met Henderson in Paris, Henderson had shot or blown up half a dozen Germans and machine-gunned a grovelling Frenchman in his bathtub. If the next figure at the end of the alleyway chose to come and investigate, Marc knew Henderson would kill them without a thought.

Henderson passed over a crowbar before screwing a silencer to the front of his pistol. Marc ran his hand along the oiled bar and glimpsed inside the suitcase: ammunition, a compact machine gun, a zipped pouch in which Marc knew lay gold ingots and a stack of French currency. The clothes and toilet bag seemed like an afterthought, squeezed into the bottom right corner. Marc found it miraculous that Henderson could lift all this, let alone carry it several kilometres through the port.

After fastening leather buckles and tipping the jangling case back on its side, Henderson faced the building and lowered his knee into the puddle. Marc leaned against the wall and stepped up so that his wet boots balanced on Henderson's shoulders.

'Now I'm really glad you didn't tread in that pile of turds,' Henderson noted.

Despite nerves and his precarious position astride

Henderson's shoulders, Marc snorted with laughter.

'Don't make me giggle,' he said firmly, walking his hands up the brickwork as Henderson stood, raising Marc level with the landing window between ground and first floors.

Marc rested his chest against the wall, then took the crowbar from his back pocket.

'You're heavier than you look,' Henderson huffed, as Marc's unsteady boots tore at his skin.

The oak window frame was rotting and Henderson felt a shower of flaking paint as Marc dug the forked tongue of the crowbar under the frame and pushed as hard as he dared. The catch locking the two sliding panes together was strong, but the two screws holding it in place lifted easily from the dried-out wood.

'Gotcha,' Marc whispered triumphantly, as he threw the window open.

To Henderson's relief, Marc's weight shifted as the boy pulled himself through the window. He crashed down on to plush carpet inside, narrowly avoiding a vase and a knock-out encounter with the banister.

Beeswax and old varnish filled Marc's nose as he hurried downstairs. The building was small, but its pretensions were grand and paintings of wigged men and naval battles lined the short flight of steps down to the back door.

Henderson grabbed his suitcase as Marc pulled across

two heavy bolts and opened the back door. Beyond the stairwell the ground floor comprised a single large room. They moved amongst desks and cabinets, separated from the waiting area at the opposite end by an ebony countertop and spiralled gold rails.

Marc was fascinated by the tools of bureaucracy: typewriters, rubber stamps, carbon papers and hole punches.

'So they keep blank passports here?' Marc asked, as he stared at the banks of wooden drawers along one wall.

'If they haven't run out,' Henderson said, as he slammed his heavy case on a desktop, tilting a stack of envelopes on to the parquet floor. 'But we can't make a passport without a photograph.'

Henderson pulled a leather wallet out of his case. The miniature photographic kit comprised a matchbox-sized pinhole camera, tiny vials of photographic chemicals and sheets of photographic paper large enough to produce the kind of pictures used in identity documents.

'Go stand under the wall clock,' Henderson said, as he worked with the tiny camera, inserting a small rectangle of photographic paper.

Henderson looked up and saw a peculiar mix of apprehension and emotion on Marc's face.

'Nobody ever took my photograph before,' he admitted.

Henderson looked surprised. 'Not at the school or the orphanage?'

Marc shook his head.

'We've got very little light,' Henderson explained, as he propped the camera on a stack of ledgers. 'So I need you to stay *absolutely* still and keep your eyes open.'

Marc stood rigid for twenty seconds, then rushed forwards on Henderson's signal.

'When can I see it?' he asked, as he blinked his stinging eyes repeatedly.

'I have a developing kit,' Henderson explained. 'There must be a kitchen somewhere. I need you to find me three saucers and some warm water.'

As Marc raced upstairs to find the kitchen, Henderson began looking around the offices for blank passports. He discovered an entire drawer full of them, along with a wooden cigar box containing all the necessary stamps and, most helpfully, a crumpled blue manual detailing the correct procedure for dealing with a consular passport application.

One of the telephones rang, but Henderson ignored it and began shaking his photographic chemicals, ready for when Marc came back with the water.

A second phone thrummed as Marc came downstairs with three saucers and a tobacco tin filled with hot tap water. Henderson found the ringing irritating, but with France in chaos it didn't surprise him that the consular phones would ring through the night.

'I need absolute darkness to develop the photograph,'

Henderson explained, as he spread out the three saucers and dipped a fragile glass thermometer in the hot water. 'Get the lights.'

Once the office lights were out and the blinds at the rear adjusted to shield the moonlight, Henderson gathered his saucers of chemicals in tight formation, leaned forwards over the desk and flipped the jacket he'd been carrying in his suitcase over his head, protecting his equipment from any remaining light.

Marc watched as Henderson fidgeted mysteriously beneath the jacket and the sweet smell of developing fluid filled the air. He stripped the rectangle of photographic paper from the camera and counted the ticks of his watch to ensure it spent the correct time in the developing fluid.

Marc had no idea how long it would be before Henderson emerged with the developed photograph. He thought of asking, but didn't want to affect Henderson's concentration.

'Have you ever made a cup of tea, Marc?' Henderson asked, once he'd moved the sliver of paper from the developer into the bleaching solution.

'Sorry . . .' Marc said weakly. 'I've never even drunk it.'

'You're a blank canvas, Marc Kilgour,' Henderson laughed. 'You go upstairs, put a kettle on the stove and I'll show you how to make a proper English cuppa while your picture dries.'

'What's a cuppa?' Marc asked, liking the word, even if he wasn't sure what it meant.

Henderson trembled with laughter beneath the jacket.

He didn't laugh for long, though. Both phones had stopped ringing, but it became clear from a loud scuffling sound that something was happening on the steps out front.

'Those gendarmes must have heard us breaking in,' Marc said anxiously, as the metal gates over the front door whined for a shot of oil. 'I bet it was them on the phone.'

Henderson remained calm. 'Ignore your emotions and use your brain,' he said firmly as he pulled his head out from beneath the jacket. 'The police don't phone up and ask burglars if they'd be kind enough to leave and the Germans certainly wouldn't tip us off with a fracas on the doorstep. I just need half a minute now to fix the image. Go up to the front window and tell me what you see.'

Marc vaulted the counter and dodged two lines of chairs in the waiting room, then peeked through a tiny crack in the velvet curtains. A white Jaguar sports car had parked up on the cobbles and an anxious crowd hassled its female driver as she unlocked the gates.

'Guessing it's someone who works here,' Marc hissed. 'She's got keys and everyone in the queue's giving her stress.'

Marc could hear what was being said, but it was all in English so he didn't have a clue.

'I have urgent consular business,' the woman yelled. 'You all need to come back in the morning. We're open normal office hours. Nine to five and noon on Saturday.'

Marc ducked behind chairs as the woman squeezed through the front door and told the people outside to mind their fingers before banging it shut.

As soon as she flicked on the lights she saw Henderson. He'd finished developing Marc's photograph and stood behind the counter with his arms out wide to make it clear that he was no threat.

'I'm sorry to startle you like this, Madame. The name's Henderson. Charles Henderson.'

Marc studied the woman from his position crouching behind the chairs. She was in her twenties, and nearly six feet tall. She wore the white blouse and pleated skirt of an office girl, but sculpted black hair and an elegant gold watch gave the impression that she lived off somewhat more than an office girl's salary.

'Charles Henderson,' the woman said knowingly. 'I decoded a transcript from London. Quite a few people are looking for you. Of course, if you're *really* Henderson, you'll know his code word.'

'Seraphim,' Henderson answered, as the woman placed her bag on the countertop then kicked on a wooden panel and ducked under. Marc's eyebrows shot up as he sighted the tops of her stockings.

'I do beg your pardon, but young Marc here needs a passport. We did a bit of damage to your landing window but it's easily fixed . . .'

'Forgive me,' the woman said, making a quick glance back at Marc before cutting Henderson dead with a raised hand. 'My name is Maxine Clere, clerical assistant to the consul. Please make use of our facilities . . . It looks like you've found the blank passports already. I know your work is important, but I have to make immediate contact with London on the scrambled telephone. We've lost the *Cardiff Bay* on the River Garonne, less than thirty kilometres out of Bordeaux – and many are dead.'

CHAPTER TWO

A quarter-hour after it had sunk, all that remained of the *Cardiff Bay* were two chunks of superstructure floating mid-river and an oily film on the water which burned the eyes of passengers making the desperate swim to shore. Fishing boats and motor launches were still picking people out of the water, but they were reluctant to use much light lest it draw back German bombers.

It was low tide and a broad mud flank was exposed along the southern embankment of the River Garonne. Thirteen-year-old Rosie Clarke was a strong swimmer and one of the first to reach the shore under her own power. The embankment mud sucked off her sandals and she fell on her face, taking a mouthful of evil brown water that combined with breathlessness to cause a coughing fit.

PT Bivott grabbed her sleeve. She'd met him on the three-hundred-metre swim to shore and got her first look at his body as he slid fingers into her armpits and hauled her up with a squelch.

Like many fifteen year olds, PT had a man's height but not the physique that went with it. His French was perfect but came with an American twist. Dark hair designed to be combed back dangled to his bottom lip.

'Keep calm, Rosie,' PT said, pulling her close and squeezing tight. Rosie's muscles burned and freezing mud slid down her dress, but all she could think about was her brother and she screamed out for him.

'*Paul!*'

Her voice wavered. Strong to start and then collapsing into sobs with her head buried in PT's life vest.

'If he's as tough as his sister he'll do fine,' PT said encouragingly, as his free hand swept hair up over his head. He'd worked hard on trying to say the right thing, but he hadn't.

'Paul's only eleven,' Rosie sniffed. 'He can barely manage a width in a pool, and that current's . . .'

'Don't cry,' PT said, tightening his grip before letting go abruptly.

The sudden break-off upset Rosie until she saw that PT had gone after a man wading up the embankment with two small boys latched on his back. As the lads slid off, their red-faced father clutched his stomach and gasped for breath. Blood streaked his chest where tiny nails had dug in.

As PT helped the father stay upright, light shone from a motorcycle headlamp on the riverbank. Rosie squinted into the beam and saw outlines of local men coming to help, while others walked victims up the beach.

'Get the boys,' PT ordered, squelching past with the gasping man's arm draped around his back.

Rosie was shattered and found it tough to stay upright. She lacked blood in her head and had mud past her ankles, but the boys were only up to her waist and the smallest was stuck fast and bawling for his mum.

'Come on, mate,' Rosie said, forcing a friendly tone as she grabbed the youngest. His sodden pyjamas and hopeful blue eyes gave her purpose as slippery fingers locked around her neck.

The older boy spoke in English as she hauled him towards dry land. 'Have you seen my mummy?'

'There are lots of beaches,' Rosie answered, as mud squirted up between her toes. She considered explaining how the currents would make people come ashore in different places, but she was breathless and doubted he'd understand. 'You'll find her in the morning,' she answered finally.

'She can't swim though,' the boy said urgently. 'She might die.'

Rosie was struggling, but PT had an even harder time

with their father, who was much heavier than PT and suffering with asthma. Eventually two men in fishing waders stretchered him across an old door, enabling PT to carry the older boy for the final stretch to the river bank.

Local men snatched the boys and guided them up a slippery ramp used to launch boats when the tide was in. The little three year old squealed and demanded to stay with Rosie, but she hadn't the energy to comfort him and found herself being pulled up the ramp by the leathery hands of an old fisherman.

People in towns had become numb to refugees and suffering, but the *Cardiff Bay* victims were lucky enough to wash up near a community of farmers and fishermen. It was their first taste of war, beyond the rumble of bombs hitting the port several kilometres east.

As a nurse attended the asthmatic father, PT and Rosie followed muddy footprints to a vaulted warehouse where trawlermen stored equipment and gutted their catch before taking it to market in Bordeaux.

The building stank of fish guts trapped in the open drains and the hosed water was bitter cold. Once the worst of the mud was gone, Rosie and PT sat outside by a hurriedly built fire. Local women rushed between their homes and the quayside bringing coffee, towels and blankets.

Rosie sat in the gravel by the fire, with her life jacket

as a seat. She was very conscious of everything showing through a wet summer dress. She caught her breath while an enamel mug warmed fingers that stung with numbness. PT squatted alongside and their bodies touched through wet clothes. Circumstances were desperate and Rosie craved this intimacy, even though they were strangers.

'Can I take your names?' a man asked from behind. The well-fed priest had pin-prick eyes behind thick glasses. He licked the tip of his pencil before impatiently drumming it on his spiral-bound notebook.

'That's my business,' PT said peevishly.

Priests expected deference, and Rosie was both shocked and impressed by PT's lack of respect. The priest raised one eyebrow before explaining impatiently.

'I'm taking all the names and where you come from. People are coming ashore at spots all along the river and on the opposite bank too. We're listing names and telephoning from the parochial houses so that people can find one another.'

'There's nobody gonna be looking for my name,' PT growled. 'But thanks all the same.'

Rosie had no idea why PT was keen to hide his identity, but the Gestapo were after Henderson, Paul, Marc and herself so she didn't want her name on any lists either. The trouble was, she wanted Paul to be able to find her and had to think fast.

'Valentine Favre,' Rosie said. 'Thirteen years old.'

If Paul saw the list he'd surely recognise his sister's age and late mother's maiden name and work out what she'd done. The Nazis would be unlikely to make the same connection.

'Were your parents aboard?' the priest asked, as he looked down his list for any other Favres.

'Just my kid brother, Michael,' she said, giving Paul's second name. 'He's eleven.'

As the priest headed away a stooped Englishwoman queuing for coffee tapped Rosie on the back. 'Excuse me,' she said, her voice barely more than a croak. 'I couldn't help overhearing. I was on a lifeboat and we pulled a boy aboard. Ten or eleven. He looked somewhat like you, but rather slimmer.'

'That's him!' Rosie smiled, bouncing up so fast that she splashed hot coffee over PT. 'Where was this? Did he seem OK?'

The woman sucked her lips into her mouth, and Rosie near burst with anxiety as she realised it was going to be bad news. 'He looked poorly,' the woman said. 'He was bloody. After coming aboard he vomited and passed out.'

It wasn't a perfect answer, but not Rosie's worst fear either.

'But he's alive?' she said hopefully. 'Do you know where he is?'

'We landed on the embankment on the other side of the harbour. If you walk back behind the warehouse and past the shop on the corner, there's a slipway heading down to the water.'

Rosie glanced down at PT, unsure about the depth of their bond. 'Are you coming with me?'

'I've no idea if he's still there,' the elderly woman interrupted, before PT got a chance to answer. 'They might have taken him to a doctor or something by now.'

Rosie had been re-energised by hope. She stepped around the bodies by the fire and followed directions, belting behind the warehouse and turning by the shop.

She found her bare soles slapping on a stone path, the Garonne on one side and a windswept field on the other. The path led down to an embankment – much smaller than the one where she'd washed up across the harbour – and a jetty used for fishing. Another barefoot runner closed in. She glanced back and was pleased to recognise PT, but didn't slow down until she reached a group of local women holding candles over a body writhing on the ground.

Rosie feared the worst, but there was a horrific moan that clearly came from a woman. As she closed up Rosie saw that she was pregnant, clutching her swollen belly and with blood streaked down her thighs.

'Is that the doctor?' a local woman shouted

desperately, as Rosie came to a breathless stop.

She didn't need to answer, because by this time PT was in plain sight and clearly too young.

'I can see you're busy,' Rosie gasped apologetically. 'But I think my brother came up here on a lifeboat. Skinny kid, eleven years old. Someone told me he was passed out.'

The pregnant woman screamed again as a bloody finger showed Rosie the way.

'On the jetty. A man named Gaston is looking after him.'

PT ran on ahead. The stone path ended and he jumped off a ledge into a splash of lapping water, with silt underfoot and two empty lifeboats bobbing a few metres offshore.

'Mind your step,' PT warned, as his hand traced the crumbling sea wall leading to the jetty. 'I don't know how deep this gets.'

The water stayed below their knees and the only danger came on the slippery steps leading up the side of the fishing jetty.

'Paul!' Rosie shouted with joy, as she reached the wooden decking and sighted her brother sat against a rotten post at the base of the jetty.

Gaston was a skinny old man who'd been giving Paul sips of water. Rosie hurried across, but she went stiff when she got close enough to see details.

Paul's left eye was open, but the right was swollen over. A vortex had sucked him deep underwater as the *Cardiff Bay* went down. When his life vest pulled him back to the surface he'd smashed into razor-sharp barnacles on a section of the ship's hull.

He'd been lucky enough not to get dragged down under the metal, but the barnacles left cuts that started on his right cheek then stopped around his chin. Shallower wounds began in the middle of his chest and ran down to his bellybutton. The lower portion of his right arm was set at a twisted angle and clearly broken.

Shock and a badly swollen cheek left Paul's face expressionless, but he raised the fingers of his left hand and quietly mouthed, '*Rosie.*'

'Are you the sister?' Gaston asked.

Rosie nodded. 'Is anyone on the way? A nurse? A doctor?'

'There is only me. I worked in an army hospital during the last war,' Gaston explained. 'I have a few supplies at my house. I can clean his cuts and set his arm, but my back is bad, I can't carry him.'

The normal thing would be to telephone for an ambulance or find the local doctor, but with German bombings, millions of refugees and many medical staff having fled further south, Rosie realised that the frail army medic was Paul's best chance.

'What about that woman down there?' PT asked.

'She's miscarrying. Judging by the blood, she could die.'

Gaston nodded ruefully. 'Wounds and broken bones I've dealt with. What do I know of a woman's problems?'

Rosie looked back at PT, slightly irritated. She wanted her brother attended to, even if the woman's plight *was* more threatening. 'Can you lift him?' she asked.

Paul made a dull groan as PT scooped him up off the wooden jetty. Gaston moved as fast as old legs allowed, leading the way through an overgrown field to a line of sagging cottages.

Paul was laid out on a dining table while Gaston's wife boiled water and found an old medic's pouch filled with yellowing bandages and dried-out creams that apparently dated from the last war. Rosie tucked a cushion under her brother's head and stroked his hand, calming his nerves and telling him that everything would be OK.

Others in the area knew Gaston had been a medic. Half a dozen injured passengers had reached the village and people began knocking at the front door asking for advice. Near eighty years old and deaf in one ear, the old man quickly grew stressed.

'I'm just one man,' Gaston shouted to his wife. 'Tell them when the boy is done I'll look at someone else.'

The elderly medic worked methodically. An electric bulb hung over the dining table, but two flickering gas lanterns were brought in to supplement it. Paul had been lifted between the lifeboat and the jetty, so at least his wounds were free of mud, but Gaston swabbed Paul's cheek with a solution of hot salt water before painting on iodine, which stung even worse.

Rosie tried not to cry as her brother sobbed in pain. Considering that Paul screamed the house down if he got shampoo in his eyes she thought he was being quite brave. But the cuts on his face filled with blood as soon as they were clean.

Gaston scratched his stubbly chin and made a decision. 'It needs stitching or he'll bleed to death.'

His wife produced a tumbler of warmed brandy, sweetened with syrup, and helped Paul to swallow it. The alcohol numbed Paul slightly before the retired medic put in five neat stitches with sterilised button thread and a sewing needle. The booze was some help, but PT had to clamp Paul's knees against the table to stop him from kicking out.

After another sweetened brandy, which left Paul thoroughly drunk, the old man moved in to set his arm. Paul trembled as he sat in a dining chair, gas lamps flickering, the handle of a wooden spoon between his teeth to prevent him biting through his tongue when the pain hit.

The bony old medic made him rest the broken arm flat against the tabletop, then prodded the swelling to feel the direction of the break.

'Been some years since I last did this,' Gaston confessed, glugging brandy out of the bottle for courage as Rosie tightened her grip on Paul's shoulder. PT and Gaston's wife stood by, fingers tense and brows dripping sweat.

Paul wailed as Gaston thumped his palm downwards. After running his fingers over the arm and satisfying himself that the bone was straight, Gaston wound some bandage around the break. They had no plaster so he improvised, splinting the arm with lengths of garden cane.

The finished tangle of sticks and tightly-wound bandages was unorthodox, but would give Paul's arm a decent chance of healing. Paul sniffed drunkenly as Rosie took him out of the kitchen and settled him on an armchair in the living room. Gaston's wife raised his legs on to a foot stool and after a wipe of his brow with a cool flannel Paul seemed content to lean on the arm and fall asleep.

'You're so kind,' Rosie said, appreciating that Paul had been lucky to receive Gaston's swift attention. By the time Paul had settled, the old man had drained his brandy and gone to the door to see if he could help someone else.

Rosie headed outside to use the toilet and found PT standing by the back door, in a great hurry to disguise something by tucking it back under his shirt. Then PT dropped an object on the ground and the teenagers almost banged heads as they crouched simultaneously to pick it up.

Rosie felt wet paper in her hands and by the time she'd straightened up she'd realised it was currency. There wasn't much moonlight and only a little lamplight leaked from Gaston's kitchen, but she recognised the wad of American bills before PT snatched them out of her hands.

'They'll dry off, won't they?' was all she could think to say, after a brief but awkward silence.

Rosie was nervous because she'd clearly seen something she wasn't supposed to. Was PT going to run off, swing at her, or what? The one thing she didn't expect was for PT to lean forwards and kiss her on the lips.

'You're beautiful,' PT said.

Rosie froze like a post. She'd never kissed a boy before and, while she didn't kiss back, she didn't shove him away either. When PT gave Rosie space her words came out like a flood.

'You!' she gasped. 'What's all that money? No wonder you didn't want to give your name to that priest. What did you do, mug some refugee? Rob a bank? And don't tell me that I'm beautiful and kiss me like that. Give me some warning or something! And what kind of name is PT? It's not even a name, it's just initials. Those were twenty-dollar bills. That's almost five pounds, each one, and you've got stacks and stacks! I mean, who on earth are you and why are you going around kissing me?'

PT smiled. 'Because you're beautiful.'

'*Don't* keep saying that,' Rosie said, though PT was tall and a couple of years older than her and probably rather elegant when he didn't have mud in his hair, so she was actually flattered.

'I *could* tell you who I really am,' PT smirked, as he drew his finger across his throat and made a choking sound. 'But then I'd have to kill you.'

Part Two

10 December 1938 – 14 December 1938

New York City, USA

CHAPTER THREE

He was named Philippe Tomas Bivott after his French grandfather, but everyone called him PT. He was the middle child in a family of three boys; both his parents were French, but he'd lived in America all his life. PT's mother died when he was ten and his father Miles moved to New York, for a job in the docks fixed up by his late wife's brother. It was secure work with medical insurance and union pay, but Miles Bivott had no taste for honest labour. He quit after seven weeks, reverting to old habits and less honest ways of earning a crust.

It was a couple of weeks before Christmas and a moderate snowfall had turned to grey slush on New York's pavements. Patches of ice lay beneath and you'd wind up bruised if you put your shoe in the wrong place, but these were the least of PT's problems.

It was three a.m. and PT needed a drill bit, specifically one six inches long and three-sixteenths of an inch in diameter. The thirteen year old walked close to the buildings, doing his best to be invisible. He was wrapped warm in black boots and sheepskin-lined gloves. A knitted hat came down over his ears and tied around his chin, and a scarf covered everything that was left, apart from a tiny slit through which you could see the bridge of a nose and dark brown eyes.

He looked both ways before cutting across the deserted alleyway. His only company was a flurry of snowflakes and empty metal cans thrown down by the garbage men a couple of hours earlier. Up ahead was a door and the sign above it said *A&H Hardware*. Being three a.m. it was closed, along with every other hardware store in Manhattan.

PT took a torch out of his heavy coat and the light showed everything he'd hoped not to find: grilles over the windows, a deadlock and two bars across the door and a burglar alarm box on the wall above it. The padlocks holding the window grilles in place were the only chink in the armour: they were the kind of locks that looked fancy, but which had nothing more than a simple lever inside.

The owner of a hardware store should have known better. After a rummage in his trousers for a metal ring fitted with various files and picks, taking the padlocks off was only a matter of insert, jiggle and twist. The window grille lifted off with a shudder and PT almost lost his footing on the ice as he lowered its weight down to the pavement.

PT knew various ways to fool alarms, but you needed to scout the location in advance and he had to be in and out fast, which left smash-and-grab as his only option. He picked up one of the empty trash cans and took a run at the glass.

Shards tumbled out of the pane above PT's head. He'd half hoped that the alarm would be deactivated or a phoney, but it broke into song as the metal can hit the floor inside the store. If there was a cop car nearby they'd have PT nailed in seconds and he rated his chances of capture at a hundred per cent if he hung around any more than four minutes.

It was an upscale area a quarter mile from Wall Street and the financial district, so the displays mounted along the wall on sheets of drilled hardboard were fancier than you'd expect: swanky bath taps, enamel light switches and brass door plates. After flicking on the lights PT stepped behind the counter and got a nose full of hardware: sawdust, key cutting and paint.

Racks of metal shelves stretched up to the ceiling, crammed with packets and tiny boxes: screws, brackets, light bulbs, a hundred different kinds of batteries and expensive top-shelf items, fronded with years of dust.

The only way to know where everything was would be to work here for a couple of decades.

'Come on you devils,' PT said desperately as he looked around for the drills. 'Where the hell are you?'

He grew more desperate as he walked between the shelves. A horrible feeling, like kittens turning somersaults in his tummy and no saliva in his mouth. Something sounded like a police siren, but the alarm was so loud he thought his mind must be playing tricks.

His elbow caught on a box of wood screws. They rolled off in a thousand directions as he moved on to a stepladder and scanned the aisles from up high.

'Jackpot!'

Right up the front where he should have already looked, PT eyed a couple of hand drills hooked on to the shelf uprights and drill bits behind. He was there in a millisecond. Small drill bits were in drawers, the longer ones came in brown card boxes, wrapped in tissue paper – but hundreds of boxes were stacked up, with no order to them.

He read the packaging and threw them down at his feet. Eighth of an inch, one-quarter, five-sixteenths, one-sixteenth. His salt-crusted boots were encircled by boxes when he eyed a pair of three-sixteenths sitting right next to each other.

PT pocketed the two bits and slid a glove back over

his hand as a flash of blue light burst across the street: cop car.

He thought about charging back through the busted window and making a run for it. He fancied his chances of outrunning the cops but not their cars or the bullets in their guns, so he gambled on a little door at the back of the shelves and prayed for a rear exit.

There was a draining board stacked with mugs and a desk covered in ledgers and hardware catalogues. The only door had a bar across, but a small window swung open easily enough and PT straddled his way into a paved yard as a cop yelled something like *Come out with your hands up* over the rattling alarm.

Buildings backed on to all four sides of the courtyard. PT's only hope was a gated alleyway at one end. The lead cop was already coming through the window and if the gate was locked he'd be looking at another three months in juvenile hall. But the catch lifted, the gate squealed and PT swept out on to the icy street.

It was a broad avenue, with shops, offices and steam rising from vents in the tarmac. PT only had twenty seconds over the cops, but he made the most of them, cutting bravely in front of a delivery truck and ending up across the street on a corner in front of Bert's Joint, a twenty-four-hour diner frequented by cab drivers and printers from the newspaper building on the opposite corner.

After cutting down a side street, PT peeked back. The absence of chasing cops was a pleasant surprise, but the escape through the courtyard had disorientated him. Whilst he couldn't be more than a kilometre from where he wanted to be, PT couldn't tell what street he was on or what direction he needed to take to get back. What's more, you didn't see many thirteen year olds on the street at this time of the morning and he'd stick out a mile if a cop car cruised by.

PT jogged to the end of the alleyway, losing his footing as he reached the next street. He skidded into a mound of snow in the gutter, but the only harm was a soggy trouser leg, and as he stood up he saw the familiar red neon glow of the sign over *Unicorn Tire Repair & Parking*, two blocks down. He looked back, reassuring himself that the cops weren't following, before striding the two blocks.

The Unicorn was a multi-storey parking lot used by Wall Street types: bankers and stockbrokers. On a weekday it brimmed with Packards and Cadillacs and the chauffeurs who drove them spent whole days smoking and playing cards in a ground-floor lounge behind the tyre shop. But when the gates were locked at midnight the lights went out and you could hear your shoes echo down the gloomy concrete ramps.

Even after three months working in the basement every night and all day Sundays, the Unicorn lot still gave

PT a creepy feeling. There were two ramps the width of a single car – one up one down – a booth where you paid to park and a sign resting on the wall that was put out when the lot filled up. PT opened a door-sized gate-within-a-gate and the instant he was through the head of his seven-year-old brother, Jeannot, popped over the brim of the down ramp.

'Took you long enough,' the boy sneered. 'Did you get the bits?'

'Like to see you try doing it quicker, you stick of piss,' PT said, rattling the two boxed drill bits under Jeannot's nose and expressing the special contempt he reserved for his little brother. 'You cried your eyes out when the cops picked you up for stealing newspapers.'

Jeannot snapped back as the boys jogged down the vehicle ramp to the basement. 'That was decades ago. You think I'd crack now? Anyway, you cried like a girl when we visited you in juvie.'

'What do you know?' PT scoffed. 'I was one of the littlest guys there. You'd shit your little dungarees if the tough guys in juvie so much as eyeballed you.'

At the bottom of the unlit ramp there was a small access door with a water hose running out. It was flung open by PT's seventeen-year-old brother, Leon. He was drowning in his own sweat and his muscular torso was streaked with clay.

'Get 'em, bro?' Leon asked.

PT waved the drill bits. 'Close thing with the cops, but I lost 'em before I got back here.'

'You sure?'

'Hundred per cent.' PT nodded.

'OK, get on the trolley and take 'em down to Dad.'

Jeannot and PT ducked under their brother's arm into a narrow room used for storage. There were buckets and cleaning chemicals on the shelves and a rail at one end on which hung jackets and caps worn by the Unicorn attendants. More unusually, linoleum floor tiles had been lifted up and there was a half-metre-wide hole in the floor at the opposite end. A rubber hose ran out of the hole, attached to a hand pump.

'How's the water level?' PT asked, as he ripped off his gloves and coat and yanked muddy blue overalls over his street clothes.

'Not great,' Leon answered. 'I've been pumping solid for the last hour and there's still a good inch and a half of water in the middle of the tunnel.'

'Should do us for tonight, and that's all we need,' PT said, as he sat over the edge of the hole and dropped down a metre and a half, clay spattering under his boots as he landed. The main shaft of the tunnel was less than half a metre wide. The ceiling was held up with heavy gauge mesh and metal hoops, while crude wooden rails ran along the floor.

PT lay chest down on a wooden trolley, head and feet

hanging off opposite ends. He checked that all four wheels were aligned to the rails and rolled his head into the start of the tunnel. After reaching blindly at the ceiling he flicked a length of wire, ringing a bell directly above his head and another at the opposite end of the tunnel.

It was possible to pull the cart through the tunnel using the walls and floor as leverage, but once someone was stationed at each end it was faster to signal with the bell and have someone pull you through on a rope.

The trolley jerked suddenly – it would disappear from under you if you got your balance wrong – and began trundling through the blackness. Water always seeped through the clay, but the snow melt made it worse than usual and drips pelted PT's neck as he rattled along with the rails centimetres in front of his face. It was pitch dark, but he'd been through hundreds of times and he knew every dip and twist, even down to the rattling noises made by the joins between individual pieces of rail.

The tunnel spanned thirty-eight metres, beneath the barbershop and beauty parlour next to Unicorn Tyre and Parking. Just beyond mid-point the clattering of the wheels changed to a rushing sound. The water was deep enough to plough over the front of the fast moving cart and give PT's chest a soaking. After a slight kink to the left, he was able to look into electric light and see his father's trousers and dirty arms pulling the rope hand over hand.

PT arrived into an underground chamber nearly two metres high and his father, Miles, reached out to stop the cart running into the mud wall.

They were directly beneath the New York branch of the Federal Reserve Exchange. The tunnel had been dug at a steady sixty centimetres per day for sixty days, and it had taken a further three weeks digging out the chamber and perfecting the running of the railway.

PT stood up, his face spattered with clay and dripping brown water that soaked him from his chest down to his thighs.

'Looking wet, son!' Miles Bivott said. 'You get the drill bit?'

'Two,' PT said. 'In case we break another.'

'Good man. Any bother?'

'A and H was alarmed. Cops went in the front but I made it out the back. I'm more worried about the water level in that tunnel.'

'It's been there near a hundred days,' Miles said reassuringly. 'We only need it for another hour or two.'

PT looked at the hole in the ceiling. This final break into the basement floor of the Federal Reserve Exchange vaults was critical: they could take their time building the tunnel, but once they broke through the floor they only had a few hours until the whole enterprise was uncovered by the morning security patrol.

'Let's get up there,' Miles said. 'Don't want fingerprints, so get your gloves on.'

There was a ladder, but PT was light enough for his father to give him a boost. PT placed his hands flat against thick marble tiles and hauled his body into the brightly lit basement.

After the tunnel it took a moment for his eyes to adjust. Apart from the hole in the floor and his father's muddy boot prints, PT found an orderly, wood-panelled space the size of two cars parked abreast. A staircase wound its way around a doorless cargo lift. At the opposite end of the room were huge metal doors, labelled *cage 1* and *cage 2*. They weren't cages at all, but basement vaults protected top, bottom and sides with thirty centimetres of battleship-grade armour plate.

The Federal Reserve supplied all currency in the United States and the cages existed because paper money wears out every few months and needs to be exchanged. When money gets tatty, banks send it to the Federal Reserve, who swap it for new bills.

If Miles Bivott's information was correct, cage one contained several million dollars in crisp new bills. More importantly, cage two contained a similar amount of dilapidated bills, which would be impossible to track down through serial numbers.

Every Monday the money in cage two was taken out

and spoiled with pink dye before being driven upstate to an incineration plant. But right now it was Sunday night and the cage might contain anything up to six million dollars.

There was no way through the armoured wall or floor, barring an explosion that would set half of Manhattan Island trembling, so Miles intended to destroy the locking mechanism inside the safe door with four expertly placed tubes of gelignite. The trouble was, the tube-holes had to be the exact same diameter as the sticks of explosive for the blast to create the correct shockwave, and he'd snapped the drill bit while making the final hole in the metal door.

'I managed to get all the broken metal out of the hole while you went on your little errand,' Miles explained. 'It shouldn't take more than five minutes to finish the drilling now.'

PT stuffed in some wax earplugs as his father unboxed a replacement bit and clamped it inside a hydraulic drill, powered from a compressed air cylinder in the chamber below. Miles aligned the bit inside the part-bored hole and used his entire bodyweight to brace the hammer action.

Drilling through toughened metal causes huge friction and the bit can easily expand and jam, so PT stood over the drill head with a jug of water. After each deafening ten-second drill burst, Miles would pull the bit out of the hole and PT would douse both the hole and the drill head with water, the first drops spitting and turning to steam as they hit.

'That's two hundred dollars' worth of drill,' Miles said, when he was satisfied with the depth of the hole. 'I'll drop in the explosives and wire up; you make up the train and get your brothers to pull all the equipment we don't need back to the Unicorn.'

'Gotcha, Dad.'

PT lowered himself through the hole in the floor and linked a pair of extra carts on to the train. Two were enough to take the drill and the last of the digging equipment. The oxygen cylinder had to be strapped to the third using a pair of leather belts.

'Ready when you are,' Miles said, lifting PT out of the hole as the three-cart train was hauled off by Leon at the other end.

Miles knew how to set gelignite and expected his tunnel to remain intact, but just in case, the pair retreated up the staircase and behind the lift shaft, with two lengths of wire trailing behind them. Detonation was a matter of bringing two bare ends together and Miles passed them across.

'You do the honours, son.'

PT trembled with a wire in each hand, not because he doubted his dad's proficiency with explosives, but because this was a moment they'd built to over more than three months' planning and gruelling labour.

On contact there was a shudder, followed by a metallic boom and flash of light. Finally a sharp breeze wafted up the stairs and glass crashed as a picture of George Washington blew off the wall.

After giving a moment for dust to settle and their ears to stop ringing, PT and Miles took out their earplugs and hurried down the stairs.

Miles leaned anxiously into the hole to check that the blast hadn't damaged the tunnel. There were externally sealed steel doors at the top of the staircase and armed security guards at the end of a long, first-floor corridor, so the tunnel was the only way out that didn't involve the inconvenience of federal prison.

'Few bits of floor crumbled into the chamber,' Miles observed. 'Looks OK apart from that.'

PT was more interested in the door of cage two. The vault was locked using three heavy-gauge pins sandwiched inside the door. Opening was via a dual-key mechanism that required two people turning locks built into the wall on opposite sides of the door. This was designed to stop a single staff member getting inside the cage and helping themselves to a handful of untraceable notes.

The array of cogs and gears inside the heavily armoured door led to a single bolt which ran through its centre. This secured the main handle locking the pins in place. Any security system is only as strong as its weakest element and while the double locking system prevented pilfering, its complexity played into the hands of any decent safe breaker.

Miles had stolen the vault plans from a lightly-guarded archive in the Federal Reserve offices above. He'd calculated that four precisely-placed explosives would create a shockwave that cracked the central lever holding the locking pins in place. If Miles had his sums right, PT only had to pull on the lever, the lock pins would slide across and the two-tonne door would glide open.

PT raised the handle. There was a clank, followed by an anxious moment as nothing happened. A more powerful tug did the trick and the huge door took on its own momentum, forcing PT backwards as it glided silently into the room.

The door opening triggered three light bulbs and they lit up steel innards – four metres deep and lined with metal shelving. PT stepped around the door and went inside. The air was stale and the thick walls ate every sound.

The shelves were full of football-sized white cotton bags. Each was stamped FOR INCINERATION, and a handwritten tag detailed the contents: *Bank of Manhattan – $9,270 mixed values. Deposited 12.4.38 counted and swapped by CLK 12.6.38.*

Miles stood in the doorway as his middle son snapped

off the tag, peered at the bundles of crumpled notes inside and broke into an enormous grin.

'So Dad,' PT said. 'How's it feel being a millionaire?'

CHAPTER FOUR

Bert's Joint had been on the same corner for thirty years, doing a good trade from one of the best all-day breakfasts in town and pies made by Bert's old lady. It wasn't unknown for Wall Street types and shoppers to come by and pick up whole pies to take home in the daytime, but most custom went to cab drivers, print workers and late-night cleaners who sat at the tables taking their time.

After dark it was a warm crowd. A fat old cop named Vernon and his young partner Perkins got friendly glances and a couple of waves as they came inside and sat at a table well away from the cold near the doorway. Vernon was hobbling and a cab driver looked over the rim of next morning's newspaper and had to ask.

'Watcha do, Vern, slip on the ice? It's deadly out there, ain't it?'

Vernon's gut squeezed between the bench and a table, while his younger colleague told the story.

'Got a call over to A and H Hardware. Skinny damned kid put a garbage can through the front window.'

'A and H.' The cabbie nodded. 'Smash and grab?'

The young cop batted the snow off his cap as he shrugged. 'Except the kid didn't grab anything. Left his scarf behind and twenty-three dollars in the register. Made a bit of a mess looking for something, then legged it out the back way.'

'You get him?'

The younger cop sniggered into his moustache, unsure whether to answer. Vernon was senior, and he wasn't certain he'd want people knowing.

Vernon raised his hands. 'Damn it, Perky, someone's gonna tell 'em, so it might as well be me. Perkins was driving, so I was inside the store first. Saw the little runt go out the back window – but let's just say I ain't as svelte as I was in the day.'

Perkins laughed. 'You'da loved it. I came in that back room, there's Vernon with his fat ass wedged in the window. *Get me outta here, Davie! If I get my hands on that little mother I'll . . .*'

Half a dozen regulars who'd tuned into the story rattled with laughter.

'And you got your ankle hurt in the window?'

'That was afterwards,' Perkins said. 'Vern was so

stirred up he came straight out on the pavement, fell on his ass and landed up in the gutter.'

This payoff got an even bigger laugh, as Bert's son put two coffees on the table in front of them. 'One black, one white,' the waiter said. 'You know, officers, I mighta seen something. If that kid came out the back of A and H, he would have emerged through the archway across the avenue, right?'

Officer Vernon waved his hand uninterestedly. 'We cruised for a half-hour trying to pick the brat up; he's long gone, and good riddance.'

'Let me finish, Vern,' the waiter said. 'I was outside, right? Maybe forty-five minutes ago. Kid came running across the street, barely looking, and I mean, you don't run in this ice unless you really have to so it *musta* been your boy. Thing is, I've seen that kid loadsa times at our other diner, a few blocks down. Kid comes in at night, always pretty late, and sometimes he's wearing this overall spattered with mud. He buys coffees and sodas, speaks with an accent – Italian or French or something. I asked him why he was out so late one time and he said he was working on a crew with his dad, digging drains.'

Perkins looked interested. 'You know where?'

The waiter nodded. 'I've seen him go in that parking place. You know, red sign – horse with the spike coming out of its head?'

'Unicorn,' Perkins said, grabbing his cap off the table

and rising up out of his seat. 'We'll go check it out.'

But Vern grabbed his partner's arm and pulled him down, before looking up at the waiter. 'Listen, no offence but you're probably putting two and two together to make five. I appreciate your trying to help, but I mean, how much can you really see of a face flashing by in the dark?'

The waiter looked affronted, but he wasn't going to start an argument with a tip-paying customer. 'I was pretty sure it was him,' he said. 'But you've got a lot of experience, Vern, you're probably right.'

Perkins looked at his partner. 'It's only two blocks down, boss. Two-minute drive. I can't see what harm it'll do.'

Vernon grunted. 'OK, we'll go over and see if anyone's working over there – but first, I'm gonna eat. I want my usual grilled steak and fries and, what pies you got today?'

'Peach, cherry, chocolate cream and key lime.'

Vernon nodded enthusiastically. 'Slice of chocolate, slice of peach, both with ice cream.'

One of the cab drivers laughed when he heard this. 'Two pieces of pie and a steak at four in the morning, Vern. No wonder you go around getting your fat can jammed in windows.'

*

PT had been waiting for months. He'd got so used to coming out every night that his nerves were numb to the whole thing: digging in the tunnel until you almost passed out from lack of air, loading dirt into the truck, dead rats, tunnel floods and curse-filled nights when it seemed the train was never going to run right.

He'd imagined the payoff a million times, but something popped in PT's head when he ripped open the first cotton bag and saw the crumpled notes inside. With the bags of money in his hands it was no longer the latest in a line of petty scams and pawnbroker's safes. This was all he'd ever dreamed of.

Everyone's role had been planned out. PT was the first link in the chain, carrying bags of money from the safe and packing them into cardboard boxes. Two boxes slotted perfectly on to a wooden carriage and when six had been passed into the chamber and stacked on board the train by his father, the bell would be rung and Leon would haul the loaded carriages through the tunnel.

At the far end, Leon unloaded the train, threw the bags up to seven-year-old Jeannot, then rang the bell for his father to bring back the train. Jeannot took the bags of money from the storeroom and threw them inside a truck parked on the exit ramp with its rear doors hanging open. By the time the train returned to the station, PT had six more boxes ready for the next trip.

*

Vernon thought checking out Unicorn Tyre and Parking was a waste of time and with his bad ankle and two slices of pie in his belly he didn't even get out of the car, which his partner Perkins had parked in front of the main gate.

'Careful on that ice, Perky,' Vernon said, as his partner got out.

The twenty-five-year-old officer had joined NYPD intending to make sergeant inside three years. It hadn't happened because it's hard to shine when you're partnered with a low-flyer like Vernon who'd sooner eat pie than bust criminals. Still, Vern was a nice old guy and Perkins earned enough to feed three kids, which is more than a lot of people could say during the worst economic depression in history.

Perkins rattled Unicorn's main gate and saw that it was locked. Peering through the bars revealed nothing except the attendant's booth and the up and down ramps. Only as he stepped back did he notice the small gate-within-a-gate. It didn't appear locked, so he slid the bolt across and stepped through. A mouse scuttled from somewhere to somewhere else and he smelled the piles of fresh rubber out the back of the tyre shop as his soles squeaked on the concrete.

It seemed dead, but the unlocked gate was suspicious, so Perkins hooked the long flashlight off his belt. He shone it along the up ramp, then on to the down ramp where he saw a truck parked halfway up with its back doors flapping open. This was an unusual spot to park, but things really got interesting when he noticed small brown shoes moving around behind the rear tyres.

'Bags are in, Leon,' Jeannot shouted. 'Ready for the next train.'

If it had been a man's voice Perkins would have backed off and called for help. But he'd look stupid if he called in extra officers for a couple of homeless kids playing trains in a parking lot. And he was intrigued by that fact that this was a kid. Maybe the waiter in Bert's had been right and he'd stumbled on a little gang that had robbed A&H Hardware. It was no career case, but it was the kind of solid police work that would impress the shift lieutenant.

Perkins flicked off his torch, backed up to the wall and stepped gingerly into the narrow gap between the side wall of the ramp and the body of the truck. He heard some thumping inside the truck and realised that the kid had noticed the torchlight and dived inside for cover.

As Perkins pushed gently to move the rear doors of the truck so that he could get past, a small bell sounded. He leaned past the end of the truck, noticing the door into the storeroom, and a rubber hose dribbling water.

He couldn't see any movement, but he could hear breathing like a man doing physical labour and there was a deadness to the sound, as if it came from below. Perkins could make no sense of it, but whatever was going on he didn't like it. It was time to back out, but as he turned around he saw two shotgun barrels aimed at his chest from the end of the truck.

'I'm not here to hurt you, sonny,' Perkins said warily, surprised by the determined look on seven-year-old Jeannot's clay-spattered face. But he didn't believe for one moment that someone so small would pull the trigger.

At point-blank range the muzzle flashed and pellets tore through Perkins' face and chest, sending him crashing back to the ground. The recoil knocked Jeannot back inside the truck into the bags of money. He found his feet and jumped down, gun still in his hands, as seventeen-year-old Leon shouted from down in the hole.

'What was that, Jeannot? What did I tell you about touching Dad's gun?'

'I shot someone,' Jeannot shouted, as he moved closer and saw an NYPD badge shining on the blood-spattered chest. 'A cop.'

Leon didn't believe what he was hearing. He wanted to pull out of the hole and investigate, but he'd almost got the train home and when it was heavy it had a nasty tendency to jump the tracks if there was a sudden change of speed.

As soon as the train clattered into the station at his feet, Leon vaulted out of the hole and found his brother frozen stiff, staring at a big red mess on the concrete.

'Is he dead?' Jeannot asked.

Leon snatched the shotgun. 'Jeannot, if your brain's spread up the wall like that, you can be sure of it.'

Jeannot's voice went all high like he was about to cry. 'But,' he blurted, after a pause, 'Dad always told us to shoot first and ask questions later.'

Leon gave his little brother a pat on the back. 'You did *exactly* the right thing, but now we need to get out of here. Did you see anyone else?'

'Just him,' Jeannot said.

Leon thought for a second. 'Cops work in pairs. I'll go look for the other one. You jump down the hole and do the emergency ring on the bell. You know how that goes?'

Jeannot nodded. 'Three rings, stop, three rings. Repeat after ten seconds if they don't respond.'

As Jeannot raced into the storeroom, Leon stalked his way around the side of the truck, clutching the shotgun and moving slow with his back close to the wall. At the top of the ramp he saw the outline of a fat man looking through the open gates.

'Perky, watcha got down there?' Officer Vernon shouted.

Leon made a dash from the top of the ramp to the rear of the ticket booth and crouched down low. The fat man heard but didn't see.

'That you, Perkins?'

Leon poked his head out and watched as the fat cop took a couple of steps. The cop was limping badly and clearly in no state to go far; he backed up to the car. As he leaned inside to radio for backup, Leon came out of hiding and rushed him.

'Officer Vernon requesting assistance, I'm at Unicorn Tyre on the corner of—

The radio operator back at the precinct heard the bang. Vernon felt a shower of pellets hitting his back and thighs, but Leon had shot from too far away and most of the pellets chinked against the car. As Leon pulled down the shotgun barrel to reload, Officer Vernon got his hand on his service revolver and shot back blindly.

The first shot went wild, but the bang made Leon jump, giving Vernon time to take aim second time around. The bullet exploded inside Leon's chest, blowing his lungs apart as he crashed backwards into the gates of the Unicorn parking lot.

A burst of adrenaline had kept Vernon upright while he was under attack, but once Leon was down Vernon succumbed to the pain of the hot pellets buried under his skin and collapsed into the snow beside the car.

Vernon tried reaching inside to grab the microphone, but gave up when he realised he didn't need to. The operator at the precinct had heard the shotgun blast at the end of his last transmission.

'Code one,' the operator yelled through the radio static. 'Possible officer shooting. All units head for Unicorn Tyre and Parking. Priority one!'

PT ran out of cage two and jumped into the hole as soon as his father yelled.

'They rung a three and three,' Miles explained. 'Time to get outta here.'

PT was startled. 'Half the money's still in there. Isn't Leon bringing us back on the train?'

Miles sounded impatient. 'If your brother was sending the train he'd have given us a four and a two. It's probably water building up in the tunnel again, but you know the rules: three and three signal means we're coming out.'

The tunnel was a thirty-second ride when you were being pulled. When you powered yourself, you lay on your back instead of your belly and propelled yourself by kicking against the ground or pulling on the ceiling props. The journey took two minutes, longer if there was a lot of standing water.

PT lay on a trolley and his father tucked a stray bag of money between his legs.

'Just in case we don't get back down here,' he smiled, before giving his son a push start.

As PT rolled head first through the blackness he hoped it really was the last time he'd have to do it. They'd pulled out two million dollars, and that was enough to be getting along with. Leon had stopped pumping water when they started running the money on the train and a waterlogged section of tunnel apparently confirmed his dad's theory that they'd have to halt operations and do a pump-out. This was a pain, but it was something they'd done a hundred times before.

But everything seemed wrong as PT sighted the end of the tunnel. Instead of Leon's muddy arms he saw Jeannot crouching tearfully in the mouth of the tunnel.

'What's the matter, squirt?' PT asked, grabbing his cart off the tracks because he could hear his father rolling up a few metres behind him.

'Cops came. I shot one, but Leon went up after and they shot each other.'

The news hit PT like a fist in the balls. 'Is Leon OK? Where is he?'

'By the gate,' Jeannot sobbed. 'He's dead.'

By this time Miles was out of the tunnel and he quickly picked up the gist. 'Why'd it have to be tonight?' he screamed. 'Of all the shitty luck you can have. Jeannot, did you see more cops out there?'

'Nope,' Jeannot answered.

Miles led his sons out of the hole. He burrowed inside his trousers and pointed at the truck. 'PT, get in the front and get the engine running. Jeannot, in the back with the money and make sure the doors are locked behind you.'

As his sons entered the truck Miles jogged up the ramp, where he found his eldest son slumped against the gate. The cop car was still parked across the exit, but Officer Vernon had passed out from the pain.

Miles wanted to stop and say goodbye to his eldest son, but he only had time to take back his shotgun and give him a quick kiss on the cheek.

Once Miles had the weapon he found a key in his pocket and swung the vehicle gate open before running down to the truck. He sat in the driver's seat and took a quick glance through the window into the back.

'You got them doors locked, Jeannot?'

'Yes, Dad,' Jeannot shouted.

Miles let the handbrake off too early and they rolled down the ramp for a couple of metres before he got the clutch in and powered up the ramp in a plume of diesel fumes.

'Brace yourselves, boys,' Miles shouted. 'We're going in hard.'

PT was alarmed to see the cop car blocking the gate and Officer Vernon sitting in the snow beside the open passenger door.

'You're gonna hit him,' PT shouted.

'Bastard shot my son,' Miles yelled, angry beyond reason.

The truck smashed into the police car, crushing Vernon and sending the vehicle spinning out into the road. PT felt the jolt in his neck, but he'd held on to the bag of money his father had tucked between his legs before his final ride through the tunnel and the crumpled notes saved him from a nasty blow against the dashboard.

Miles hadn't anticipated the forces involved when they hit the police car. His face hammered into the steering wheel, knocking him cold.

'Dad!' PT screamed, jerking up in his seat as the truck ploughed on.

It rolled on across the street on to a median planted with flowerbeds and bushes. Hitting the cop car had taken most of their speed off and knocked the engine out of gear. The bags in the rear shifted about and Jeannot got thrown into the truck's metal side as PT reached between the seats and grabbed the handbrake, bringing them to a complete stop with shrubbery lodged between the wheels.

He turned back and looked through the hole into the cargo area. 'Jeannot, you all right?' he shouted.

One of the back doors had flown open and there was enough light to see Jeannot slumped amidst the money bags. PT jumped out of the cab as he heard the police sirens closing from a couple of blocks south. He had to run, but wanted to take Jeannot if he could.

'Jeannot?' PT yelled, leaning in the back and scooping cash-stuffed bags out of the way.

Jeannot had a bloody nose and a nasty split in his lip. He was breathing, but unconscious, and PT wasn't strong enough to carry his brother much more than a few metres.

The sight of Jeannot and the thought of his other brother lying dead by the gates across the street broke PT's heart. But there were two dead cops on the scene and PT knew if he stuck around he'd be on the wrong end of a savage police beating.

'You'll be all right,' PT said, reaching out to give Jeannot a quick pat on the ankle as the sirens grew louder. Then he turned back towards the street and started to run, with a single white cotton bag in his right hand.

CHAPTER FIVE

PT read the label on his cotton bag and saw that he had $3,800* in twenties, tens and fives. He tucked it into his waistband, ran north through the ice and took a cab up to Grand Central Station. After ditching his overalls in a toilet cubicle and a quick splash to wash clay off his face, he caught one of the first subway trains running out to Queens. Being a Sunday, the cars were empty and his heart thudded, imagining that the cops were gonna jump aboard and nab him at every stop.

Miles was a known bank robber who would have been identified within minutes, so PT didn't dare head home. His outdoor clothes were in the storeroom at the Unicorn and he got looks as he walked through

*Equivalent to roughly $55,000 in 2009.

temperatures below freezing in a short-sleeved shirt. He ordered breakfast at a near-empty diner but only pushed it around his plate and got a raised eyebrow when he paid with a torn-up twenty.

'My dad hit the numbers,' PT explained, as the waitress eyed him suspiciously. 'Told me to spoil myself.'

He'd only glanced at Leon as the truck came up the ramp, but the image was glued in his head: clay-spattered torso, blood pooled in the snow and the *What, me?* expression on Leon's face like he got when you caught him cheating at cards.

Leon didn't have PT's brains, but he was the kind of big brother you looked up to: he'd stick up for you in the neighbourhood and only had to look at a girl to get what he wanted. The horror of his death was too big to grasp, but PT had to get on top of it and deal with his situation.

Cold was the most immediate problem. PT knew a Sunday flea market and bought new gloves, a second-hand overcoat and a clean shirt. But the cops around here knew his face so he took a bus south to Brooklyn.

He hopped off in a spot he didn't know. Apartment blocks ran up both sides of a hill, breaking only for a kid's playground and a Laundromat standing on its own. An old man from the neighbourhood played good Samaritan, shovelling a path through the overnight snow.

Vending machines on the next corner were filled with the final edition of the *Sunday Post*. Blood and guts sold newspapers and the main picture was a gory shot of Officer Vernon spattered over the side of a police car and the headline: *TWO COPS, TWO ROBBERS DEAD IN $10-MILLION TUNNEL HEIST.*

Two robbers.

PT scanned the article until he came to it. *Notorious Chicago bank robber, Miles Bivott, died after a struggle with police officers trying to restrain . . .*

The cops would have arrived less than a minute after PT ran off and his dad was in no state to struggle, but the news was no great shock. PT had mixed with bad people his whole life and every crook knew the score: if you kill a cop they'll either kill you or make you wish that they had.

Next he scanned the columns for his little brother:

Bivott's youngest son was found in the back of the truck and is being questioned by police. A third child, believed to have been Bivott's middle son, Philippe, escaped the scene and is being hunted . . .

PT wanted to cry as he imagined little Jeannot in a cell, scared witless. With two dead officers on the scene they'd be pressuring him, most likely with some hard slaps and the threat of worse if they didn't like what he said. But Jeannot's age counted in his favour: at seven years he was too young to be locked away and hopefully they'd see him more as a victim than a perpetrator.

Unlike Jeannot, PT was old enough to cop a murder

charge. NYPD had his photo and fingerprints on file and if they caught him he had more than juvenile hall to worry about this time. There might be an outcry if both he and his father died at the hands of the police. So they'd be unlikely to kill him, but they'd beat him senseless. The judge wouldn't do him any favours either and the prison guards would ensure that he did the hardest time possible when he got to juvenile hall.

PT had to run, but where?

*

He waited until darkness on Wednesday evening. After four days on the street, PT was in a real state. Boots and trousers crusted with rock salt and dirty snow. Black face, black fingers and dried-out clay itching like mad beneath half a dozen layers of clothes. He dreamed of heading west to California, but he was scared of the cops picking him up at a train station and his picture had been in Monday's paper, which made hitchhiking an invitation to get busted.

After three freezing nights huddled in an unheated garage, PT couldn't bear a fourth. He'd have to throw the dice and hope they didn't land him in a police cell. PT's aunt and uncle – the brother of his late mother – lived in an apartment on the lower east side of Manhattan, close to the docks.

The cops had probably figured that they were PT's only surviving relatives, so he approached cautiously and used what his father had taught him on surveying a joint before a robbery.

He walked purposefully down both sides of the street, checking that nobody was sitting in any cars, then vaulted a wire fence and used the back fire stairs up to the third floor. A couple of kids stood on the landing, sharing a bag of monkey nuts and flicking shells over the side.

Number eighteen was the fifth apartment down the hallway. PT checked the rim of the door and when he saw light shining through listened out for a few seconds before knocking. It was a rough neighbourhood, so his Aunt Mae put a chain on the door before opening up.

Her jaw hung, but much to PT's relief her expression quickly warmed and she ushered him into a living room that was even warmer.

'Darling,' she said, looking suspiciously up and down the hallway before slamming the door. 'My god, the state of you!'

Mae couldn't have kids and her substitute was a cage stuffed with chirping canaries against the back wall. Their noise and the smell of seed cake brought back memories of his first ever visit: six years old with his mother and Jeannot just a baby. Mae had bought him a die-cast fire engine with ladders that came off along the sides.

'You let someone in?' Uncle Thierry said, leaning curiously out of the kitchen.

Thierry had worked the docks his whole life and always wore a sweat-stained, white vest, showing off the dragons and sea serpents tattooed up his arms. His reaction to PT couldn't have been more different.

'Well, well, well,' Thierry said, giving a mean shake of the head that turned PT's stomach. 'Look what sprang out of the gutter.'

'Would you like something to eat?' Mae asked. 'I've got stew.'

PT nodded eagerly, and found himself across the table from Thierry as his aunt ladled out a stew thick with potatoes and stringy lamb and bread sliced from a fat loaf.

'Where you been?' Thierry grunted.

'Around,' PT said. 'Garage over in Brooklyn. Ducking and diving, you know?'

'Can't say as I do,' Thierry said. 'Never shot no cop myself. Never been on the run.'

PT felt small. Twenty years labouring the docks had turned Uncle Thierry into a side of beef, and PT got the feeling that not only could his uncle rip him in half with his bare hands, but that he was actively considering the idea as they spoke.

'Had the cops here giving me the third degree Sunday afternoon,' Thierry said. 'You seen the paper? That poor widow, with three kids under seven. Who did the shooting, your father?'

PT's hand trembled as he raised a spoon to his mouth. 'Leon, I think.'

'Federal Reserve too. I always said your father was a dumb bastard.'

'There's no call for that language, Thierry,' Mae said sharply. 'He's your sister's boy and he's thirteen years old. His father brought him up to this life. You can't blame PT for what Miles led those boys into.'

'I did everything for that man when your mother died,' Thierry said, eyeballing PT as he crammed a fat slice of bread between his teeth. 'Called in a dozen favours to land him easy work loading the mail on the transatlantic ships. Do you know how many men shovel coal in the docks for twenty years and still don't get a job like that? And then the asshole doesn't even last two months and leaves me looking the fool.'

PT couldn't answer for his father's sins and turned to his aunt. 'Have you seen Jeannot?'

'They let me visit this morning,' Mae said, nodding. 'He's real sad, but the police are done with him and they've moved him to a children's home. I'm going to try bringing him to live here, but there's a procedure. I've got to petition the court and apparently it could take a month or more.'

'We're his next of kin,' Thierry explained. 'And he's young enough not to have too many of his father's bloody stupid ideas in his head.'

'I've got some money,' PT said. 'Maybe I can help you out.'

Thierry interrupted with a huge laugh. 'You think I'm gonna lay a hand on that dead-cop money? If I start showing cash around the cops'll have me locked up faster than a longshoreman drinks his wages.'

'Do you still have influence in the docks, with the union and that?' PT asked, although he already knew the answer. For all the complaints about his brother-in-law being a criminal, Thierry was a well-paid representative for the dockworkers' union, which was a thinly-veiled front for the New York mafia.

'I'm sure we could help with a lawyer and things, PT,' Mae said. 'But after what happened, you're going to have to accept a severe punishment and there's not much we can do about that.'

Thierry smiled again, and much to PT's relief it had a touch of sympathy to it. 'That's not why you're here though, is it?'

PT shook his head. 'I thought, with your influence in the docks, you might be able to get me on a boat.'

'You were always smarter than your brothers,' Thierry said. 'I thought you might turn up here sooner or later. I've already put out feelers, just in case.'

PT smiled, but only until Thierry yanked his head across the table and nearly twisted his ear off.

'Uncle,' PT gasped. 'Please.'

'When cops get killed there's a *lot* of heat,' Thierry growled. 'I dearly loved my sister. She wouldn't have wanted you to rot in prison so I'm doing this for her – but once you're gone you can't *ever* come back to the United States. Not next month, not next year, not even when you're a hundred years old.'

'I understand,' PT moaned weakly.

'If the cops ever find out that I helped you, I'll be in so much shit that even my union connections won't help. So you keep your mouth *shut* and if you ever mention my name or even try to contact me or your little brother – god help you.'

Thierry let go of PT's ear.

'Thanks, Uncle.'

Thierry explained more as Mae refilled his bowl of stew. 'A stolen French passport and identity documents will cost you a hundred and sixty dollars. I can get them sorted in a few hours. I assume you can cover that cost?'

'I've got money.' PT nodded.

'And you speak good French?'

PT nodded again. 'Dad always spoke it at home.'

'There's a cargo ship sailing for Bordeaux tomorrow evening. Captain's a man I've known for many years. He'll put you on crew as a cabin boy, but I expect he's gonna want a few hundred dollars for his trouble.'

'And there's no bother getting me into the docks?'

Thierry shook his head. 'The crossing takes around

eighteen days. Once you arrive in Bordeaux you'll be on your own, but you've got money, and the captain may even be able to help you some. We'll make your documents so that you're fourteen. Plenty of boys that age work on the ships, so you should have no bother getting yourself a room in a hostel. When your money runs low there's always gonna be work on a boat or around the docks.'

'I appreciate this, Uncle,' PT said, as tears started welling in his eyes.

Thierry was a hard man, but he stood by you when it mattered.

Part Three

3 July 1940 – 5 July 1940

Bordeaux, France

France signed a formal surrender agreement with Germany on 22 June 1940. The country was to be divided into two zones. The industrialised north and a broad strip stretching along the Atlantic coastline down to Spain would be occupied by Germany. The rural south and the Mediterranean coast were to be ruled by a puppet French government based in the small spa town of Vichy.

Under the terms of surrender the French Navy was under Vichy Government control, but the British feared that its fleet would eventually fall into German hands. On 3 July the Royal Navy surrounded the main body of the French fleet at the North African port of Mers-El-Kebir and delivered an ultimatum. The French could either scuttle their ships, join the British in the fight against Nazi Germany, or be destroyed.

Meanwhile in Berlin, the German High Command was jubilant at the rapid capitulation of France. Hitler had no desire for a long battle and expected to reach a diplomatic settlement with Britain that would end the war within months.

CHAPTER SIX

Once he'd met up with Paul and Rosie again, Henderson wanted to take the kids by ship from Bordeaux or across the border into a neutral country. But Paul was too sick to travel for a week after the *Cardiff Bay* sank and by that time German forces controlled the entire Atlantic coast, including all ports and the borders with Spain and Switzerland.

Henderson couldn't risk getting arrested at a port or border crossing and decided to lie low. Hopefully the Germans would assume he'd left the country if a few weeks went by without any sightings.

They needed somewhere to stay and consular official Maxine Clere provided it. The half-English daughter of a Bordeaux property developer, Maxine let Henderson and the four youngsters move into a house she'd inherited from a great-aunt. It was a grand affair, but its location on hilly ground several kilometres out of the city made it unlikely the Germans would pay much attention.

The exterior was pink. A balcony ran the length of the first floor and the interior was richly decorated with antique furniture and a spooky array of animal skins and native artefacts that Maxine's great-uncle had brought home from France's African colonies. But while the house remained impressive, the substantial grounds were shabby, because the gardener had been conscripted into the army.

On a sunny day you could sit out on the overgrown lawn, listen to nothing but birdsong and bake in the height of summer. At least you could until PT and Marc decided on a bout of tag wrestling and all hell broke loose.

Barefoot and bare-chested, the pair squared off with one arm behind their backs and handkerchiefs tucked into their back pockets. The game's object was to snatch your opponent's hanky and, despite three years in age and a huge difference in height, the pair were a surprisingly even match.

Marc was like a bull. With broad shoulders and solid limbs, he tended to stand his ground while his opponent danced about. PT loomed over him, circling on fast feet, swooping in all directions and hurling abuse. Sometimes PT managed to grab Marc's tag, but mostly Marc would evade PT until he tired. He'd then use his strength to charge forwards and knock PT on his back.

Today was no different. Paul and Rosie watched from garden loungers a few metres away as PT crashed backwards on to the shaggy lawn. Rosie enjoyed having the two testosterone-fuelled boys riling the place up, and they both flattered her with their attention.

PT was brazen about his attraction, though Rosie hadn't let him near enough for a second kiss. Marc's interest was more innocent, but she often caught him glancing at her chest or staring jealously when she was deep in conversation with PT.

Paul was less comfortable with Marc and PT. He was a quiet boy who'd sooner draw than wrestle and he didn't like sharing the attention of his big sister. It was nineteen days since the *Cardiff Bay* sank, but he still couldn't close his eyes to sleep without his imagination sucking him underwater. His broken arm ached relentlessly and his swollen face gave him regular headaches.

'Hah!' PT yelled triumphantly as his long arm zipped the handkerchief out of Marc's shorts. 'Thirty-five-twenty-eight to me.'

They'd been keeping score since day one and the running tally was hotly debated.

'Thirty-three–thirty-five to *me*,' Marc yelled back.

PT gasped theatrically. 'You can't count those stupid bouts up in the bedroom. I was half asleep and there was no room to move about!'

'Aww, crap,' Marc scoffed. 'The only reason you don't count them is that I pinned you five times running.'

'Get stuffed,' PT said. 'You couldn't pin a sheet of newspaper to a horse's arse.'

'Wanna bet?' Marc jeered as the two squared off again, this time without tags or any pretence of rules.

Rosie smiled and sat up so that she could see better. Paul sighed and stood up. 'I'm going indoors for a rest.'

Rosie looked concerned. 'You OK? You want me to get you an aspirin, or a drink?'

As Paul headed inside, PT and Marc slammed into each other.

'Lying son of a whore!' Marc shouted.

'Box baby!' PT shouted back.

PT got his long arms around Marc and slapped his bare back hard. Marc ploughed forwards and shoved PT on the grass beneath him, then pinned one shoulder beneath his knee.

'Fifteen years old and you're such a weed!' Marc grinned, as sweat trickled down his brow. 'If we were the same age I'd crush you.'

But PT knocked him off and they somehow ended up fighting head to toe, this time with PT on top. He got his knee across Marc's chest and squashed him, but PT's foot was right in Marc's face and the younger boy opened his mouth wide.

'AAAARGH!' PT shouted, springing into the air and hopping on one leg. 'Toe-biter! What kind of wrestling is that? Christ almighty, it's bleeding.'

'Victory is mine!' Marc shouted, thumping his chest before picking his shirt off the lawn and using it to wipe PT's blood from his front teeth.

Rosie found the whole performance hilarious, but as she laughed she turned and saw that Paul had come back out on to the lawn.

'You OK, mate?'

Paul smiled mischievously before pointing his thumb at an upstairs window. 'I was heading upstairs when I saw something. Henderson's got Maxine up there. They're kissing and they've not closed the door properly.'

'Gotta see this,' Marc hooted.

PT's eyebrows shot up and he gave Marc an almighty shove before leading the way inside and racing up the marble staircase. Paul, Marc and Rosie followed a few steps behind, stifling giggles as they hurried down the hallway and slowly poked heads around a half-open door.

The master bedroom was more than ten metres deep, with a parquet floor and four-poster bed. Maxine lay across a chaise-longue set in the bay window, wearing nothing but black stockings. Henderson sat at the end, massaging the stockinged feet in his lap.

'I bet he's gonna fertilise her,' Marc whispered with a snigger.

PT stuck his hand in front of Paul's eyes. 'You can't watch this, you're too young,' he hissed.

'Get off,' Paul said, gritting his teeth and batting the hand away. 'You wouldn't even know if I hadn't come down and told you.'

Oblivious of the fascinated audience, Henderson leaned over Maxine and kissed her on the mouth before standing up and starting to unbutton his shirt.

'What's fertilising, anyway?' Paul asked as quietly as he could.

PT stifled a laugh as Marc explained in a whisper. 'We did it on the farm where I used to work. The cow gets put in a little pen, then Henri the bull comes in. His penis blows up until it's about a foot long and he shoves it right inside her.'

'A bull's thing is a foot long?' Paul gasped. 'But why would Henderson do something like that?'

PT found Paul's innocence hysterical. He couldn't control his laughter and had to back off down the corridor.

'This is private,' Rosie said. 'We shouldn't be watching. Especially you, Paul.'

She gave Paul a tug but he was determined not to look weak in front of the older boys and as he pulled away from her his shoe squealed on the hallway floor. Henderson's head turned sharply towards the noise.

'Goddammit,' he shouted, steaming towards the door with one hand holding up his trousers. 'What the hell are you playing at out there?'

PT was out of sight and took to the stairs, but the three younger kids didn't have time to scarper and looked worried as Henderson closed in. He shook his fist as they shrivelled into the hallway.

'Shoo!' he yelled furiously. 'If I catch any of you spying on me again I'll take a switch and thrash your arses raw.'

The quartet was in fits of giggles as they poured back into the garden.

'The dirty old sod,' Rosie said indignantly. 'He's got a wife back in England too.'

*

Paul slept for most of the afternoon and was woken by Maxine stroking his face.

'You OK?' she asked gently.

Paul's eyes were gluey and dancing shadows on the wall told him that the sun had dropped behind the tall trees out front. Maxine was beautiful in a rather severe way, while her height and taste for dark clothes gave her the air of a movie star who only got to play baddies.

'Better for a sleep,' Paul yawned, before remembering what he'd seen immediately prior to his nap and drawing an anxious breath. 'I'm sorry we spied on you. I know it was rude.'

Maxine stroked his hair. 'It's natural for children to be curious. Charles has made some dinner, so go wash your face and hands.'

PT and Marc sat at a mahogany dining table while Rosie helped Henderson carry plates dished up with an English-style roast: a chicken wrapped in bacon, with roast potatoes and local vegetables. Although food was short in cities and towns this was mainly down to transport problems. Food remained in plentiful supply to a well-connected local like Maxine.

'Warm up the radio,' Henderson said, glancing at his watch. 'We'll catch the seven o'clock news.'

Paul reached out and switched on an elderly radiogram in a huge wooden cabinet. The valves that amplified the sound took a minute to warm up. Maxine allowed the kids a single glass of wine and there was light conversation and light music until the Radio Paris bugle blasted seven o'clock. The station had fallen under Nazi control and its broadcasts now had an unsubtle pro-German bias.

'Good evening, France,' the newsreader said urgently. 'This is Radio Paris. News has reached us this evening of the greatest naval defeat since Trafalgar. Despite a personal guarantee from Adolf Hitler that the French fleet could continue to operate independently in the defence of our colonies, the British Navy today surrounded our Atlantic fleet at Mers-El-Kebir in North Africa and attacked mercilessly. Fifteen-inch guns from the battleships Hood and Valiant opened fire without warning, slaughtering thousands of innocent French sailors . . .'

'I need to hear the other side of that story,' Henderson said, shooting backwards in his chair before realising that Paul was much closer. 'Paul, tune the BBC up, right now.'

Paul moved the dial as quickly as he could, but BBC France was broadcast from London and its signal was always weak. Everyone stepped away from their food and struggled to pick out words between bursts of static.

'*In a statement to the BBC, Prime Minister Winston Churchill this evening expressed his sadness at the tragic loss of a small number of French sailors who had fought alongside their British allies for the past year. However, he stressed that the French fleet was a risk to British interests in the Mediterranean. Furthermore, the French fleet had been amply warned and her ships were given sufficient time for crews to disembark before the Royal Navy opened fire.*'

When the broadcast ended Marc scowled at Henderson. 'Why are you Brits sinking French ships? What have we ever done to you?'

Maxine was more sympathetic to the British cause. 'It's not that simple, Marc. Hitler isn't trustworthy. He's reneged on every agreement he's ever made and the only thing the British can count on right now is their dominance of the sea.'

Paul couldn't resist taunting Marc. 'French army got creamed by the Germans. Now your navy gets blasted out of the sea by us Brits. Face it, France is rubbish at everything.'

Marc was no great patriot, except when a foreigner taunted him. 'You wanna see what this piece of French rubbish does when his fist encounters your front teeth?'

'We're half-French, Paul,' Rosie noted diplomatically.

'You lot, *calm* down!' Maxine ordered. 'Otherwise I'll take your plates and send you up to bed.'

Henderson sat himself back at the head of the table, ignoring his food and drumming his fork on the mahogany. It was several minutes before he spoke decisively.

'Maxine, how badly damaged was the radio transmitter you rescued from the consulate?'

'It fell from a tabletop when the bomb hit the jeweller's shop,' she explained. 'Several valves shattered and the metal casing took a dent, but I'd say it's fixable with some new valves and a bit of soldering.'

Henderson nodded. 'I need to re-evaluate my strategy. After France fell so easily I thought Churchill was posturing: trying to make the best of things before making a diplomatic settlement with Germany. But destroying the French fleet like that shows that they're really in for the long haul.'

Maxine didn't look convinced. 'But the Germans have swept everyone aside. Poland, Czechoslovakia, Austria, Denmark and now France. What chance does Britain have?'

PT butted in. 'It's not just Britain though. There's

the whole British Empire: Canada, Australia, India, half of Africa. Britain has eight times as many battleships as the Germans.'

'But the Germans rule the skies,' Marc said. 'I travelled from Beauvais all the way down to here. The Germans were bombing the hell out of everything and I didn't see one British plane. Not *one*.'

Henderson looked at Maxine. 'Are you taking food into the shelter tomorrow?'

Maxine nodded. 'I'll take your van if that's OK. Do you need a ride?'

'I'll take a look at the radio tonight,' Henderson said. 'If it looks fixable I'll go into Bordeaux tomorrow morning and try finding some tools and parts. Any radio communication that I make is a risk: it could give our location away to the Germans. But I'm quite possibly the only British agent operating in France right now and the government may need me.'

'What about us though?' Rosie asked nervously. 'I thought you said we were lying low until Paul was well enough and then we'd try crossing over the mountains into Spain.'

'I know what I said,' Henderson said irritably. 'I've no plans to abandon you, but you're perfectly safe here and the British Government may need a job doing before we leave the country.'

CHAPTER SEVEN

Maxine's Jaguar was a thirsty beast and with fuel hard to come by they drove into Bordeaux in the small truck Henderson had stolen in the south of Paris a few weeks earlier. Maxine and Rosie sat up front and Henderson rattled around with Marc in a cargo compartment that also contained two wicker hampers stuffed with eggs and vegetables.

The British had ordered Maxine to destroy any sensitive documents and close the consulate. She obeyed the first part of this order, but ignored the second and on her own initiative reopened the offices as an unofficial refuge and missing children's bureau.

The rooms upstairs, including the consul's wood-panelled banqueting suite, now housed children who were mostly aged five and under, while the kitchen that once prepared food for local dignitaries specialised in warm milk and toddler-sized meals.

The chaotic exodus south had split thousands of children from their families. Thirty kids lived on the consulate's first and second floors, while two hundred others, ranging from babies to young teens, were divided amongst local church halls, private homes and classrooms. Some had got lost amidst the chaos, while others had seen mothers and siblings killed or horrifically injured in bomb blasts.

There was a shortage of everything from food and clothes to bedding and medical supplies. After carrying the food hampers in from the truck, Rosie hurried upstairs to be greeted by a bunch of surprisingly cheerful youngsters, who hugged her legs and begged her to play games.

Maxine had recruited several women refugees, who looked after the children in return for regular food and a safe place to sleep. Caring for so many youngsters in a space not designed for them was hard work, but Rosie mucked in with the washing, feeding and laundering.

Rosie had grown to know the kids over the past two weeks, but looking after them was exhausting and at times she hated it. Several of the children were ill and after all they'd been through it was only natural that several sets of pee-stained sheets had to be washed each morning. But Rosie continued to grieve for her own father and the work gave her life some purpose.

Other parts of the job were more pleasant. On bright afternoons she'd take a group of five kids to chase around the grounds of a nearby church and once in a while she'd witness a minor miracle: an auntie or mother turning up and taking one of the children away.

Maxine worked downstairs in the offices. She kept records on every missing child in the Bordeaux area and published a list of children and adults who'd lost track of someone. Each day the long list was typed on to stencils, then duplicated on a hand-cranked Mimeograph machine.

After lunch she'd walk around town putting up copies in a dozen prominent locations such as the main railway station, police stations and churches. In many spots Maxine's list was met by a crowd, anxious to check if the names of missing relatives had been added.

Her final stop was the local newspaper, which printed new additions to the list and occasionally found space for a story with a happy ending.

*

There were several radio repair shops in Bordeaux, but Henderson judged that the one situated in the docks would be used to repairing maritime transmitters and more likely to stock the items he'd need to repair the consul's radio transmitter.

The situation around the port was even grimmer than

three weeks earlier. Several coal barges had arrived enabling the backlog of ships to sail, but there was still a shortage of fuel for trucks, and the railways had been crippled in the final phase of German bombing. This left mountains of goods rotting on the dockside with no route to market.

The Germans wanted France to return to normality and asked refugees to go back home, but people faced the same transport problems as the produce and German military needs were given priority on the few trains that ran.

The presence of food in the docks also attracted thousands more hungry refugees. They were short of fresh water and without shelter or toilet facilities, so the streets stank in the summer heat and it was only a matter of time before typhoid or cholera broke out.

As Marc stepped down from Henderson's stolen truck, the refugees sprawled out in doorways seemed barely human. Some kept clean by washing in the sea, but many had given up all pretence of decency. If you were healthy you could head out into the country and steal from farms, or start making your way home on foot. Those who stayed around the docks tended to be old, sick or burdened with several children.

Radio Maritime had a conspicuously modern shopfront in a street of seedy bars and hostels. The front door had been boarded over following one of the many bomb blasts around the docks, but a sign pointed to a side entrance down an alleyway and Henderson was pleased to discover a large workshop and storage shed.

'Should stock plenty of spares in a joint like this,' he noted.

Henderson knocked on the steel door, but had already begun sizing it up for a break-in when a bolt finally thunked across the inside. A young man opened it and as he let Henderson and Marc inside it became clear that a club foot had kept him out of the army.

'I was down in the basement,' the young assistant said apologetically. 'I keep the door locked because you get people wandering in, wanting food or begging to use the toilet. Not that the toilet even works now. There's so many refugees out there that all the sewers are backed up.'

Henderson pulled a crumpled sheet of paper out of his jacket. 'I need to replace a couple of valves. Got the part numbers written down here.'

The assistant sucked air between his teeth. 'Not a valve on the shelf, I'm afraid. Valves are fragile beasts and when the bombing started we had more repair work than we could handle. Once the Boche[4] arrived they came and took what little stock we had left to repair military equipment.'

---

[4]Boche – offensive slang term used to describe Germans.

'Figures,' Henderson said sourly. 'I suppose that means nobody else in town will have any either?'

'You suppose right, sir. I can't even sell you one of the new sets in the window because they've all been stripped out. With no parts, the only work I can do right now is cannibalising: making one good set if you bring in a pair of damaged ones.'

'And I don't suppose you've kept any stock back for a customer who can pay a good price?' Henderson asked.

The assistant shrugged. 'You know, my father owns this shop. He said I should have tried to keep a couple back from the Boche. But when two big uniforms with guns came through the door and started ripping stuff off the shelves I didn't fancy playing the hero for the sake of a few glass tubes.'

Henderson looked deeply disappointed. 'Supposing a man *had* to have a valve, is there anywhere he might get one?'

The assistant laughed. 'Short of robbing the Germans in their barracks, I doubt it.'

Henderson's eyes lit up. 'Would you know where that is?'

'Sure, my dad and my sister are helping them repair equipment up there now. They took over the university building across the river, but you're wasting your time. They won't give you anything.'

'Guess you're right,' Henderson said sadly. 'I'll let you

get back to your cannibalisation.'

The smell of the street hit Marc again as they went out into the alleyway.

'Looks like we're buggered on the radio front, boss,' Marc said sadly.

Henderson smiled determinedly. 'Marc, if there were no valves in Bordeaux we'd be buggered. All we're facing is a minor difficulty.'

Marc laughed as they turned back on to the street and approached the truck. 'You're probably the most wanted man in France. You're not seriously gonna try robbing a German barracks are you?'

Marc stopped by the truck, thinking they'd be climbing back inside, but Henderson kept going towards the docks.

'Come on,' Henderson said. 'I'll bet you ten francs that we don't head home empty-handed. All we need do is find a boat with a German name written on the bow.'

*

While Maxine, Rosie, Henderson and Marc travelled into Bordeaux in the truck, PT and Paul stayed back at the pink house.

Paul hated the noise and chaos of the toddler-packed consulate and Henderson had made it clear that he only wanted Marc for company during his quest for radio spares. The pair had formed a strong bond travelling south from Paris together and Henderson made no effort to hide the fact that Marc was his favourite.

Maxine had put bread and jam out in the kitchen before she left and Paul scoffed three thickly buttered slices. Bread and jam was his favourite breakfast and he planned on having the same for lunch if Henderson wasn't back by then.

After eating he headed upstairs to get an artist's pad and a small pack of coloured pencils Maxine had found for him. He'd owned a more elaborate selection of inks and pastels, but they'd gone down along with all his other possessions on the *Cardiff Bay*.

The three boys shared the second largest bedroom in the house, and PT had taken advantage of Marc's early departure to spread himself over the double bed. PT was usually moody until lunchtime, so Paul crept around making sure he didn't wake up.

When Paul and Rosie's parents were alive they'd worried about Paul being so shy. His mother made Paul go to birthday parties when he didn't want to, while his father had enrolled him in manly activities such as the Boy Scouts and a boxing club.

Despite Rosie taunting him for being a wimp and a couple of thrashings from his father, Paul resisted with violent tantrums until both schemes were dropped and his parents came to accept him as a quiet boy who enjoyed his own company.

Having his right arm in a sling made it awkward to

carry his pad, pencil tin, a slice of bread and jam wrapped in greaseproof paper and a hip flask filled with water. It was impossible for Paul to feel truly happy – with his father having recently died and his future uncertain – but as he sat by a stream just beyond the grounds of the pink house with the sun on his back he felt warm and relaxed.

A friend of Paul's late father was a Professor of Art at a Paris university. The professor had recognised Paul's talent and on several occasions allowed him to sit in on studio sessions with his students. Paul had been intimidated by the much older students, but loved being in a place where art was the centre of everything and having the chance to try out pastels and charcoal for the first time.

Paul used one of the techniques he'd learned from the professor and timed himself making three-minute sketches. A duck on the lake, a vista of the pink house and surrounding hills and a frustrating attempt to capture the sheen of a ladybird's shell. Conscious that he only had twelve precious sheets left on his pad, he kept all the drawings on a single side.

After ninety minutes drawing, Paul took a break and lay back on the grass. He ate the slice of bread and drank water that had baked in the metal hip flask. He'd planned to stay out all morning, but his bowels had other ideas and he strode briskly back to the house and locked himself in the toilet.

It was still only half-past eleven, so he decided to head back out. But as he passed down the hallway he noticed Marc's pigskin bag leaning against the wall in the hallway.

'Marc, you back already?' he shouted.

But Paul knew Marc hadn't taken the bag with him: he'd seen it in the wardrobe upstairs when he fetched his pencils. Paul loosened the draw-string and saw that it contained one of Marc's shirts and several days' worth of food.

Paul checked the rooms downstairs, looking for PT. When he didn't find him he headed up, stepped into their bedroom and saw that PT had packed his things.

PT was old enough to make his own way in the world, but Paul didn't like the fact that he'd taken Marc's bag and found it suspicious that he'd chosen to sneak out of the house when nobody else was around.

As he stepped out of the bedroom, Paul heard a thump in Henderson's room along the hallway. He crept up to the door and saw PT leaning over the bed, going through the equipment in Henderson's suitcase.

Paul watched as PT turned over the guns and equipment, then gasped as the older boy found the leather pouch in which Henderson kept gold ingots and currency.

'Put it back,' Paul blurted, charging in through the doorway and wondering if he'd done the right thing as his words echoed into the huge room.

PT jolted with fright, but was relieved to see that it was only Paul, who presented no physical threat to him.

'I thought you were out drawing,' PT said peevishly.

'What are you doing?'

'What does it look like?'

'But why leave?' Paul asked. 'I thought you liked it here.'

'All I want is a quiet life,' PT said. 'It was nice hanging out with you guys. I liked the idea of crossing the mountains to Spain. But now Henderson's changing it all. I mean, radio transmissions? Contacting the British Government? That's dangerous shit and I'm staying away from it.'

'So leave then,' Paul said indignantly. 'But after all Henderson and Maxine have done for you these last three weeks, how can you steal his stuff? You've got loads of money. Rosie saw it.'

'I'm not taking everything,' PT said as he pulled three gold ingots out of the pouch. 'But in troubled times like these a lot of people prefer gold to dollars or francs.'

'Come on, put it back,' Paul begged.

PT pocketed the three ingots. 'Paul, I've got my own problems and I can't afford to get into trouble. Tell Henderson that I'm grateful for everything he's done and sorry I had to take some of his gold.'

Paul didn't like PT much, but Rosie would be upset if she came home and found him gone. 'Why don't you stay until tonight and talk about it?' he said. 'Put the gold back and I'll not mention it, I swear.'

'I'm leaving as soon as I'm packed.'

There was a pause as the two boys eyed each other warily.

'So I guess it's goodbye,' Paul said uncertainly, reaching out to shake hands.

PT smiled as they shook. 'I guess it is.'

Paul mustered a smile but felt uneasy as he backed out of the room. His brain worked hard as he headed downstairs. On the one hand, Paul had no great liking for PT and wouldn't miss him, but sneaking off and stealing from Marc and Henderson left a nasty taste.

Paul considered what he knew about PT. PT claimed that he'd run away from a father who beat him, worked as a cabin boy and made several thousand dollars beating crewmates at poker. But PT always got shifty when you asked about his background. No one really believed his story and Henderson had openly speculated that the money was stolen.

So, PT was a liar and a thief, and after three weeks living in the pink house he'd heard enough of Rosie and Marc's stories to work out that Henderson was a British agent. Paul guessed PT could walk to Bordeaux in about an hour, or maybe get there even quicker if he hitched a lift. The important question was, what would he do when he got there?

If PT approached the Gestapo and offered them information in return for a reward, there could be a German reception committee waiting for Henderson and the others when they got home. Although Paul doubted that PT would go to the Nazis with information, he wasn't trustworthy and the consequences would be terminal if he did.

Henderson and Maxine would be tortured and executed as British spies and the fate of Marc, Rosie and himself was unlikely to be pleasant. Marc had already had one of his front teeth ripped out by a Gestapo officer.

Paul took the decision to act, but what could he do? PT was four years older and with one arm in a sling Paul had no chance in a direct physical confrontation. He'd have to take PT by surprise, and he only had minutes to come up with a plan.

CHAPTER EIGHT

The Bordeaux Institute of Science and Medicine made an ideal base for the town's German garrison. Student accommodation housed soldiers, there was a dining hall, sports facilities and a university hospital for the wounded. Tanks and artillery pieces suffering after two months' campaigning were being refurbished in the institute's main square, while handheld weapons and communication equipment got serviced in the laboratories.

Across the street from the main gate a café did a good trade serving off-duty Germans. Marc and Henderson jostled through cigarette smoke and green uniforms and made their way towards the most important looking men in the room.

Henderson's language skills were considerable. He not only spoke all five major European languages but could conjure a variety of local accents. Marc stood alongside as Henderson became Captain von Hoven, from the merchant ship SV *Hamburg*. His bearing grew stiffer and his accent belonged to a German aristocrat.

After flamboyantly offering to buy the three senior officers brandies, he raised a toast to German conquest, congratulated them on their role in the collapse of France and expressed regret that an injury sustained while falling over on the deck of a ship had kept him out of the fighting.

'France is a backwards nation,' Henderson said, loud enough for half the bar to hear. 'All its glories are in the past. Today it's a nation of peasants, foul toilets and broken telephones. The French might not know it yet, but this invasion is probably the best thing that's ever happened to them.'

The officers nodded in broad agreement.

'We've been here two weeks and not had a squeak out of the locals,' one officer noted. 'My men are under strict orders to behave decently towards them and the French are reciprocating.'

'All the French care about is food in their bellies,' another officer slurred. 'They haven't had a leader worth the name since Napoleon. That's why we broke their backs so easily.'

The barman didn't understand German, but his face gave the impression that he'd spit in their glasses given half a chance. Henderson poured three rounds of extra-old brandy down the officers' necks and refused to let them return his favour.

'I can afford it,' he insisted. 'And it's the least I can do for men who fought for Germany while I dragged a shipload of Brazilian timber across the Atlantic.'

Marc was briefly introduced to the German officers as a cabin boy aboard Captain von Hoven's ship. While Henderson socialised, Marc sat at a wobbly table, choking on cigarette smoke and taking his time over a baguette and a coffee. He could follow most of Henderson's conversation, thanks to a gift for languages and a kindly teacher who'd given after-school German tuition to his cleverest pupils.

After half an hour, during which one officer left but two others got drawn to the free brandy, Henderson made a discreet thumb signal.

Marc came over and spoke meekly in broken German. 'Captain von Hoven, sir, I don't mean to be impertinent, but we need to find the spare parts if—'

'What?' Henderson roared, grabbing Marc by the scruff of his shirt. 'You know I hate it when you mumble. Speak like a man.'

Marc started over, speaking firmly. 'We need to replace the broken valves, Captain. Perhaps if you're going to stay here drinking *all* afternoon you could give me some money and I'll go and look for them.'

The four Germans laughed at Marc's sarcastic tone as Henderson crouched down and yelled right in the boy's face. 'Do you fancy a week in the ship's brig, my boy?'

'No, sir,' Marc said meekly.

Henderson grinned at the German officers. 'My ship has a *marvellous* brig,' he explained. 'It's right down in the hull, directly beside the main boiler. It's all bare metal and it gets so hot that they emerge covered in blisters.'

'Would you like that, boy?' a drunken colonel jeered, as Marc acted suitably scared.

'I'm sorry, Captain.'

The Germans were amused by Marc's squirming, but Henderson looked at his watch and gave him a friendly shoulder squeeze.

'He's a good lad, really,' Henderson said. 'Nags worse than my wife, but he puts in a good day's work. Quite remarkable, when you consider that he's French. And we really do need replacement valves for our shipboard radio. We've walked all over this godforsaken town and drawn a complete blank.'

The youngest of the four officers gave a friendly smile. 'What are you looking for exactly?'

Henderson pulled the crumpled piece of paper from his jacket. The German snatched it, read it and then tilted it towards the colonel.

'You think we can help a fellow German?'

The colonel passed the note to Marc. 'We'll keep an eye on your captain for you,' he smiled. 'Take this across the street. When you get to the gate, tell them Colonel Graff said you can have whatever you require.'

Marc nodded politely, but he was awed by Henderson's powers of manipulation. As he headed out of the café the barman poured out more brandy and Henderson raised another toast.

'Long live the Fatherland,' he shouted.

*

Paul exited the front of the pink house and sat near the entrance steps, grinding palms against his cheeks as he tried to think straight. Apart from two unwilling excursions into a boxing ring and occasionally getting thumped by Rosie, his main experience of fighting came from movies.

In a flash of genius he remembered seeing a film about American gangsters where a prison guard had been floored using a sock stuffed with billiard balls. There were no billiard balls around, but Paul reckoned his long grey socks and the loose pebbles fringing overgrown flowerbeds would do the trick.

It wasn't easy with one hand. His shoe and sock came off without difficulty but he had a rougher time holding the sock open with his splinted arm and dropping in rough stones that snagged on the grey wool. When the sock felt sufficiently heavy Paul gave it a couple of test swings.

He decided that the best technique was to wrap most of the sock around his wrist and flick it like a cosh, but doubts surfaced as he crouched beside a tree trunk a few paces from the house, awaiting PT's exit. Ensuring that PT didn't leave seemed good in theory, but the reality of his slight frame and a broken arm made Paul wonder if surprise would be enough of an advantage.

PT looked solemn as he left the pink house, a small brown suitcase in one hand and Marc's pigskin slung over his back. He turned and took a few backwards steps, looking at the house and clearly torn about leaving.

Paul considered dumping the sock and making another attempt at persuading PT to stay. But he had no new arguments and his idea was fuelled more by cowardice than any realistic belief in success.

As PT crunched down the gravel driveway, Paul felt himself sweating in places he barely knew he had. He found courage from somewhere, however, and when the moment came the sock belted the side of PT's skull with a horrid thunk.

'Shit!' PT yelled, as the blow and the weight of his luggage pulled him over.

Stone chips spewed up as PT landed heavily in the gravel. A streak of blood broke through his hair as he rolled on to his back, but to Paul's alarm the blow hadn't knocked him out.

'What are you doing, you little idiot?'

'You know too much,' Paul shouted back. 'Stay down or I'll whack you again.'

But PT reared up defiantly. Paul feared a beating if PT got back to his feet, but the sharp-edged stones had shredded his sock and as Paul swung a second time they burst out through a hole in the toe. A few hit PT but the big ones all missed.

'Stop it,' PT shouted. 'Do you want me to beat you up?'

PT tried standing up again, but his head swirled and a stone chip was jammed in one eye. Paul reckoned a handful of dirt in PT's other eye would even the odds, so he scooped up loose gravel and threw it hard.

As PT tried to shield his eyes, Paul kicked him in the gut. The shoe connected, but PT grabbed the flying ankle and twisted Paul's foot around. Paul crashed down into the gravel, groaning with pain as he landed on his bad arm.

Blood dripped off PT's chin as he loomed over the younger boy. Paul winced, expecting a hammering as PT's knee pinned his thighs to the ground, but as PT's fist bunched, Paul's flailing hand found a large stone and he swung upwards.

The face of the rock hit PT in the temple. Paul wriggled as PT's fist glanced off his head, but a second later PT's shoulders drooped and he listed sideways. The churning gravel had thrown up clouds of dust. Paul coughed violently and his stomach burned with pain as he sat up – but he'd finally knocked PT out.

*

There was a warm atmosphere as the quartet rode the van back towards the pink house under late afternoon sun. Rosie was exhausted after her day at the refuge, but it was a good kind of tired: the kind you get when you feel you've accomplished something.

Maxine was cheerful. She made a point of driving fast over bumps because she knew Henderson was feeling the worse for half a dozen brandies. Marc sat in the rear compartment with a German mechanic's satchel resting on his lap. It contained a reel of solder, a soldering iron and the four precious valves.

Paul was a sobbing mess as he bolted out of the pink house to meet them. He'd tried to wash up and fix the splints on his arm but hadn't done much of a job. Henderson feared the worst and pulled his gun as he jumped out the back of the truck.

'I tied him up,' Paul blurted as he led Henderson through to the kitchen.

Paul wasn't sure he'd done the right thing and feared that he'd get shouted at, so it was a huge relief when Henderson looked proudly at him.

'You reasoned all that through by yourself?' Henderson smiled. 'And he's a damn sight bigger than you.'

'So I'm not in trouble?'

'Absolutely not,' Henderson replied, as they arrived in the kitchen together. 'Sneaking away, stealing my gold. Let's see what the little bugger's got to say for himself.'

PT was sprawled over the terracotta floor with a bloody pillow under his head. Paul had bound his arms and legs with washing line and hauled him up the driveway in case his body was spotted by a passerby.

'That's Marc's bag and the suitcase he packed,' Paul explained, as he pointed towards the kitchen table. 'I wanted you to see what he'd done, so I didn't touch it.'

Henderson saw the gold ingots as Marc walked in behind. 'Traitor,' Marc spat, furious that PT had planned to steal his bag and his only spare shirt.

The two females were more rational. Rosie was torn between compassion for PT's pathetic state down on the tiles and loyalty to her distraught brother. Maxine took one look at Paul before rushing to light the wood-burning stove so that she could heat a pan of water to clean his arm and remake the filthy dressing.

'Why'd you try to leave?' Henderson bawled, as he hoisted PT off the floor and slammed him down in a dining chair. 'Guess I was a fool trusting you, eh? Stealing my gold, eh? What were you gonna do? Walk into town and try selling us out to the Gestapo?'

PT's head rolled forwards. Henderson thrust his chair up to the table to stop him flopping forwards.

'You gonna tell me straight, or would you prefer me to

thrash the truth out of you?' Henderson shouted.

A string of dried blood and snot hit the wooden table as Henderson closed up behind. The other three youngsters watched nervously from the opposite end of the table.

'I just wanted out of here,' PT explained through a bloody mouth. 'I thought we were going across to Spain. Then yesterday you started talking about spies and fixing radios and stuff. I'm not up for any of that. All I want is a quiet life.'

Henderson grabbed a handful of hair and slammed PT's head against the tabletop. 'Why should I believe you?' he bellowed scarily.

Maxine turned sharply away from the stove. 'For god's sake, Charles. He's a kid!'

'Why did you try sneaking off?' Henderson demanded. 'Why did you steal my gold?'

'The same reason that *you* carry gold,' PT sobbed indignantly. 'There are some things that only gold can pay for: including the gypsy guides who help people across the mountains and into Spain.'

'You're a liar,' Henderson snarled, keeping up the pressure even though he knew PT was right about the gypsies. 'You were going straight to the Gestapo in town. You were going to rat on us, grab a fat reward while the Gestapo tortured your supposed friends Rosie, Paul and Marc to death.'

'Bull crap!' PT shouted. 'A quiet life, that's all I wanted.'

Henderson smiled slightly. 'The thing is, PT, I can't trust you any more. I can't let you go, because you know too much, and I haven't got any prison to lock you up in. That only leaves me with one real choice, doesn't it?'

Henderson slipped the pistol out of his jacket and flipped off the safety. PT swivelled his eyes towards the gun in a state of complete terror.

'You can't kill him!' Rosie screamed.

'Why the hell shouldn't I kill the little traitor?' Henderson shouted.

Marc was torn up. He knew what Henderson was capable of and he hated that PT had betrayed them and tried to steal some of his meagre possessions, but PT had been his friend and wrestling partner for the last three weeks and that still counted for something.

'Please, Mr Henderson,' PT sobbed, as the muzzle pressed against his bloody temple. 'I haven't been into town since the *Cardiff Bay* sank. I don't know where the Germans are, or if they'd pay a reward. And believe me, I wouldn't go near the authorities. They'd be as likely to arrest me as you.'

'So why's that?' Henderson asked.

'I didn't win that money gambling,' PT explained. 'Check my notebook. It's in the brown case with a newspaper article folded up inside. That's who I really am. If you read it you'll see why I'd never go near the cops, the Gestapo, or anyone else.'

Rosie was nearest the case. She quickly found the notebook and a water-damaged sheet of newspaper folded between the pages. She unfurled it and read the headline aloud, '*Hunt for tunnel-heist boy continues.*'

Beneath the headline was a short article, and a family picture.

'They must have searched our apartment and found the photo,' PT explained. 'That's the only picture of my family I've got.'

'So you didn't win the money gambling on board a ship?' Henderson asked.

PT shook his head. 'Two cops died in that robbery and the Feds issued an international arrest warrant. If they haul my ass back to the USA I'm as good as dead. I'm on the French-police wanted list, so believe me, I'm the last person on earth who'd go anywhere near the Gestapo or the cops.'

Henderson wiped the bloody muzzle of his gun on a handkerchief before putting it back into its holster. PT gasped with relief, but Henderson shocked him by banging his head against the tabletop again.

'You're still a liar and a thief,' Henderson said. 'Maybe you wouldn't have gone to the Gestapo, but you still tried sneaking off with my gold.'

'What do you want me to say?' PT shouted desperately.

'I did what I did. If you're gonna shoot me, shoot me, you twisted old buzzard.'

'You're *damned* lucky you're not a year or two older,' Henderson snarled, as PT buried his face in his hands. 'I've killed spies, traitors, soldiers and thieves, but I've got this little twinge of conscience telling me it's wrong to blow a fifteen year old's brains across this nice old table.'

Marc and Rosie exchanged relieved glances. Maxine seemed angry at the way Henderson was behaving, but she concentrated on heating the water to clean up Paul's arm.

Henderson looked at Paul. 'Is there any more washing line about?'

Paul nodded. 'Quite a bit.'

'OK,' Henderson said, crouching down so that he was speaking right into PT's bloody earhole. 'I'm gonna take you out to the garden shed and truss you up. I'm gonna think about your situation overnight. In the morning I'll come out and let you know if there's any *possible* circumstance under which I can let you live.'

Something seemed to be on PT's lips, but he didn't say it.

'What about food and drink?' Rosie asked.

'He's getting neither,' Henderson said as he wrenched PT up by the scruff of his shirt and shoved him towards the back door. 'Little hunger and thirst might make him more cooperative over any questions I decide to ask come morning.'

CHAPTER NINE

Henderson set the broken transmitter on the dining table and unfolded a wiring diagram next to it. Paul offered to help, but Henderson was in a mood after dealing with PT and impatiently told him to clear off.

Paul spent an hour sitting in the living room reading a book about Ancient Greece while Henderson crashed about the dining room, his language getting fouler and fouler.

'My dad was a salesman for Imperial Wireless,' Paul said warily, as he stood in the dining-room doorway, studying Henderson's berry-red face. 'They had engineers, but my dad would do simple repairs himself, to keep customers happy, and I helped a few times.'

'If you're so smart, come look,' Henderson sighed. 'You can't make any more of a hash of this than I am.'

Paul moved towards the huge table. The soldering iron was plugged into the light socket above and the smell of smoke and metal stuck to the air. Henderson had replaced two of the broken valves, but had made a horrible job joining up some damaged wiring.

'That's messy,' Paul said, as he dug his thumbnail under a huge silver blob of solder and picked it away.

'I didn't say touch it,' Henderson growled.

'You won't get a good connection if you use that much solder,' Paul explained, picking more off the end of the loose electrical wire and leaning over to study the wiring diagram. 'You've put it back on the wrong terminal anyway.'

Henderson pushed Paul aside, made a careful study of the diagram and then said, 'Oh . . .'

'You'd have blown all sorts of things if you'd powered up like that,' Paul said, braving a tiny smile. 'I built a transmitter two summers ago.'

'With your dad's help?' Henderson asked.

'Some,' Paul admitted, as he pulled off another of Henderson's mis-soldered wires. 'My dad found a diagram for a simple radio and got me all the parts, but I did the work myself over the summer holidays. Except for a couple of *really* fiddly bits.'

'Quite impressive,' Henderson admitted. 'You must have only been nine back then.'

'It's not that difficult really. As long as you have a

wiring diagram and all the right parts. It's sort of like a jigsaw puzzle, except the end result is more useful than some stupid picture of kittens.'

Henderson watched as Paul lined up the wire with the correct terminal. 'I've only got one good arm, so you hold the wire and solder together and I'll make the new joint.'

Paul took the hot-tipped soldering iron off its stand, leaned awkwardly over Henderson and fused the wire to the circuit board by melting the end of the solder into a neat metal drip.

'You need enough to make a strong connection, but *never* use too much,' Paul explained, as the dot of solder hardened into a strong joint. 'My dad always said that having little fingers helps.'

'I'm sorry I snapped at you before,' Henderson said. 'When you asked if you could help, I thought you'd be sitting with your elbows on the table asking me annoying questions. I'm starting to realise that children are capable of a lot more than people give them credit for.'

Paul had felt like an outsider ever since they'd arrived at the house and Henderson's compliment meant a lot to him. 'People think I'm stupid because I never say much,' he explained. 'But I was always the cleverest in my class.'

'We live in a technological age,' Henderson said, smiling. 'Brains matter more than brawn these days.'

'I tried to tell myself that every time some bruiser pinned me to the floor in the school toilet,' Paul answered, smiling back cheekily before eyeing something inside the radio casing and zooming in to study it.

'There's your biggest problem,' Paul said, as he pointed to one of the broken valves. 'The valve mounting itself is fractured. But there's that broken radio upstairs in the master bedroom. If we took a valve casing out of there it would probably do the trick.'

Henderson leaned forwards. 'Are you sure it's cracked?'

Paul wobbled the top of the glass tube. 'You can't see the crack because of all the dust and grease, but you see how much play there is when I jiggle it? It's doing that because the insulation underneath is cracked. So it's either got to be replaced or taken out and glued. But even if we've got glue, it won't harden until tomorrow morning at the earliest.'

Henderson shook his head. 'My transmission window for today is between nine forty-five and ten.'

'What's the window for?' Paul asked.

'I have a special coded sequence. You take my codeword, the date and run it through a special formula that gives you a radio frequency and transmission time for every day of the year. Someone back in Britain should be listening out for my transmission at that time on that frequency each day.'

'Who?' Paul asked.

'It should be my assistant, Miss McAfferty. Although as I've been out of contact for a month she may have been reassigned, in which case her job will have been passed on to the MI5 monitoring centre.'

'Clever,' Paul said, nodding. 'So we've got about ninety minutes to get this set powered up.'

'How do you rate our chances?'

Paul loved the fact that Henderson was suddenly asking him for answers. 'You've already wasted an hour,' he said pointedly. 'And I can't work fast with this arm, but we can give it a go.'

*

Marc glanced up and down the hallway, before looking into the kitchen and whispering to Rosie. 'Go for it.'

Rosie grabbed a plate, then rushed to the larder. She cut a chunk off the end of a garlic sausage and peeled a few leftover strips from the previous night's roast chicken before adding an apple, a carrot and two small tomatoes.

'He'll want something to wash it down with,' Marc noted.

As Rosie poured tap water into an enamel mug, Marc opened up the back door and made sure nobody was in the garden.

'Henderson's concentrating on the radio,' Marc said, as they moved out on to the back lawn. 'It's only Maxine we have to worry about.'

Rosie gave Marc the mug to hold before she spoke. 'Maxine hasn't said much, but she clearly doesn't like the way Henderson's dealing with this.'

It was nearly eight p.m. and the sun was in their eyes as Marc led the way down the gently sloped garden towards a tatty metal shed. He turned the padlock key and the door squealed.

PT lay on his back, his head-wound caked in dry blood. His mouth was gagged, his ankles bound and his wrists hooked around a thick wooden post supporting the roof.

Marc approached warily. 'If I take this gag off, you've got to keep the noise down, OK?'

PT nodded and Marc pulled the gag down until it hung around his neck. Rosie could hardly look at the dried blood and the tears welling in PT's eyes.

'We brought you some food,' she said.

PT nodded. 'What is it, my last meal?' he asked bitterly.

Neither Marc nor Rosie could answer such a bleak question.

'I can't eat it unless you undo my hands.'

Rosie shook her head. 'I'll feed you. What do you want first?'

'Water.'

Rosie held up the mug and a good portion dribbled down PT's chin as he drank greedily.

He'd drunk nothing since Paul knocked him out

eight hours earlier and the drink re-energised him. 'Why won't you untie my hands? Or do you both think I'm a traitor too?'

'Henderson's being cautious,' Rosie explained softly.

Marc's tone was more hostile. 'Rosie talked me into coming out here, but you ripping me off like that was *way* out of order. You've got more than a thousand dollars – all I've got is that pigskin bag and a change of clothes.'

Rosie fed PT one of the tomatoes.

'I'm a thief,' PT admitted. 'If it's there, I nick it. I'm sorry to say I was brought up that way. I took the gold because I thought I might need it to get into Spain, but I didn't take all of it. I took your pigskin because I liked it . . . but you've been a mate, so I guess that was plain wrong.'

'Why'd you run, anyway?' Rosie asked.

'I don't care which side wins this stupid war,' PT said. 'I've been on the run for two and a half years, stealing from here and there, working a few weeks on a boat or unloading on the docks whenever I get bored. It's not a bad life, but I've kept out of trouble by keeping my head down and not taking stupid risks.'

'If it's OK here, why did you want to go to Spain with us?' Marc asked. 'Why did you come back here when Maxine invited you?'

'Germans give me the creeps,' PT explained. 'And

besides, the winters are warmer down in Spain and I feel like a change of scenery.'

'The Germans seem to be behaving themselves,' Rosie said. 'Maybe they're not as bad as everyone was saying.'

Marc bared his missing front tooth and glowered at her. 'Was it decent when the Gestapo ripped that out? Or when they dropped a bomb on your dad?'

'I know,' Rosie said, raising her hands defensively. 'I've got as many reasons to hate the Germans as anyone.'

'I worked a few weeks on the *Cardiff Bay*'s sister-ship late last year,' PT explained. 'A lot of passengers were Polish Jews, crossing the English Channel before heading to America. The stories they told about what the Nazis were doing were horrific. So maybe they've got reasons for treating the French OK right now, but I don't want to stick around and see if it stays that way. And when Henderson started going on about radio transmissions and undercover missions . . . That's not for me, and I decided to leave the first chance I got.'

'Henderson saved my life,' Marc said. 'He's a good guy. He proved that when he had the chance to abandon me at the port and travel on the *Cardiff Bay* with Paul and Rosie.'

'He's good to you, maybe,' PT sighed. 'You're his golden boy, after all.'

'You stole from Henderson,' Marc said sharply. 'You stole from me. It's your own stupid fault that you're sitting here all tied up and covered in blood.'

Rosie tried to lighten the mood as she fed PT the last piece of sausage and another mouthful of water. 'The thing that amazes me is my scrawny little brother knocking you out.'

PT's mouth was full, so he took a moment to answer. 'Little swine came out of nowhere.'

Marc laughed. 'Paul's *so* weedy. You're miles taller, and his legs are like little twigs!'

'Oh, well.' PT shrugged. 'If Henderson puts a bullet through my head in the morning at least I can't stay embarrassed about it for long.'

He tried to make it sound funny, but the reality of Henderson's threat pricked everyone's mood.

'He won't kill you,' Rosie said determinedly.

PT spoke bitterly. 'Henderson's a professional spy. He can't risk someone like me being on the loose and knowing his business.'

'I'll speak to him,' Marc said. 'Maybe if you apologised and offered to stay with us . . .'

PT smiled. 'And we can all eat tea and toast and live happily ever after. What planet are you from, Marc? The only way that I'm gonna live is if you guys untie me and let me escape.'

Marc and Rosie looked uneasily at one another.

'All our mucking around and stuff over the last few weeks,' Marc said. 'I thought you were a friend. But, to be honest, after you tried to steal my bag I don't trust you any more than Henderson does.'

Rosie had tears down both cheeks. 'We can't let you go, PT. But I'm going to speak to Maxine and Henderson and try to sort this out.'

'You might as well put the bullet through my head yourself,' PT yelled furiously.

'Keep your noise *down*,' Rosie ordered, as Marc grabbed PT's gag, raised it back over his mouth and tightened the knot.

'Come on,' Marc said, grabbing Rosie by the arm. 'Food and water, that's all we came here for.'

Marc worked hard to hide his feelings, but both he and Rosie were upset as they crept back towards the house.

*

Paul's soldering expertise meant they got the set powered up just before nine. Henderson's next step was to encode his message.

'How's it work?' Paul asked as he watched Henderson scribble numbers on to a pad of squared paper.

'Simple key phrase,' Henderson explained. 'It's relatively easy to decode so it's only suitable for transmissions of up to about fifty words. For instance, suppose my key phrase is *Mary had a little lamb*, and I want to send the name *Charles Henderson*. M for Mary is the thirteenth letter of the alphabet and C for Charles is the third. Three and thirteen is sixteen so I send the sixteenth letter of the alphabet in Morse code.'

'P,' Paul said. 'What if it adds up to more than twenty-six?'

'You subtract twenty-six from the total. So for example, the fourth letter of my name is R and the fourth letter of my key phrase is Y. R is the eighteenth letter of the alphabet, Y is the twenty-fifth. So I add eighteen and twenty-five, then minus twenty-six equals seventeen. So I send the letter Q.'

'So you have to do that for every single letter?'

'Every one.' Henderson nodded. 'And the message that comes back from headquarters will be encoded using a different key phrase.'

'So we won't get a response straight away?'

Henderson shook his head. 'There'll be an immediate acknowledgement if they receive our signal. I've got another transmission window on another frequency that'll be open between midnight and three a.m. for them to send a reply. If we don't get a reply tonight, I'll listen out again tomorrow.'

The pink house had steep hills rising up behind and Henderson reckoned they needed higher ground for their transmission to reach London.

Maxine found a blanket upstairs and made a flask of coffee. Paul had been through a long and stressful day, but he'd worked hard on repairing the transmitter and was keen to come along and see whether it worked. Henderson also suspected that Paul might be useful if they had trouble getting a good signal out of the transmitter.

It was a heavy device, intended to send secure transmissions from within the consulate rather than being dragged around hillsides by spies. The Germans had imposed a nine p.m. curfew on the entire occupied zone. This ruled out using the truck, or even walking on the dirt roads that led to the farms uphill.

The pair had to stay off-road. They cut through a hedge at the bottom of the garden, crossed the stream and began to ascend the hillside, which was planted with long rows of vines. At this time of year they bulged with unripened bunches of grapes.

While Henderson strained with the weight of the radio, Paul carried the Morse key, a lead acid battery, a blanket, flask and some bread and pâté. It hadn't rained in more than two weeks and the evening breeze whipped dust off the dry ground.

After a quarter-hour they were near the hilltop. At this height it was too windswept for cultivating vines and the uneven grassland was grazed by sheep, who took no notice as the pair found shelter behind a moss-covered boulder.

Paul glanced down the slope, seeing a moody orange sunset illuminating the pink house at the base of the hill. But there wasn't time to admire the landscape. They'd already hit the fifteen-minute transmission window and even if some part hadn't worked loose on the trek uphill it would take several minutes to rig up the battery and wait for the valves inside the transmitter to warm up.

Much to their relief the orange bulbs illuminating the signal gauges lit up when Henderson plugged in the Morse key.

'Nice,' Paul said, as Henderson manically tapped his coat pocket.

'Dammit,' Henderson growled. 'I've left the coded message and my pad on the dining-room table.'

Paul's mouth dropped open. 'Are you sure?' he gasped, knowing they'd never get down to the house and back up the hill before the end of the transmission window.

'Gotcha!' Henderson smiled as he pulled the notepad out of his trousers and wafted it under Paul's nose.

'Git,' Paul complained. 'You totally had me there.'

'I'm no radio operator,' Henderson said, as his hand hovered over the Bakelite knob of his Morse key. 'Read me the letters, slowly.'

'You should have got Rosie up here,' Paul said. 'She learned Morse code at Girl Guides, back in Paris. She got the highest mark in her whole troop.'

'*Now* you tell me,' Henderson said, as he pulled on a set of headphones. 'Well, here goes nothing.'

'Q,' Paul said. 'T, M, L . . .'

He carried on reading the letters as Henderson stared

intently at his Morse key, tapping out dots and dashes.

When decoded Henderson's message would read: *SERAPHIM ALIVE, BORDEAUX AREA. BLUEPRINTS LOST AT SEA. PREPARING TO LEAVE VIA SPAIN WITH COMPANIONS BUT WILLING TO ACT UPON ALTERNATIVE INSTRUCTIONS. OUT.*

Although the message was just twenty-three words long, it took Henderson more than two minutes to tap out. After waiting several minutes for someone to verify his message and encode a reply, Henderson grabbed a pencil and began jotting down the letters he heard in his earpiece.

Paul watched anxiously as Henderson used a different key phrase to decode them.

'RAU, McAfferty,' Henderson said, with obvious delight. 'She got it!'

'What's RAU?' Paul asked.

'Received and understood,' Henderson said, before squeezing Paul gently and reaching out to shake hands. 'Couldn't have done it without you. Put it there, little man.'

As Paul shook hands, he looked over Henderson's shoulder and saw a trio of curious sheep behind him.

'I hate sheep,' Paul said seriously. 'Those beady black eyes just stare at you.'

'They make a lovely Sunday lunch though,' Henderson laughed, as he spread out the blanket. 'It's two hours until our next transmission window. I'm all set up. You can go back down to the house and get some sleep if you like.'

Just thinking about sleep made Paul yawn, but he'd bonded with Henderson that evening and didn't want to go. 'I'll wait up here in case anything goes wrong with the radio.'

Henderson poured some coffee and studied the sunset for a few moments. They only had a single cup that screwed on top of the flask, and when he turned to ask Paul if he wanted some he saw the boy sprawled over the blanket with his eyes closed. He thought Paul was asleep, but one eye came open as Henderson settled on the blanket beside him.

'I think PT's basically a good guy,' Paul said. 'Don't you?'

Henderson sighed deeply. 'I don't think he was planning to snitch, but he knows all our business. It's my fault: I should have been more careful about what was said around PT, but he was getting on so well with Marc, and he's got a crush on your sister. I never thought he'd try doing a runner like that, not for a second.'

'*Please* don't kill him,' Paul said.

Henderson rested a hand on Paul's chest and stared down at the patterned squares on the blanket. 'I've done a lot of bad things in my time,' Henderson said softly.

'You can't avoid them when you work as a spy. I don't want to kill him, Paul. But the question is, what do we do with PT if I don't?'

CHAPTER TEN

Nobody slept much in the pink house that night. Rosie was up with the sun and walked a few hundred metres to a batty old neighbour who supplemented her pension by keeping chickens. She thought about stopping by the shed on the way back to give PT more water, but Henderson's bedroom overlooked the garden and his curtains were already open.

Yellow light streamed through the kitchen windows and Paul sat at the dining table, licking jam off a knife, as she placed the basket of eggs on the countertop.

'You'll turn into bread and jam one of these days,' Rosie said with a smile. 'How'd it go last night?'

'Good,' Paul answered coyly, before tearing another bite from his slice of bread. 'The radio worked. We got a response.'

'What time did you get to bed?'

'It was gone two by the time we'd lugged that blasted set down the hill, but I did doze off for a while between transmissions.'

Rosie was expecting more information. She folded her arms and scowled. 'Have I got to drag it out of you? What did their message say?'

Paul shook his head, reluctantly. He didn't like holding things back from his sister, partly out of loyalty and partly because she was inclined to thump him if he pissed her off.

'Henderson told me not to discuss the message with anyone until he'd dealt with PT.'

Rosie sighed. 'Well, was the message good news or bad news?'

Paul enjoyed knowing something his sister didn't. 'You're not gonna wheedle it out of me. And it's not really good or bad. Just interesting.'

'You want scrambled eggs on toast?' Rosie asked. 'Or are you full of bread and jam? You've pigged half a jar since yesterday.'

'Yeah, I could go for some eggs,' Paul said.

Rosie looked into the basket and tried working out how many eggs she needed to cook. 'Who else is around?'

'Marc's up and about and I heard Henderson running the shower.'

'Maxine?'

Paul shook his head. 'She stayed at her own place. I think they had a row.'

'She certainly wasn't happy with the way he treated PT,' Rosie said. 'I heard them upstairs yelling before dinner.'

Marc came in with wet hair and a bare chest. 'Morning,' he said, before spotting the basket. 'Oooh, eggies!'

Paul looked horrified as Marc cracked an eggshell on the countertop, flipped his head back and drained raw egg into his mouth.

'That's so gross!' Rosie said.

Marc poked out his tongue, which was covered in strands of yolk. 'Give us a kiss, darling!'

She picked a wooden spoon off the worktop and whacked Marc hard on the elbow. 'One step closer and you see what you get.'

'You and whose army?' Marc teased, as he lunged at her.

Rosie screamed, but the fun ended abruptly as a length of metal chain clanked down on the table behind them.

'Good morning,' Henderson said firmly. 'You all doing OK?'

'You want eggs on toast?' Rosie asked, as the two boys shrugged.

'I surely could,' Henderson said. 'Make some for PT too. I expect he'll be hungry.'

Marc smiled. 'Are you letting him off?'

Henderson rattled the chain. 'If he behaves himself, I've got a couple of options for him. Marc, I want you to go cut PT loose and bring him up here. Let him know that I've got my eye out and I'll shoot if he tries to run.'

Marc got a sharp knife from a drawer and jogged down to the shed. Rosie checked that the hotplate over the wood-fired oven was up to temperature before starting to crack the eggs into a saucepan.

'Paul tells me you got a reply last night,' Rosie said, still bursting to know. 'Was it good news?'

'I'm not going through the whole thing six times,' Henderson said. 'I'm going to deal with PT. Then we'll deal with the message and our new plans.'

'So what's the deal with the chain?' Paul asked.

Henderson had a sly way of not answering awkward questions when he didn't want to. He ignored Paul and wandered over to see if there was any hot water on the stove. 'I'll make some coffee,' he said, as he peered out towards the shed, making sure that Marc was OK.

PT came in a minute later and sat at the table. The shed was stuffy and he'd not washed since his tussle with Paul on the driveway. Dry blood caked his shirt, his head-wound had dried up into an unsightly scab and the smell of his sweat was stronger than eggs or coffee.

'Manna from heaven,' PT said, tucking in greedily as Rosie put a plate in front of him.

Marc and Paul brought their plates over to the table, but Henderson told them to eat standing up by the cabinet with Rosie.

'I *should* kill you,' Henderson said to PT. 'Letting an untrustworthy worm like you live is a risk that could lead to the slow painful death of everyone in this room – but you're not much more than a kid.'

PT glanced up from his eggs, but after his ordeal he resented Henderson and refused to show any sign of being grateful.

Henderson pointed at Paul, Rosie and Marc. 'I thought they were your friends, PT.'

PT shrugged. 'I've got nothing against any of you, just no appetite to go around spying on Nazis.'

'Two options,' Henderson said dramatically, as he raised one end of the coiled chain. 'This chain is the first. I can't let you split from us until we're a day or so ahead of you. So I'll put you upstairs, chain you to a bed and give you a knock-out pill. I'll leave some food, some water and a file.

'You'll come around after eighteen to twenty-four hours, and I reckon it'll take you another eight to ten to file your way through the wooden bedpost. By the time you set yourself free, we'll be at least a couple of hundred miles away. I'll leave you your money. You won't have the gold you might need to get into Spain, but you've got experience working on boats. If you're alone you'll be better off getting a job on a steamer heading for the Mediterranean and jumping ship.'

'I'm right off boats after the *Cardiff Bay* sank under me,' PT sighed. 'I like the idea of crossing a land border.'

Henderson scratched his head and thought for a second. 'How about if I sell you two gold ingots for six hundred dollars? The trouble is, I hear it's a nightmare getting into Spain at the moment. There's tens of thousands of refugees. The official border's closed and if you're lucky enough to find a guide to take you through the mountains there's every chance that they'll escort you up to some remote spot, steal anything worth having and push you off a cliff. Especially if you're travelling alone.'

'Sounds like a bag of laughs,' PT said, burying his face in his hands. 'Where do I sign up?'

'Must be better than me putting a bullet through the back of your head,' Henderson observed.

'What's my other option?'

'We all make bad decisions,' Henderson said. 'Especially when we're fifteen years old and on the run. I'm prepared to wipe the slate clean. You can come with us.'

'Come where?' PT asked.

'I have a very important job to do before we can leave France,' Henderson said. 'I'm not going to pretend that it doesn't involve significant danger to all of us, but at the end of the operation we'll be in an ideal position to travel back to Britain. I can't tell you any more than that without compromising the security of the plan.'

'It's not much to go on,' PT said, smiling awkwardly.

'Everything in life comes down to trust,' Henderson said. 'If you travel with us, I'm trusting you not to run off again. *You'll* have to trust that I'll look after your best interests.'

'Which option would *you* prefer?' PT asked.

Henderson shrugged. 'I honestly don't mind, although I guarantee you won't be alive to get a third chance if you betray my trust again.'

Rosie stared at PT. 'You should stick with us,' she said. 'We all look out for each other. What's so great about being off on your own?'

Marc nodded in agreement. 'I travelled to Paris alone before I met Henderson. I wouldn't recommend it. Everywhere you go there's people trying to rob you or rip you off.'

PT allowed himself to smile. He'd tried getting away because he'd baulked at the idea of Henderson being a spy. If anything, the beating and a night tied up in the shed had made him more hostile towards Henderson, but the way Rosie and Marc had sneaked out food showed that he'd made two real friends.

'People only forgive if they care about you,' PT said, finally looking Henderson in the eye. 'You've got nothing to gain by letting me live.'

Henderson smiled. 'Except a clear conscience – and the fact that Maxine and Rosie would never have spoken to me again.'

'It's lonely out there on your own,' Paul said.

'Indeed,' PT replied.

'So you're with us?' Rosie smiled.

PT liked the idea, but he wasn't ready to commit himself.

'Don't rush him,' Henderson said. 'PT needs a bath and a few hours' rest. I'd rather he took his time and made the right decision.'

Part Four

16 July 1940 – 20 July 1940

'Despite her hopeless military situation, Britain shows no sign of willingness to come to terms. I have decided to prepare, and if necessary to carry out, a sea-based invasion against her.

'The English Air Force must be reduced morally and physically so that it is unable to deliver any significant attack during the German crossing.

'Preparations for the landing operation must be completed by the middle of August.'

Adolf Hitler, 16 July 1940.

CHAPTER ELEVEN

Natural History Museum, London, UK – Intelligence Ministry wartime HQ

Eileen McAfferty stepped out of the lift and found herself in a shiny-floored basement corridor, barely wide enough for two people to pass. She was thirty-one years old, but dressed like someone older, in cardigans and floral prints. Her shoes, as always, were flat, with their tongues cut open because she was overweight and her feet swelled in the heat.

It felt desperately hot as McAfferty read the room numbers off, door after door. Some were left open to circulate the air, and sounds of chattering typewriters and telephone conversations came from inside. People swooped in and out holding folders or occasionally pushing a trolley piled with files. They all looked so purposeful that McAfferty was afraid to ask for directions.

Finally she spoke to a pencil-thin man in a three-piece suit, her accent heavily Scottish.

'Room eighty-three is to the left,' the pencil replied. 'Double doors. That's the Minister's office, you know that?'

You could see on his face that he thought someone like McAfferty had no business going into the Intelligence Minister's office.

'I'm late,' she explained. 'Signal failure on the Piccadilly line.'

'Really?' the man said unsympathetically. 'I'd hurry up, if you're late for the Minister. He's been biting people's heads off all week.'

Twenty minutes behind schedule, McAfferty found herself in the Intelligence Minister's office. It was a grim space with oak furnishings, moved from less secure offices in Whitehall. The walls were peeling and the only natural light came through a slot window near the ceiling.

'Ahh.' The man behind the desk smiled at her. 'I'll have a strong tea and a shortcake. And these gentlemen . . .'

'This is Miss McAfferty, your Lordship,' the Minister's secretary said. 'The tea lady will be along shortly.'

'Oh,' the Minister stuttered. 'Terribly sorry. I'm Lord

Hawthorne. This is Colonel Jackson, Deputy Director of Army Intelligence and Eric Mews, Deputy Minister from the Department of Economic Warfare.'

McAfferty shook the important hands and swept her skirt beneath her legs before taking a seat. Jackson and Hawthorne were establishment men, with posh accents. Mews was more common stock: a Labour Party man, with a north-east accent and an unlit pipe.

'I'm new to this intelligence malarkey,' Mews said bluntly. 'My job is to set up a new organisation known as the Special Operations Executive. I'll have to be honest with you, ducks. I've not even heard of your Espionage Research Unit and nor have quite a few people who've been in this game for a lot longer than I have.'

McAfferty nodded. 'I believe the ERU dates back to a rivalry between the Army and the Navy during the last war. The Army had a small espionage unit that concentrated on German military technology. When the Navy found out, they set up their own equivalent. The ERU had a few dozen operatives at its peak in 1918, but has rather withered on the vine since then.'

'The plan is for all branches of the intelligence service to come under a single command structure for the duration of the war,' Lord Hawthorne explained.

'That sounds sensible.' McAfferty nodded.

'So what manpower does the ERU have?'

'There's me and Betty at the office in Greenwich,'

McAfferty explained. 'Then there are three operatives. Mr Gant was injured on an operation in Norway last summer. Then there's Mr Moon who's based in Gibraltar and Mr Henderson.'

'And you run this organisation?' Colonel Jackson asked.

'Officially I'm a field assistant. But our chairman Captain Partridge suffered a stroke last summer and hasn't been back to work since.'

'And he wasn't replaced?' Hawthorne gasped. 'What the devil are the Navy playing at?'

'I'm not party to decisions at senior level,' McAfferty explained diplomatically. 'I mucked in when I returned from working with Henderson in Paris two months back.'

'Do you have much experience in espionage work?' Hawthorne asked suspiciously. 'Henderson is an important resource and an operation like this needs expert handling.'

'He's the only active British agent in France,' Colonel Jackson added. 'The Boche are planning an invasion. Any information he can provide us on German strategy will be hugely important.'

'What's your background exactly?' Hawthorne asked.

'My father worked as a riveter in the Clyde shipyards,' McAfferty replied. 'I went to my local grammar school and won a partial scholarship to Edinburgh University. I got a double first in Economics and French, then spent three years with the diplomatic service – first stationed in France, then a two-year posting in Malaya. Unfortunately, the opportunities for ladies in the diplomatic service are limited to secretarial work. I found typing tiresome so I came back to London and joined the Espionage Research Unit.'

Hawthorne pushed his chair back, clearly rather impressed. It was rare for a working man's daughter to go to university in the 1920s. Obtaining a first-class degree and joining the diplomatic service without a public-school background or family connections was positively stunning.

'Do you like intelligence work?' Colonel Jackson asked.

'Somewhat,' McAfferty admitted. 'The ERU is very small, so you get lots of responsibility. A big cog in a small machine, as they say.'

'Sounds like you're a smart lass to me,' Mews said, resting a hand on McAfferty's shoulder with a gesture that she found warm but patronising. 'There certainly doesn't seem any reason to bring some naval officer with no intelligence experience in over your head. I'll assign you rank and status in line with your role as the leader of an intelligence organisation.'

'What ranks are Henderson and Moon?' Colonel Jackson asked.

'Commander,' McAfferty said.

'You'll have to be a captain then,' Lord Hawthorne

said, before laughing aloud. 'How does that sound, Captain McAfferty?'

'Not Captain,' Colonel Jackson said. 'The equivalent rank for a Wren[5] is Superintendent.'

'Mr Henderson might not be happy,' McAfferty noted. 'I mean, I worked as his assistant. He's been in the Navy for more than ten years . . .'

'There's a war on,' Mews said firmly. 'I'm creating a new intelligence organisation from scratch and I have the power to assign civilians whatever rank they require to get their jobs done. The ERU is a naval department, so you'll receive naval rank and naval pay. I'll send the papers through for your commission and you have my number. If you need more people, larger offices or anything else, just let me know.'

'Well, I suppose,' McAfferty said warily. 'But my feet tend to swell up, so if I'm to wear a uniform, I hope the Navy has some shoes that fit comfortably.'

'Men's shoes,' Colonel Jackson suggested. 'Extra-wide fitting or something. I'm sure they'll dig up something suitable.'

Lord Hawthorne cleared his throat. 'Leaving Miss McAfferty's footwear aside for a moment, perhaps we should discuss Henderson's position in France.'

---

[5]Wren – a female member of the Royal Navy, derived from WRNS (Women's Royal Naval Service).

'Yes,' McAfferty said, stifling a smile as she marvelled at the turn her day had taken. 'Henderson has spent most of the last week laying plans for the trip north. He's arranged French papers for himself, his lady friend Maxine and six children.'

'*Six* children?' Mews said. 'Where the hell did all that lot come from?'

'I'm not certain,' McAfferty said. 'I believe he's taking two orphaned toddlers home to their grandparents, but to minimise the risk of our communications being intercepted and/or decoded, we keep messages short and only ask questions if we have to know the answer.

'They've obtained fuel for a truck and a car, and I believe they've arranged accommodation on a farm near Calais. Once they arrive, Henderson is going to scout the coastline and German military bases to find out whatever he can about the invasion plans. If possible he'll also try to sabotage them.'

'*Very* good,' Lord Hawthorne said, nodding enthusiastically. 'Although I suppose there's a limit to how much sabotaging a single agent can do.'

'What about the secondary objective?' Mews asked.

'Minister, our secondary objective is to gather information on the German occupation,' McAfferty said. 'As you of course know, the Special Operations Executive wants to start sending agents into occupied France as soon as they're trained, but we have little idea what's going on over there.

'We need basic information on everything from curfews and train times to permits, landing spots and German security measures. When Henderson leaves France, he'll bring back as much original documentation as he can muster so that SOE's forgery department can get to work making copies.'

'Well,' Lord Hawthorne said, glancing at his watch before making a sweeping gesture to indicate that the meeting was over. 'Colonel, I expect I'll be seeing you at the club this evening. Superintendent McAfferty, a huge amount is riding on Commander Henderson's operation. The future of Britain could hinge upon his ability to give us advance warning of a German invasion.'

McAfferty was overawed and her feet hurt so much that she dreaded the long walk back to the lift. She reached across the desk and shook the Minister's hand.

'Henderson is an outstanding agent,' she said. 'I have every confidence in his success.'

CHAPTER TWELVE

Northern France

Lucien Boyle was four years old. He had dark hair, serious eyes and currently stood at the roadside fifteen kilometres north-east of Abbeville, facing the side of a burned-out tank.

'Come on then,' Henderson sighed. 'What are you waiting for?'

The boy looked back over his shoulder. 'You have to undo my button,' he explained.

Henderson leaned forwards and caught an unpleasant smell. They'd been on the road for two and a half days, sleeping at the roadside or in the back of the truck. Everyone was grubby, but Lucien was the worst because he sometimes wet himself in the night.

Henderson jerked Lucien's shorts and underpants

down with a single movement. The instant the youngster's penis was exposed he blasted the tank tracks.

'Crikey,' Henderson cursed, as he flicked beads of the youngster's urine off his hand. 'Couldn't you wait two seconds?'

Lucien looked a touch upset, but Henderson staved off tears by giving him a quick kiss on the forehead. 'You're a good boy,' he said reassuringly. 'Run back to the truck.'

As Henderson unzipped to pee himself, Marc reached out the back of the truck and lifted Lucien over the rear flap. The little boy wandered to the middle of the floor and settled on a mound of pillows and cushions. His five-year-old sister Holly shoved him away.

'You stink!' she blurted. 'Get off me.'

Once Henderson was back in the cab he blasted the horn, telling Maxine to lead off in her convertible Jaguar, with the truck trundling behind. In the back of the truck, Rosie grabbed Holly and pulled her away from her brother.

'Don't even *think* about starting another fight,' Rosie said, as Holly scowled at her.

'He keeps weeing himself!' Holly said, stamping her heel on the metal floor. 'He stinks.'

'I *don't* stink,' Lucien stormed.

'Both of you, calm down,' Rosie said. 'It's not long now. We should reach the farm before dinnertime.'

Marc sat up near the rear of the truck and called Lucien over. 'Come sit with me, mate.'

Lucien was tired and grumpy. He cuddled up and closed his eyes as Marc looked out the back of the truck, awed by the carnage on all sides.

The countryside north of Abbeville had seen some of the heaviest clashes between French and German troops during the first phase of the invasion. The road had been patched up and cleared of debris, but the surrounding countryside was littered with mangled weapons. Many dead horses and humans had been piled up and cremated before they putrefied, but the blackened pyres remained and you didn't have to look too hard to spot rat-gnawed flesh rotting in ditches or between bushes.

The bombing here had a more intense focus than in the south and anything left standing had been crushed by tanks or artillery as the Germans raced westwards in their successful attempt to split France in two and cut the most powerful battalions of the French Army from their supply lines.

Marc tried to imagine what kind of hell the local people must have experienced, hiding out in fields or sheltering in basements as bombs and machines ripped their world apart.

The truck and the Jaguar drove on six more kilometres. The late afternoon sky threatened rain and they had little company, except for German military vehicles coming in the opposite direction. They eventually reached a tiny settlement that had escaped the worst of the fighting. The row of five peasant cottages appeared unoccupied, but German vehicles were parked out front and a security post manned by two armed guards stretched across the road.

The barrier marked the divide between the Somme and the Pas-de-Calais regions. The Germans wanted France back to normality and were encouraging people who'd fled south to go home and resume normal life, but the Pas-de-Calais, at the northernmost tip of the country, was an exception.

This area had been designated as a special military zone. A dozen Luftwaffe[6] bases had been constructed from which regular attacks were being launched on Britain and a huge number of soldiers had been sent in to the area for training exercises.

The Pas-de-Calais was exactly where you wanted to be if you planned to spy on German invasion plans, which is precisely why the Germans were being cautious about who got in or out.

'Out, out, out and line *up*,' a German roared, making a fair stab at the French language. 'Hands in the air. No sudden moves.'

Maxine and PT stepped out of the Jaguar, Paul and

---

[6]Luftwaffe – the German Air Force.

Henderson from the cab of the truck, while Marc and Rosie jumped off the back before helping the little ones.

Henderson had spent a week bribing and cajoling, first obtaining forged identification papers for everyone except Lucien and Holly and then taking on the much more complex business of securing paperwork required to enter the military zone.

'Monsieur Boyle,' a German grenadier[7] said, as he stood in front of Henderson inspecting his driver's licence. 'Aged thirty-two. Why are you not in military service?'

'My back was injured in a farm accident some years ago,' Henderson lied. 'My military exemption certificate is in your hand.'

'You look healthy enough to me,' the German sneered as he looked at it.

'I have good days and bad days.'

'And a very friendly doctor, no doubt,' he snorted. 'Are these all your relatives?'

Henderson nodded. 'My wife, Maxine. Paul, Rosemarie and Marc are my children. Philippe Tomas and the two little ones are my brother's children.'

'Where is your brother?'

'We've not heard – but he's a German prisoner, most

---

[7]Grenadier – the lowest rank of German soldier, equivalent to a private in the British Army.

likely. His wife died in a bomb blast during the invasion.'

Hearts thumped in the line-up in front of the truck as the officer snatched more documents from Henderson and asked him to step across to a wooden table set in the dirt alongside the barrier.

Their documentation was all filled out on stolen forms, carefully crumpled and indistinguishable from the real thing, but anyone who interrogated Henderson's 'family' for any length of time would realise that they had widely differing accents. A thorough search of the truck would reveal the radio transmitter, several guns and a variety of espionage equipment, hidden in a compartment beneath a false floor.

'You are a farmer?' the German said suspiciously, waving to attract his superior as thunder rumbled. The sun was vanishing under dark clouds.

'Is there some problem with that?' Henderson asked.

The officer was a stooped man with wisps of grey hair. He looked at the grenadier and spoke in German.

'I'll have to telephone headquarters,' he said, unaware that Henderson could understand him.

'You get back in line,' the grenadier barked as his boss disappeared into a cottage with the paperwork.

Henderson gave the others a reassuring smile as he walked back, but it didn't fool anyone.

Time passed, with Lucien and Holly fidgeting, army vehicles passing and a truck filled with labourers skimming through after a ten-second inspection of documents waved from the driver's cab. Then it started to rain.

Drizzle became a torrent, blasting the grey road in windswept sheets as trees buckled and air howled through blast-damaged cottage windows. The sky was almost black when Maxine finally stepped out of line.

'Can we put the children in the back of the truck, at least?' she asked. 'I don't want them catching a cold.'

'Back in line,' the guard yelled as he waved his rifle at her. 'I have to stand here day and night, rain or shine, in this French shithole. You can do the same.'

After nearly three hot days inside the metal-sided van, Marc found the rain refreshing. Lucien was in a playful mood after his nap and ducked beneath Marc's untucked shirt to blow a raspberry on his belly. Normally this would have been funny, but Marc was on edge and the isolated setting freaked him out.

There was nothing in any direction except for the checkpoint, the cottages and the road cutting through overgrown fields. He tried not to imagine what would happen if their true identities were unearthed, but knew that the Gestapo would subject everyone to terrible torture before they were shot.

The entire party was drenched when the officer finally came outside and waved to Henderson. 'Get in here.'

Henderson felt behind his leather belt, making sure he

could feel a small hunting knife hidden within. The two armed guards made it useless out in the open, but once inside Henderson thought he might be able to attack the officer with the knife, snatch his gun and shoot one or perhaps both of the grenadiers standing outside before they knew what had happened.

The cottage had been home to a peasant family. It had no electricity and a dirt floor. The Germans had thrown the living-room furniture into the street and the officer had taken a table from the kitchen to use as a desk. He'd lit an oil lamp because of the sudden darkness. His telephone was clearly a new addition, with its woven cable running out through the front window.

'Sit,' the officer said, as Henderson dripped on the dirt floor.

The officer's French was well below the standard of his subordinate. 'I phone Calais and they say no. Where you get documents?'

'Bordeaux. I was assured—'

'You have permits correct,' the officer interrupted. 'But your reason for entry says *Farmer*. That is not sufficient to enter military zone.'

Henderson cursed in his head, though it was tempered with relief because his worst fear was that he'd been recognised as a spy.

'You have to go back.'

Henderson sighed. 'But I received these documents

from the office in Bordeaux. They were sealed by a major and I was assured that everything was in order before I set off. Is there someone else I can speak to at the office in Calais or something—'

The German raised up his hands. 'Stop!' he said dramatically. 'You speak *much* too fast. My French is not good.'

Henderson knew he'd need all of his persuasive skills so, to the officer's surprise, he explained again in German, deliberately adding a strong French accent.

'You speak my language well.' The officer smiled. 'Where did you learn?'

'I worked as a salesman for a German company before I returned to the family farm,' Henderson explained.

For some reason the officer found this hugely amusing. When he stopped laughing he gave Henderson another smile and picked up the telephone again.

'We have a lot of Germans, a lot of French and nobody understands each other,' the officer explained. 'Hold on, I'll phone Calais again.'

The cottage was warm and Henderson's wet clothes stuck to his skin as the German explained that he'd unearthed a local farmer who spoke fluent German. Henderson worried that this ability might raise suspicions, but after a few sentences the German put the telephone down.

He took Henderson's travel permit, crossed out the

word *Farmer*, wrote *Translator* in its place, belted it with a rubber stamp and scribbled in a set of initials.

'You can drive to your farm,' the officer said. 'Tomorrow morning you must arrive in Calais before ten a.m. Find the German headquarters and report to the Office of Translation for a skills assessment.'

Henderson realised that this was an order rather than a request. A translation post would bring him into close proximity with German operations and was a stroke of luck, but no farmer would be happy at being taken off his land, so he made a fuss.

'I've been away for five weeks,' Henderson said. 'My land will be in a poor state. We need to rescue as many crops as we can before winter.'

The German's lips thinned. 'You have a wife and three boys,' he said impatiently. 'They can work the land. You're lucky to be getting into the military zone at all!'

'Of course, sir,' Henderson said. 'I didn't mean to seem ungrateful.'

'And now I've phoned Calais. The office will be expecting you, so make sure you arrive – or you'll be arrested and punished.'

Henderson offered his hand.

'Soft hands, for a farmer,' the officer noted, as he shook.

CHAPTER THIRTEEN

It was possible to walk around Bordeaux for half a day without sighting a German patrol. By contrast, the countryside between the ports of Calais and Boulogne bristled with German trucks and Kübelwagens[8]. At one point a curve in the road unveiled an entire hillside with hungry French soldiers dotted over it like grazing sheep. Less than a dozen bored-looking Germans kept them in place, but the prisoners didn't bother escaping because they expected to be sent home within weeks.

The truck and Jaguar's destination was a rural spot near the coast a few kilometres south-west of Calais. This last stretch of a seven-hundred-kilometre journey dragged, with a break to top up Maxine's Jag from the

[8]Kübelwagens – open-topped German cars, similar to American Jeeps or British Land Rovers.

last can of petrol and a second security stop.

Lucien and Holly Boyle grew hugely excited when they recognised their home village, then turned through the gates of a small country house with an eccentric brick turret at one end.

'Nanny, Granddad!' Holly squealed, as an old man lifted her off the back of the truck.

Marc and Rosie basked in the emotional reunion as they dropped on to the driveway and walked off the stiffness from a day cooped up.

'Mummy died in a bomb,' Holly explained anxiously, as she nuzzled her grandfather's neck.

Luc Boyle welled up as he hugged his granddaughter. His wife Vivien squeezed Lucien and kissed his grubby face. The couple were in their late fifties and wore typical peasant clothing, but small touches such as Luc's Swiss watch and his wife's soft shoes betrayed the fact that they owned land, rather than working it themselves.

'I thought I might never see you two again,' Vivien sniffed. 'We *finally* had a card in the post yesterday. Your daddy is being held prisoner in Lille, but he's safe at least.'

As they ran into the house, Lucien hugged a fat servant before roughhousing with the Boyles' youngest son, a sixteen-year-old named Dumont.

The party from Bordeaux took turns bathing in the house's impressively large tub while one of the Boyles' servants scrubbed their filthy clothes. Vivien pulled a half lamb from her oven and served up a meal extraordinary in both quantity and quality. Wine flowed and the adults turned a blind eye as Marc, PT and Dumont competed to drink as much as possible.

When everyone was stuffed the kids went into the back garden to enjoy the last of the sun. Lucien and Holly chased around, Paul and Rosie pushed them on a rope swing, while the three older boys crashed out on the lawn.

While the kids mucked around, Henderson and Maxine went into the drawing room and discussed more serious matters with Vivien and Luc over brandy.

Luc puffed on a small cigar as he quizzed Henderson about his life and his family. Henderson was the worse for half a bottle of wine, but still had to remember details of a complicated back story that tangled fact and fiction.

The truth was that after identifying a list of lost children from the Pas-de-Calais region using Maxine's missing-person records, Henderson selected Lucien and Holly because documents found on their mother's body showed that they came from a village situated between the ports of Calais and Boulogne that would be ideal for spying on a German invasion of England.

He'd also found a diary containing a telephone number for the dead woman's parents-in-law. This not only made communications easier, but indicated that they were wealthy and likely to be in a position to help him out.

Over the course of several phone calls, Henderson had explained his position and thrashed out a deal with Luc Boyle. Henderson had told Luc that with so many refugees marooned in southern France there was no work and he needed a job to feed his four children.

He'd heard that there was plenty of work in the north for those who could get there and said he could obtain the paperwork required to enter the military zone. Henderson offered to bring Boyle's two grandchildren home. In exchange Boyle would provide Henderson with a few months' free accommodation on a farm.

'There's one minor detail I couldn't discuss on the telephone,' Henderson said awkwardly, as Vivien poured him another cognac. 'My German contact told me that it would be easiest if we all travelled under one name. So my name and that of my family is now Boyle. It will be best if you tell the locals that I'm a distant cousin, or something.'

Vivien raised an eyebrow as she passed back Henderson's glass. 'Even people who've lived here their whole lives can't get back into the area,' she explained. 'So people are sure to ask where you've come from.'

'The Boche are short of translators,' Luc said. 'It's *remarkably* lucky that you turned out to speak such excellent German.'

Henderson knew that the presumption of using his family name was likely to stick in Luc Boyle's throat and the couple clearly sensed that there was more to Henderson than met the eye, but they were ecstatic at the safe return of their grandchildren and apparently happy to let the matter slide. At least, for the time being.

*

Marc woke on a bare mattress in a musty room with sunlight shining through a crack in the roof and a puddle in the far corner. A burp sent acid surging up his throat and for a horrible instant he thought he was going to puke over his blanket.

His head thudded as he looked around and saw PT's boots on the floor beside him. Marc remembered the wine and a bumpy midnight ride in the back of the truck, but had no recollection of the building in which he'd awoken.

If anything, the holey-roofed bedroom was a high point of the cottage. Green stalactites of mildew hung from the ceiling in the cramped hallway and damp seemed to be consuming the building from within. A step and a door that scraped along the floor because the top hinge had rotted loose led into a kitchen.

'Eggs?' Rosie asked brightly, as she thrust a sizzling pan in his face.

'Get off,' Marc groaned, clutching a hand over his mouth before scrambling past PT and Paul and running out the back door where he spewed red vomit over a honeysuckle bush.

PT yelled through the open door, 'Dirty beast.'

'Poor lamb,' Maxine said sarcastically, stepping out into the fresh air behind Marc. She'd swapped her usual stockings and smart blouses for rubber boots and an overall. 'Looks like someone can't handle their wine.'

Marc's only reply was a desperate, 'Oh god,' as he leaned forwards and threw up for a second time.

Rosie was more sympathetic and passed out a glass of tap water for him to wash his mouth with.

'Why didn't someone stop me drinking?' Marc groaned, as he staggered back indoors, clutching at his aching sides.

'If you're stupid enough to try out-drinking a sixteen year old who's twice your size, you can deal with the consequences,' Maxine said.

Marc looked up at the rotting roof beams, tattered chairs and rusted kitchen range. 'How did we end up in this crap-hole?' he asked.

'You should have seen Henderson's face when we arrived here last night,' PT said, grinning. 'He was raving, saying that Luc Boyle was a lying bastard and all sorts. There's no electric and the farm buildings are in an even worse state than this heap.'

'It'll clean up well enough,' Maxine said optimistically, as Rosie dished eggs for Paul and PT which made Marc heave again. 'And we're well out of harm's way.'

'Where is Henderson?' Marc asked.

'He's taken the bike into Calais to meet with the Germans,' Maxine explained.

'How far's that?'

'About thirteen kilometres,' Maxine answered. 'But there's no petrol left for the Jag and turning up in a lorry might look peculiar.'

'We'd better get the roof fixed in that bedroom,' Marc said. 'Judging by the size of the hole, me and PT might drown in our sleep if it rains again.'

'I've made a list,' Maxine announced. 'Rosie and I are going to scrub this rotten house top to bottom and then unpack everything from the truck. PT said he saw some sheets of metal in the back courtyard and he'll try patching the roof. Charles wants to transmit this evening, so Paul's job is to unpack the radio and find a good spot for a transmission. Which leaves Marc to deal with the animals.'

Marc looked slightly stunned. 'What animals?'

Maxine smiled. 'According to Luc Boyle, this land was abandoned three months back and it hasn't been worked properly since the tenant farmer and his son got conscripted into the army almost a year ago. Now, I'm led to believe that you're our resident farming expert.'

Marc baulked. 'I did some labouring for a farmer when I lived at the orphanage, but I'm no expert. I spent a few months working in the fields before I got assigned to mucking out cows.'

'I told you he understood cows,' Rosie said brightly. 'You can go and sort out Muriel and Sarah.'

'Please,' Marc begged. 'Anything but dirty stinking cows. All they're good for is eating and shitting. And how do you know their names?'

'I don't,' Rosie said. 'I named them this morning when I went out for a look around.'

'Besides, I'm not an expert.'

'You might not know much,' Maxine said, 'but I've never set foot on a farm, Charles certainly hasn't and PT, Paul and Rosie are all city kids. So you're an expert compared to any of us.'

'Why bother anyway?' Marc said. 'Henderson and PT have got loads of money. We can just buy food.'

'We're supposed to be a poor family living on a farm, you idiot,' Rosie said. 'How suspicious is it going to seem to the locals if we leave the land to grow wild and start splashing money around?'

Marc ate half a slice of bread and sipped at a cup of cold water before Maxine drove him out to work by slamming doors and deliberately banging metal pots around as she cleared out the kitchen cupboards.

His first proper look at the farm was a shock. Marc had worked with a farmer called Morel when he lived at the orphanage and was used to neat barns and carefully tended crops. Here, all he could see in every direction was backbreaking work: two fields up to his neck with stinging nettles, a rusted hand-plough, a well with no bucket and a shed-over-a-hole toilet set in a bog filled with buzzing flies.

Animals had been released to fend for themselves when the tenants left three months earlier. The chicken cages were crusted in lime and the overgrown grass around them was strewn with feathers where hens had fallen prey to foxes. There was a goat pen, but no signs of life within, and two pathetic cows fenced inside the field furthest from the house.

As Marc walked an overgrown footpath towards the cows he caught the familiar smell of manure and was surprised to find that this infused his head with an odd nostalgia for the days he'd spent on Morel's farm near Beauvais. In particular he remembered Jae Morel, the farmer's good-looking daughter, who'd been the closest thing he'd ever had to a girlfriend – until he accidentally knocked her into a manure pit.

The cowshed was large enough for eight animals, but the better stock had either been sold off before the owners left or pilfered afterwards. Of the pair that remained one was a calf with a deformed back leg that Marc guessed was six to eight months old. Its mother appeared in reasonable health, except for a tick infection that left raw patches on her coat.

Marc crouched down to inspect the older beast's udder and saw that she was still producing milk for her calf. He found a pot inside the cowshed, washed it out in a trough overflowing with the previous day's rainwater, then nervously approached, patting the cow's side to gauge whether she was comfortable with his presence before going down on one knee and inspecting the udders for any sign of infection.

As the cow hadn't been milked for some time there was a chance of a violent reaction, but Marc moved his hand gently down the teat and a blast of warm, creamy milk hit the bottom of the pan.

'Good girl,' Marc said soothingly, stroking the cow's side as she mooed.

CHAPTER FOURTEEN

After six days on the farm the fake family had established a routine. Henderson complained to Vivien and Luc Boyle about the state of the farm, which pressured the couple into action. They arranged for a local handyman to do some repairs on the cottage, donated a goat, some chickens and a third cow.

The land was still a mess, but the cottage was now sealed from the rain, while warm weather and fanatical ventilation were gradually clearing the stench of damp and mildew. The previous tenants had sown a vegetable patch and two fields of potatoes in the spring and, while the crops had been neglected, there were still enough vegetables for a family to get by on.

The chickens gave eggs and Marc had cleaned out the cowshed and got the two adult cows into a regular milking schedule. He felt proud because they were the first things he'd ever been entirely responsible for.

On weekdays Henderson left at seven and rode into Calais, where he worked as a translator at German headquarters. Maxine and the kids did small jobs around the farm each morning, though their lack of expertise meant that they concentrated on tidying up rather than any serious attempt to clear the overgrown land and bring the farm back to full-scale production.

The local schools had closed before the invasion and because there were few pupils and even fewer teachers they showed no signs of reopening. So after making lunch Maxine would set the kids free. Paul liked to wander off on his own, with a large pad and a tin of coloured pencils and pastels that Henderson had bought from a Calais pawnbroker.

Paul had lived in Paris all his life and he was fascinated by the coast. There was a stretch of pebble beach a few minutes' walk from the farm and a craggy expanse of white stone behind it. He liked to sit alone and draw, but he liked it more when the Germans arrived.

They came in convoys of open trucks, formed lines and did light physical training exercises before stripping to their shorts and heading down to the sea. Paul buried himself behind rocks, and sketched the men.

He'd always thought of the German Army as a mighty force packed with muscle-bound brutes, but stripped of boots and guns they reminded him of a school gym lesson. Confident bodies threw themselves at the waves, while big men with flabby arms looked embarrassed and skinny ones who didn't like walking on the pebbles hobbled.

Paul drew men quickly, in a few rapid strokes, trying to capture expressions and postures of the sea-front drama. A non-swimmer was dragged out yelling and screaming as his mates on the shore jeered. They yelled phrases that Paul didn't understand; their bullying tone matched that of boys who'd pushed him around at school in Paris.

Paul found it depressing to think that when he finally escaped from education, he was sure to be conscripted into the military and would have to put up with the same bullying crap all over again. As Paul wallowed in this train of thought he failed to hear the German officer clambering over the white rocks in the blind spot on his left.

The first he knew was when a boot crunched a few metres from his face, sending chalkstone clattering down the shallow cliff-face. The officer was a good-looking man, with a square jaw and spindly fingers.

Fearing a slap or kick, Paul dropped his pad and covered his head.

'Don't be scared.' The officer smiled, speaking in decent French, 'I see you have the sling off your arm today.'

Paul was shocked. He thought he'd been invisible, but the German had clearly seen him before.

'Max— Er, my mother took the splints off last night,' Paul explained warily, as he held out a lower arm with a distinct kink in it. 'It hasn't set straight, but luckily I draw with my left hand.'

'Like me,' the German said, still smiling. 'I'm left-handed, but every time I took the pen with my left at school the teacher would rap me on the knuckles.'

'Same with me.' Paul nodded, feeling more comfortable now it was clear that he wasn't in trouble. 'It's really stupid. What difference does it make if you write with your left hand?'

'Beats me.' The officer shrugged. 'So what do you think of today's swimmers?'

Paul sat up on the rocks as he answered. 'They're not as good as the ones you had here last week.'

'That's an understatement,' the officer laughed. 'They're a mountain battalion. Half of them can't swim and most have never seen the sea before.'

Paul couldn't think what to say in reply and there was a brief silence before the officer bent over and took Paul's pad. He burst into laughter as he saw the sketches of men struggling in the water and doing their exercises.

'These are really good,' the officer said. 'You really capture their . . . I don't know the French word. The *sense* in their body.'

Paul enjoyed the compliment. 'Their emotions,' he smiled.

'Yes,' the officer said, nodding as he began flicking through the pad. 'Emotions. It's *very* clever how you convey so much with just a few lines. And I see that you work well in other styles too.'

Paul cringed as the German turned the spiral-bound pages. He hated people looking at his drawings because he sometimes liked to draw really dark stuff like dead bodies or people being eaten by giant bugs. But the German held the pad open at a pastel drawing of Rosie, depicted with a hammer in her hand as she helped PT to repair the cottage roof.

'Is that your girlfriend?' the officer asked teasingly.

Paul shook his head. 'My sister.'

'You draw beautifully,' the officer said as he reached into his pocket and pulled out a small bar of chocolate. 'Here. I have plenty.'

Paul had a sweet tooth and was a huge fan of chocolate. This was the first he'd seen since leaving Paris a month earlier, so he snatched it keenly. 'Thank you *so* much, sir.'

'I've seen you up here several times,' the officer said, as he passed back the pad and took his wallet from inside his coat, 'but I had no idea that I was in the presence of such a talent. Have you ever tried drawing from a photograph?'

Paul nodded. 'It's not as good as real life, but I used to do it all the time. When I was little I used to draw cars and aeroplanes from pictures in magazines, but I mostly draw people and animals now. They're more interesting for some reason.'

The German took a photograph from his wallet. 'My wife, daughter and I. If I gave you this could you make a small drawing of it?'

Paul liked being free to draw whatever he fancied, but he was intimidated by the tall officer and grateful for the chocolate.

'You don't look sure,' the officer said. 'But you do like chocolate, yes?'

'The only thing better than chocolate is bread and jam.'

'OK,' the officer said, laughing. 'In our storeroom we have boxes of good Belgian chocolate. Twenty-four bars in each box. If I gave you one of those would you draw my family from this photograph?'

'We're almost out of jam,' Paul said. 'Do you have jars of jam?'

The officer held his hands about thirty centimetres apart. 'The army gets it in cans about this size. Mixed berry or apricot.'

'I'll draw your picture for a can of mixed berry,' Paul said, smiling.

'Deal,' the German said, as he passed over the

photograph. 'It's my only picture of them, so be sure you don't lose it.'

*

Henderson was in decent shape but the Germans seldom let him off work much before seven and the thirteen-kilometre ride home along the coast road was no fun when he was tired. Waves crashed and occasional gusts sent his bike wavering dangerously close to military vehicles. The German drivers ignored speed limits and knew they'd face little more than a rebuke if they squished a French cyclist.

Halfway between Calais and home, the Germans had set up a snap checkpoint. These cropped up at random locations throughout the region and comprised two cars or two trucks parked on opposite sides of the road and anywhere between three and six soldiers.

This was the third checkpoint Henderson had encountered in the six days since they'd arrived in the north. French traffic queued, while Germans were waved through. The wait varied, depending upon the level of traffic and how methodical the soldiers were, but even a ten-minute delay was irritating at the end of a ten-hour shift.

The Germans had forbidden the sale of petrol to Frenchmen, effectively banning private vehicles in the process. The queue comprised a single farm tractor, eight bicycles and a similar number on foot. The soldier inspecting documents spoke less than a dozen words of French, but took great pains over each piece of paper and held it up to the sun, presumably to check for some mysterious sign that it was a forgery.

Although the Germans were on the lookout for spies, their everyday targets were French soldiers who'd escaped from the weakly guarded prisons. As a result, men got a harder time than women and men of military age such as Henderson could expect a thorough grilling.

After a fifteen-minute wait, during which less than half the queue in front of Henderson disappeared, a Mercedes limousine with a Nazi flag at the end of its long bonnet drew up alongside. Henderson got the horrible feeling that he was being called back to translate at some ghastly late-night meeting, but instead the back door was thrown open revealing Oberst[9] Ohlsen, the Deputy Commander of the Pas-de-Calais region.

'Mr Boyle,' the Oberst said warmly. 'Perhaps I can offer you a short cut?'

Henderson nodded as he recognised the balding Oberst. He'd met him the previous Friday whilst translating at a meeting with a director of the French railways.

The Oberst thumped on the glass panel that separated the passenger compartment and ordered his driver to

---

[9]Oberst – a high-ranking German officer.

strap Henderson's bike to the rear of the car. Henderson walked around to help the driver, but the Oberst ordered him brusquely inside the car.

The vehicle's interior was panelled in walnut, with two comfortable chairs at the back and two pull-down seats facing the other way. Henderson settled in next to the Oberst, separated by a leather arm rest which flipped open to reveal two crystal decanters and a row of tumblers.

'Drink?' the Oberst asked.

Henderson was thirsty after a six-kilometre bike ride and needed cold water more than whisky or wine, but an opportunity to socialise with such a senior officer was a rarity so Henderson accepted a glass of red.

'Heading home, Mr Boyle?' the Oberst asked.

Henderson nodded. 'A long day,' he said. 'At least my wife will have a meal ready.'

The driver pulled away and the engine of the huge limousine was so remote from the back seats that they could hear the click of German heels as the soldiers on the checkpoint saluted their deputy commander.

'I envy you home cooking,' the Oberst said. 'It's four months since I saw my wife.'

This comment made Henderson feel guilty. It had been more than four months since he'd seen his real wife back in England, and Maxine wasn't the first woman he'd slept with during the interlude.

'This beats the bike.' Henderson smiled, spreading himself over the padded leather as the German raised his glass and made a toast.

'Cooperation,' the German said, and Henderson copied him.

'It is actually a pleasant surprise to bump into you, Mr Boyle,' the Oberst said. 'Your translation at the meeting on Friday was immaculate and I've found that a good translator can make my life a lot easier.'

'Thank you, sir,' Henderson said.

'I've received orders from General Rufus today. He's put me in charge of the overall planning for Operation Sea-lion.'

Henderson had nosed around and picked up details from documents he shouldn't have seen, but he pretended to be mystified. 'Sea-lion, Herr Oberst?'

'The operation to invade England,' Ohlsen explained. 'The logistics are fearsome: eleven battalions, twenty thousand horses, eighteen thousand tanks, artillery pieces and god knows how many vehicles have to be transported across the English Channel on barges. The battle between the Luftwaffe and the Royal Air Force is going in our favour and Berlin demands that we're ready to invade as soon as we control the skies.'

'A task you can really sink your teeth into,' Henderson said, as he wondered whether to ask a bold question. 'Is there a target date set for the invasion?'

The Oberst smiled. 'There's no firm date, but once the destruction of the Royal Air Force is complete, the die will be cast.'

'Before winter, I assume,' Henderson said.

'Of course.' The Oberst nodded. 'You need daylight and good weather for this kind of operation. It has to be before the end of September. Otherwise we'll have to wait until next spring and who knows what fortifications the British will have built by then?'

'Absolutely,' Henderson agreed, as he drained the last of his wine.

'Another?' the German asked, but Henderson shook his head and the Oberst continued. 'Anyhow, Mr Boyle, getting back to your excellent translation services. I actually dictated a memo to the translation department earlier today, requesting that you be permanently assigned to my office. Operation Sea-lion has absolute priority, which means that I'll need a highly capable translator, rather than whatever incompetent the translation department decides to assign me.'

'Well, Herr Oberst,' Henderson smiled, 'I'm flattered.'

*

Henderson kissed Maxine as he waltzed into the kitchen whistling the hymn *All Things Bright and Beautiful*.

'You're late,' Maxine said. 'So – why the good mood?'

'Oh, you won't believe.' Henderson smiled, as he nodded to Paul and Rosie who sat at the table. 'Short of a direct order from the Führer's office in Berlin, putting me in personal command of the German invasion of Britain, I couldn't be in a better position to steal information.'

'How did that happen?' Maxine asked, as she opened the oven and took out the remains of a sausage casserole.

'You're now looking at the personal translator to Oberst Günter Ohlsen, who is in overall command of the invasion planning for the entire Pas-de-Calais region.'

Rosie looked at her brother. 'That sounds even better than Paul scoring the big tin of jam from that Boche on the beach.'

Henderson sat at the head of the table and was so excited by his stroke of luck that he barely thought as he scooped a huge mouthful of sausage and potato into his mouth.

'Hot!' he yelled, as he spat the food back into the bowl. 'Holy Mary mother of god! Maxine, get me some water!'

'Fool,' Maxine laughed, handing Henderson a cup of cold water as Paul and Rosie killed themselves laughing. 'You watched me pull it out of the oven half a minute ago. Were you expecting it to be cold?'

Once he'd guzzled water and taken a couple more cautious mouthfuls of casserole, Rosie spoke seriously.

'It's quarter to eight,' she explained. 'Tonight's transmission window is eight-fifteen to eight-thirty, so if you've got a message for McAfferty I'd better start encoding now.'

Henderson slid a small document pouch across the table. 'It's not much,' he said. 'At least not compared to the kind of information I'll get when I start working for the Oberst's office. It's information on barge movements and more delays getting the railway lines into the docks at Boulogne repaired.'

Rosie had developed a knack for encoding. To minimise the risk of their radio signal being detected, she had to pack all the information Henderson gathered into the shortest message possible and then convert it into the code using Henderson's key phrase.

'I practised my Morse code again this afternoon,' Rosie said proudly, as she scanned the documents and began making notes with a pencil. 'I'm up to twenty-two words a minute.'

'Excellent,' Henderson said. 'Just remember that accuracy is the most important thing when you're transmitting in code. You only have to miss one letter and the poor soul unravelling the message will have the devil's own job setting things straight.'

'I know.' Rosie nodded. 'I was thinking, actually. Seeing as you're always tired and you have to get up halfway through the night to listen out during the reply window, maybe you could take a rest after your meal tonight. Paul and I can easily handle the transmission.'

Henderson considered this over a mouthful of potato. Paul knew more about the workings of the radio than he did and Rosie was better at sending Morse code, plus he *was* tired after his long day working in Calais.

'I'd be grateful for that,' Henderson said. 'I could do with an early night. But remember what I taught you. Transmission is the riskiest part of this operation. We've got no clue if the Germans have radio-detection teams working in this area, or how good they are at their jobs if they do. One of you has to sit outside and keep lookout during transmission and if you're even *slightly* suspicious you abandon the receiver and run. Is that understood?'

'Absolutely.' Rosie nodded.

Paul nodded too, but he felt uneasy because he'd be the lookout and he recalled how effortlessly the German officer had managed to sneak up on him at the beach earlier in the day.

'I'd be even happier if Marc or PT went with you,' Henderson said. 'Two sets of eyes are better than one.'

But Maxine shook her head. 'They went out after dinner with Luc's son Dumont.'

'Really,' Henderson said suspiciously. 'What are they up to?'

'Hunting rabbits with a catapult,' Paul explained. 'They brought two back with them this afternoon and Dumont showed us how to skin them.'

Maxine shuddered. 'It was horrible,' she said. 'I felt

queasy when I saw the blood on the floor of the barn.'

Henderson laughed. 'Well sweetheart, if you want to eat an animal you've got to kill it.' But his tone got more serious as he looked out the window, 'Mind you, I can't see how they're hunting rabbits in this light. You can barely see out there.'

'It's going to rain,' Maxine added. 'I just hope they muster the sense to get indoors before it starts to pour.'

CHAPTER FIFTEEN

Dumont was a chunky sixteen year old. He was light in the brains department, but PT and Marc thought he was a laugh and he knew a lot about hunting and fishing.

With so many people unable to re-enter the military zone the boys had free run over hundreds of abandoned farms. The former tenants were poor, but Dumont claimed to have broken in and stolen all kinds of valuables they'd left behind.

But Dumont claimed all kinds of things, and the only houses he took Marc and PT into contained nothing more valuable than tools and bottles of wine. When they got bored of hunting and burgling they threw stones through windows and Dumont got annoyed because Marc was a much better shot.

PT enjoyed learning about the countryside, but he'd

survived on his own wits for more than two years and found Dumont's bragging and destructive appetites childish. Marc had less reservation. After growing up in the regulated environment of an orphanage he prized nothing more than freedom.

Whilst Marc's conscience told him that some day people would come home to find busted doors and wine bottles smashed against their walls, he loved the sense of power you got roaming around the empty buildings doing whatever the hell you liked.

It was turning dark as the trio sat on a low wall in the heart of the village. There was a duck pond set in a square, but two shops and a post office were boarded up and the grass on the lawn around the pond was up to knee height. Apart from the wind, the only noise came from a small but lively crew of German soldiers sitting outside a bar across the square.

They were young intellectuals, ranging from late teens to early twenties and from grenadiers to junior officers. They drank wine and smoked cigarettes while they discussed arts and politics and teased each other about their love lives. The bar served good food and they enjoyed the fact that they'd found a secluded spot, away from boorish colleagues who preferred to down half a dozen beers and start throwing punches.

The boys had walked ten kilometres since they'd met up early that afternoon, so their feet ached and they were all hungry, but while the village was only a couple of hundred metres from Dumont's house, PT and Marc faced a three-kilometre trek back to the farm.

'You reckon your dad would give us a lift?' Marc asked.

'No hope,' Dumont laughed. 'He's only got half a tank of petrol so I reckon his car's gonna rust before he uses it again.'

'We'd better shift then,' PT said, looking up at the sky before turning to Marc. 'We're gonna get drenched and I'm *starving*.'

'My mum gets pissed off if we let our dinner sit in the oven,' Marc added.

Dumont fought with his dad and never wanted to go home. 'C'mon,' he said. 'Stop being such mummy's boys. It's like, barely eight o'clock.'

'*We're* mummy's boys?' Marc said incredulously. 'You still hold your mummy's hand when you cross the road.'

PT smiled. 'She still holds his dick when he takes a piss.'

'Screw you,' Dumont said, as he jumped off the wall. 'You two don't know shit. You both practically turned green when I slit the innards out of that bunny.'

Marc tutted. 'At least we don't chuck the shits over drinking a few glasses of wine.'

'I told you I can't help that,' Dumont moaned. 'Wine disagrees with my stomach.'

PT imitated Dumont's voice. '*Wine disagrees with my*

sto-mach. Boo hoo, you big fanny. You're all talk, all mouth. I've been listening to you talk bull since lunchtime and I'm going home for some grub and to give my eardrums a break.'

Dumont looked offended. '*I'm* all mouth? What have you two peckers ever done?'

'More than you,' Marc said, as he started walking after PT. 'Catch you around some time tomorrow, I expect.'

'Have you still got them American dollars?' Dumont asked.

'What's it to you if I have?' PT asked back.

'Green open-topped Boche car,' Dumont said, as he pointed. 'Parked over beside the bar. You see it?'

'So what?' Marc said.

'I'll go over there, pull out my cock and piss all over the inside if you give me a ten-dollar bill.'

Marc found the idea hilarious, but PT didn't like trouble and wasn't having it. 'Don't be stupid. If they catch you they'll crack your skull open.'

'You just don't want to cough up ten dollars,' Dumont sneered. 'Because you *know* I'll do it.'

'You're an idiot,' PT said. 'I'm going home.'

'I guess that shows who's really all mouth,' Dumont said. 'Tell you what, *forget* your money, I'm gonna do it anyway.'

PT grabbed Marc's arm as Dumont charged through the long grass and skirted the duck pond. 'He's such an 'idiot,' PT said. 'Let's get out of here.'

'He'll chicken out,' Marc said with certainty.

PT started walking, but despite his better instincts part of him wanted to know if Dumont really would do it. So Marc and PT dived behind the wall and peered through cracks in the brickwork.

'Bugger me,' Marc gasped, as Dumont reached the side of the bar and stood alongside the open car.

Dumont pulled down the front of his trousers and aimed a powerful yellow streak inside the open-topped car. He started off peeing in the back, then took a step and urinated over the driver's seat and steering wheel before giving the inside of the windscreen a wash down.

'What an *idiot*,' Marc laughed, as Dumont buttoned up and disappeared into trees behind the car.

'Come on,' PT said, as he tugged Marc's arm. 'They won't be happy when they find out.'

*

There was a heavy military presence in the Pas-de-Calais region. As well as roadside checkpoints Henderson had learned that the Germans sent random search squads into the countryside. Their main aim was to hunt down the escaped prisoners and guns that posters in every village promised would lead to a death sentence for those who harboured them.

The bulky radio transmitter was impossible to hide in the small cottage, so Henderson had stashed it on the upper deck of a barn on an unoccupied neighbouring farm.

It was dark by the time Rosie completed a four-minute transmission to London and received McAfferty's acknowledgement. After covering the radio with heavy tent fabric and mounding it over with straw, she grabbed the handle of her oil lantern and climbed down the ladder, carefully skipping the broken fourth rung.

Paul heard her coming down and leaned inside the barn door. 'All good?' he whispered.

'Good.' She nodded as she picked up the heavy ladder and placed it in a precise spot, leaning against the side of the barn.

This was one of several security measures devised by Henderson. The ladder was always put in a specific spot so that you'd realise if anyone had moved it to climb into the loft. Two garden rakes were placed inside the door ready to flick any unwary intruder in the face, and a small piece of slate wedged in the doorway would drop out if the door was opened. Finally they watered the ground around the entrance so that the soft mud would register the boot prints of anyone who came by.

Paul jammed the slate into the bottom of the door frame and hopped across to dry ground before levelling the mud with a spade.

It was a remote area and, with the surrounding farms unoccupied, it was pitch black with nothing but natural sounds around them. After tossing the spade, Paul followed his sister into the long grass and spoke thoughtfully.

'I've been thinking,' he said. 'What will we do if the Germans invade Britain? I mean, we'll have nowhere left to go.'

Rosie walked ten paces, pondering her answer. 'I don't think the Germans can defeat Britain. The British are much more powerful than the French.'

Paul humphed. 'They were saying France was invincible three months ago and look where we are now.'

'Who knows anything about anything these days?' Rosie shrugged. 'At least Henderson's smart. If Britain lost, he'd find a way for us to get into Spain or something. And who knows, maybe Britain and Germany will sign a peace treaty and by Christmas nobody will even remember that there was a war.'

Paul liked this idea. 'I can't help thinking about it at night,' he admitted. 'All the different things that could happen to the world. It keeps me awake for hours.'

'I know what you mean,' Rosie said. 'I'm the same sometimes, but I can't think of anyone I'd rather have looking after us than Henderson.'

'HALT!' someone shouted, as bodies crackled through the long grass on either side. Then in gruff German, 'Put up your hands.'

Paul spun around and yelped, but he slammed into an unseen body. Before he knew it he'd been shoved backwards through the undergrowth and had a pair of knees pinning his shoulders to the ground.

'Gotcha!' Marc grinned, before tweaking the end of Paul's nose and letting him up. 'I bet you've got big brown streaks in your pants.'

'Dick-heads,' Paul said furiously, as he stumbled up. 'That's not funny.'

'Looked pretty damned funny from where I'm kneeling,' Marc grinned.

A few metres away PT had performed a similar stunt with Rosie. But Rosie was no pushover and they whipped about in the grass until PT straddled Rosie's thighs. Once they were face to face she relaxed her upper body and cracked a smile.

'That was a mean trick,' she said, but with an expression that showed she thought it was actually kind of cute.

PT felt a blast of lust as he closed in to kiss Rosie's lips. Although Paul and Marc were only a couple of metres away, the dark and the tall grass gave them privacy. Savouring the moment, PT paused with his lips millimetres from Rosie's and moved his hand up her chest to cup the bottom of her breast.

But the boys weren't the only ones who could play a trick and the instant PT's weight shifted off her thighs Rosie brought her knee up, hitting him hard in the kidneys.

'Arsehole,' Rosie hissed, as PT groaned with pain. She bunched her fist and thumped him in the eye before rolling him away. 'This isn't a game you know, you goddamn moron.'

It wouldn't have been appropriate for PT to hit back at a girl, but this was academic because as Rosie stormed back towards home he was rolling around in the grass, howling like a wounded dog and seeing nothing but blurs of light from his right eye.

Paul grinned proudly as Marc gave PT a hand up.

'Henderson's right, you know,' Paul laughed. 'My sister *definitely* has a crush on you.'

CHAPTER SIXTEEN

Paul liked his daily walk down to the beach. After heading off the farm, he crossed the heavily trafficked coast road and found the chalky stone path with reed beds on either side. You didn't get to see the water until you'd walked up a slight cliff, then four kilometres of coastline broke out in front of you.

The weather had been stormy the previous day and German swimming lessons had been cancelled, but today's sky was clear and sunlight dazzled off a sea that was as calm as Paul had ever seen it.

The beach was abuzz and Paul crouched down low, doubting that every German would be as welcoming as the slim officer he'd encountered two days earlier.

Today was clearly a special occasion. There were double the usual number of troops and no sign of old men or fatties. Every soldier seemed to have big shoulders and blond heads, as if they'd been hand-picked for a photo-shoot.

A wooden pathway stretched down to the sea. There were several artillery pieces, each tethered to horses made uneasy by the stones underfoot and the unfamiliar crashing waves. Three barges hovered off shore. The largest was a self-powered beast with a huge cavity, designed for hauling coal. The other two were tied behind a Dutch harbour tug which bobbed uncomfortably, even in such a modest sea.

Paul waved as the slim officer emerged from the crowd and raised a thumb. 'Come to watch the show?' he asked cheerfully when he neared the top of the shallow cliff.

'I've never seen all this lot before,' Paul noted.

The officer handed Paul his set of binoculars. 'Look on the pier over there,' the officer said. 'The fat man in the pale blue uniform.'

Paul's dad had always refused to give him a coin to look through the telescopes on weekend visits to the Eiffel Tower, so the enlarged view was a minor thrill in itself.

'You can see *so* much detail,' Paul said excitably. 'All the yellow braid on their uniforms and everything. Who are they?'

'The pale blue uniform belongs to Reichsmarschall Hermann Goering, supreme commander of the

Luftwaffe. There's also an admiral or two, three generals and the fellow in black is a Standartenführer from the SS[10].'

Paul shuddered slightly as he saw that the group of VIPs were guarded by black SS uniforms. These were a rare sight in the military zone, but he knew from experience that the SS and their Gestapo police units were the most dangerous Germans of all.

'So what's all this for?'

'A little show,' the officer explained. 'We've begun converting river and canal barges into landing ships for the invasion. Goering has moved to Luftwaffe headquarters in Beauvais to coordinate the air attacks on Britain and the generals are putting on a little show for his benefit.'

Paul turned the binoculars around and studied the barges bouncing on the relatively small waves. 'Is it me, or do those things look dodgy?'

'They're river barges. We've been assured that they're seaworthy,' the officer said. 'Not that I'd fancy crossing the channel in one on a stormy night.'

Paul handed the binoculars back to the officer and picked his pad up off the rocks. 'I did your drawing, sir.'

---

[10]SS, or Schutzstaffel – the elite military division of the Nazi party. SS personnel were selected on grounds of racial purity and fanatical devotion to Hitler.

The officer was delighted when he saw it. Paul had drawn portraits before and knew that people were happiest when the image flattered them. He'd made a notebook-sized pencil drawing with thousands of neat strokes. The daughter and wife were both recognisable, but somehow more beautiful than in the original photograph.

'I hope you like it,' Paul said. 'It's from a photograph, so I had to guess all the colours.'

'It's fabulous,' the officer said, beaming. He clearly missed his family and seemed genuinely touched. 'I was going to send it to my wife, but you know what? I think I might keep it in my quarters.'

'I can see there's a lot going on today,' Paul said. 'I can get the jam another day if you're busy.'

'No,' the officer said. 'I want to put this drawing back in my car before it gets crushed. You can walk with me.'

The officer's car was parked at the kerb of the coast road, half a kilometre away. The exercise had brought a huge amount of traffic into the area and the parked trucks and cars were causing horn blasts and frayed tempers.

As they walked, three huge Panzer tanks blasted along the pebble beach. Their tracks spun, throwing stones and grit in a huge plume as the engines revved and diesel smoke billowed through the exhaust towers at the rear.

'Have you ever driven a tank?' Paul asked.

'No, thank god,' the officer said. 'I've ridden in one a few times and they're merciless: hot, smelly and you wake up the next morning with a backache and twenty bruises.'

The officer's car was a Renault with French number plates that had presumably been commandeered from one of the locals. After laying Paul's drawing flat in the glovebox, the German opened the boot and pulled out an aluminium can with a small brown label.

'It's more like a paint can,' Paul smiled, as the weight dragged on his arm. 'It's really lucky because all I've got left is a tiny blob in the bottom of the jar and my mum can't find any more in the village shop.'

'My pleasure,' the officer said. 'Go straight home with it. It's best not to get seen running around with a big tin of German jam with all these SS officers around.'

Paul looked disappointed. 'But I wanted to watch the barges.'

'Run it home and come back,' the German suggested. 'And when you do, stay at this end of the beach. I wouldn't stray too close to the VIPs and their bodyguards if I were you.'

There were so few civilians in the area that Paul decided it would be safe to cross the coast road and hide his jam behind a tree on the path back to the house. Once this was done, he retreated to his usual spot amongst the rocks as the empty barges headed towards the beach.

*

While Oberst Ohlsen stood on the pier behind Hermann Goering and a line of SS guards, his staff back in Calais were enjoying his absence. As well as working as Oberst Ohlsen's personal translator, Henderson had been tasked with giving six senior officers a basic grounding in French.

The classroom at the Calais headquarters had formerly been the executive dining room of a French shipping line. The walls were hung with pictures of steamships, although the one over the fireplace had been taken down and replaced with a swastika.

Henderson had never taught languages before, but rather than bore a roomful of busy officers with written exercises he made them take turns enacting scenes such as ordering drinks from a bar, or speaking to a telephone operator.

When the class grew bored, he'd liven things up with blue jokes or more risqué scenarios, such as what to say to a Frenchman who aims a shotgun at you when he catches you in bed with his daughter.

This teaching technique worked well, but Henderson's style was all part of his real intention, which was to get friendly with as many senior German officers as possible.

'Now our beloved Oberst is at the beach in his little

pink trunks,' Henderson said in German, as he looked at his watch and saw that it was a quarter to one. Then he switched to French, 'So I suggest that we all adjourn for a very long lunch break.'

It took the six officers several seconds to grasp what he was saying and rise up from their desks.

A young major smiled at Henderson. 'If my teachers at school had been as much fun as you, Mr Boyle, I never would have ended up in the bloody army.' A few of his colleagues laughed in agreement as they headed out the door. 'Would you care to join us for lunch?'

Henderson shook his head. 'I have a pile of translations to type up. Another time, perhaps.'

As the officer's boots clattered down the marble stairs outside, Henderson gathered his papers into a briefcase and took a side door through a disused kitchen. He then cut across a thickly carpeted corridor and found himself in the reception area outside Oberst Ohlsen's office.

The reception was usually manned by the Oberleutnant who worked as Ohlsen's assistant, but Henderson had sent him to lunch, so he opened the double doors and peered cautiously into the empty room. The office was opulent, with models of steamships in glass cases and a private bathroom behind a huge desk with marble columns for legs.

Hitler gave a reproachful look from the wall and a vase was filled with the miniature swastika pennants that were usually attached to the bonnets of cars. They reminded Henderson of the paper flags he'd pushed into sandcastles as a child.

In the two days since becoming Ohlsen's personal translator Henderson had taken part in half a dozen meetings with city officials, directors of the local ports and railways and a variety of shipyard and dock owners.

All of these produced intelligence and gave clues about the German invasion plans. However, the highest level meetings between military officers took place entirely in German, which meant there was no reason for Henderson to sit in. The only way he'd get his hands on the actual plans would be to steal them.

At the end of the room nearest the double doors was a huge plan chest with more than thirty slim drawers. It had been designed for naval charts and blueprints belonging to the steamship company, but served as well for maps of German positions and diagrams of the invasion plans.

Henderson checked the corridor outside before opening the assistant's desk and snatching a bunch of keys from the top drawer. Back inside, a tiny key unlocked the plan chest, allowing Henderson to slowly open the top drawer. He drew a terse breath, awed at what lay within.

Henderson had seen the plan laid out on the Oberst's desk, but had been ordered to stand well back as he was told to deal with a dispute over a car repair with a garage in town.

The original map had been drawn on linen-backed paper by a German draughtsman. The English Channel and the French and British coastlines ran top and bottom. There were hundreds of markings and symbols, denoting everything from towns and sea lanes to the locations of German tank divisions and British coastal defences.

Corrections had been added. Some were drawn over patches of correction fluid. In other places sections of the map had been sliced out with a craft knife and everything redrawn on fresh paper. This had happened several times in some spots, turning the map into a delicate collage of postcard-sized pieces held together with sticky tape.

It was unacceptably risky to view the map in the open office, so Henderson carried it quickly to the bathroom where he pushed the bolt across, laid one of the Oberst's thick bath towels over the floor tiles and put the map on top of it.

There was a mass of details and so many markings that it was difficult for anyone other than the person devising the plan to distinguish between truly important information and notes and crossings-out jotted during telephone conversations with Berlin.

But as Henderson studied the whole map it became

clear that the invasion plan had been scaled back since it was first conceived. The Germans had originally planned to invade with 250,000 men, launching out of a dozen occupied ports stretching from Bruges to Cherbourg. This had now been downsized to a force of just 100,000 troops which would land on a strip of England's southern coast between Portsmouth and Dover, with the aim of rapidly advancing to London.

The plan to invade across the sea with less than a fifth of the manpower that had taken France was undeniably bold. The physical reality of the map, with the names of German divisions written over English towns, stirred up Henderson's sense of patriotism and made him even more determined to do all he could to stop it.

He began his work by writing as many details as he could in shorthand and sketching a rough outline of the main landing zones and current locations of German troops.

Balancing risks is the heart of a spy's job. If you take too many you'll be caught, but you'll achieve nothing if you take none at all. Henderson could have spent his entire lunchbreak noting more details from the map, but he'd personally known spies who'd ended up dead after hanging around too long, or going back to steal a few extra sheets of discarded carbon paper from a waste bin. And the knowledge that the lives of Maxine and the kids would be at risk if he were caught made him more cautious than if he'd been acting alone.

After no more time than a man can reasonably spend locked in a bathroom, Henderson checked that the office and the room outside were empty before sliding the plan back into the chest.

As he pushed shut the drawer he noticed a faint scribble in the bottom right corner of the map: *S-Tag 16-9*. He realised it was probably the most important snippet of information he'd find in his whole life: the Germans were planning to invade Britain on 16 September.

*

The huge coal barge had been cut open at the front and fitted with a drop-down ramp. Paul got a good view as the hand-picked troops with full kit strapped on their backs waded through half a metre of seawater and climbed aboard. They were followed by two pieces of horse-drawn artillery.

Everyone seemed edgy as the first Panzer III tank rolled up. The tracks clattered against the slippery ramp and the barge tilted forwards as twenty-two tonnes of metal crept aboard.

As the middle of the tank passed the crest of the ramp, it tilted forwards and slammed the hull. The entire barge slumped in the water, and a powerful half-metre wave sent the second half of the boarding party charging up the pebbles, seeking higher ground.

There were shouts of alarm, then the barge crew paused the loading procedure – the weight of the tank had brought the vessel dangerously close to grounding on the pebbles. Orders were yelled down to the stern, where a bemused Dutch captain stood in an open-backed wheelhouse.

He fired the two diesel engines and the craft began drifting backwards. But moving a coal barge designed for a river in a tidal sea was an imprecise business. Waves were already pushing the craft towards shore, so the captain had to briefly run the engines up at full power to move it backwards and prevent grounding.

Confusion reigned as the barge moved slowly away from shore. At first senior officers yelled at the last troops, making them wade out into waist-deep water with their heavy kits. Four made it up the ramp, but as the barge headed backwards the crew realised that the entire hull would flood if the ramp wasn't raised before they got into choppier water.

The winch was engaged and the last soldier to board arrived head first, sliding down the ramp and taking his comrades down like nine pins. Soldiers in the water were knocked backwards by the wash created as the five-metre-wide ramp came out of the water. With heavy kits strapped on, several who lost their footing found themselves anchored to the seabed.

As the barge continued to drift out, troops on the

beach threw down their kits and dived in to rescue the drowning men. Paul looked down towards the pier to see how the VIPs were reacting to the chaos. As he did so he noticed a vague hum high above – but this was nothing out of the usual, as the RAF and Luftwaffe had been dog fighting over the Channel for several days.

Reichsmarschall Goering faced the barge, first throbbing with anger, then turning and laughing to his bodyguards. An army general, flanked by two Obersts – including Ohlsen – was storming across the pebbles towards some nervous subordinates, including the slim officer for whom Paul had made the drawing.

The noise in the sky grew louder, but people had other things on their minds.

Paul spoke no German, but was rapidly developing familiarity with the ruder end of the language. All of the troops were out of the water and the barge floundered. Nobody seemed to know whether to try bringing it back to shore to finish the loading operation, or to complete the planned demonstration by backing a few hundred metres out to sea before landing the troops and weapons in a natural harbour on the opposite side of the pier.

As everyone concentrated on watching each other the sound overhead grew. Paul had drawn hundreds of aircraft and although it was the first example he'd seen in the flesh, Paul instantly recognised the four engines and square tailplane of a British Halifax bomber. A

Hurricane fighter hovered off either side.

As the son of a British man Paul felt a certain pride, but he'd seen enough German bombs fall to know that explosions didn't take sides. He sprang up from between the rocks and began running towards the road. By the time he'd made five steps the Germans had also recognised the threat and four hundred men, from teenaged grenadiers to the Reichsmarschall himself, were running for cover.

At over three hundred miles an hour, the Hurricane's transition from a silhouette to a beast strafing the beach with machine-gun fire took less than twenty seconds. Paul had made it across the road and dived for cover in the trees beside his tin of jam. He looked up and saw the second Hurricane making its attack run.

From less than thirty metres, he could see the pilot's moustache and read the side markings as it flew level with the reed tips on the clifftop. A few Germans fired handguns while others ran into the road or yelled for medics.

Paul thought about running deeper into the trees, but fear glued him down as the British bomber approached. He'd seen plenty of bombers on his route south, but the Germans had nothing even half the size of the four-engined Halifax.

Time crawled as he glanced up between the trees. His body felt like it was floating as the plane cruised forwards. Its height was less than a hundred metres and its bombing doors were open. A soldier rushed past, his trousers soaked in seawater and his huge boot barely missing Paul's ankle.

The bomber dropped its load and Paul imagined death. He saw his parents' faces as he shut his eyes – but there was no explosion, just German shouts and a rustling on the sea breeze. He looked up and discovered thousands of folded brochures catching sunlight. They pelted the cliffs and the road like a rainstorm. A few made it as far as the trees and Paul snatched one that jostled the branches above him.

The blue and red cover bore a cartoon drawing of a huge bulldog. It wore a Union-Jack waistcoat and carried Hitler in its mouth like a bone. The title was in German, but Paul flipped through and realised that it was a spoof guide, giving the Germans tips on how to invade Britain.

CHAPTER SEVENTEEN

Paul got on OK with PT and Marc, but Dumont had a big mouth and liked throwing his weight around so Paul tried to avoid him. Today was an exception, because he wanted Marc to tell him what the leaflet said. He found the three older lads easily enough, just a few hundred metres from the house, checking rabbit traps they'd set the day before.

The leaflet had been prepared by the British Propaganda Ministry with the aim of demoralising German troops and was entitled: *A Guide to the Invasion of Britain*. The first section was an English phrasebook containing handy phrases such as '*Help me, I'm drowning*,' and '*Please don't bayonet me again, I wish to surrender.*'

There was also a section of jokes and Marc sat in the

grass and read one aloud, pausing occasionally to translate the words.

'Hitler recently set up a meeting with the Chief Rabbi of Berlin. He was desperate to cross the English Channel and threatened to demolish every synagogue in the city unless the rabbi told him the secret of how Moses parted the Red Sea. The rabbi replied that Moses' magic wand was currently on display at the British Museum.'

Paul and PT laughed, but Dumont looked baffled. 'I don't get it.'

Marc tutted. 'Hitler wants the wand,' he explained. 'But it's in the British Museum, in London, where he can't get it.'

Dumont scratched his head. 'But if the British have this wand, why don't *they* use it?'

'For god's sake,' PT said, as he thumped on the grass in distress. 'Dumont, it's a *joke*.'

'Sometimes I think he's putting it on,' Marc said, grinning. 'But then it turns out that he really is that thick.'

'I'm smarter than *you*,' Dumont said. 'My mum says I'm practical, rather than being good with words and numbers.'

Paul couldn't resist teasing, 'And your mum's bound to be totally unbiased . . .'

Dumont reared up. 'Unless you want your head

mashed into the nearest cow pat, I'd suggest you shut your weedy little mouth.'

Paul stepped back, but wasn't too worried because he figured Marc and PT would stick up for him. The tension subsided a moment later when Marc turned to the centre of the invasion guide.

'Phwoarr!' he spluttered. 'Now that's rather nice.'

PT and Dumont zoomed in on the leaflet. Paul had already seen the image of two topless girls with *Something for you to look at while other men are taking care of your wives and daughters back home*, written beneath it.

'You guys are so dirty,' Paul complained. 'You'll burn in hell for sure.'

'Some things are worth going to hell for,' PT said, smiling. 'You said these leaflets were scattered all over the road?'

'Are there any different ones?' Marc asked excitedly, before Paul could answer. 'Like, with different pictures of girls in them?'

'Let's go down there and find out,' Dumont said.

The idea of Halifax bombers dropping topless pictures didn't fit in with Paul's image of how the RAF was supposed to behave, but the older boys' reactions made him realise that a leaflet with topless girls in would get ten times the exposure of one without. He thought about going back to the house but tagged along behind the others.

An hour had passed since the raid and there was no sign of Germans except a gruesome spray of blood on the chalk cliffs. Orders had been given to clear the leaflets and the only ones in open sight were soggy examples that had washed ashore after the Germans left. The trees beyond the road proved a better hunting ground and Marc ripped off a branch and used it to knock down dozens of copies stuck in the canopy.

'So what about that house I was telling you about?' Dumont asked, once the boys were satisfied that there was only one version of the leaflet. 'It's a fair way, but the people who lived there were loaded. I'm telling you, we'll bag heaps of stuff.'

Marc sighed. 'You said that when we walked miles to that other place three days ago.'

'We had fun catapulting all the old gramophone records, didn't we?' Dumont said. 'And what else are we gonna do?'

Most of Dumont's schemes hinged on this point. There wasn't much to occupy the boys' time, and even if Dumont's promises of loot never materialised, it wasn't as if there were any more exciting alternatives.

Marc looked at Paul. 'You fancy it?'

Paul screwed his face up. He suspected he wouldn't enjoy it, but was curious to know what the trio of older boys got up to when they disappeared for half the day.

'I guess,' he said warily.

It took an hour to reach the house, taking things slow and stopping to skim stones off a pond along the way. Dumont laid into Paul because he was useless at it and by the time they arrived Paul wished he was sitting on his own somewhere with his pencils.

The house they'd come to rob was double the size of the pink one they'd stayed at in Bordeaux. It was surrounded by unkempt fields of wheat, but the large front garden was immaculate.

'That's been mowed like *yesterday*,' Marc said. 'There's no way it's empty.'

'Yes there is,' Dumont said. 'The old caretaker who lives here mows it. But he came staggering into our neighbour's house last night and they put him on the back of a wagon and hauled him to the hospital in Calais after curfew. Burst appendix.'

'We're gonna rob a house while an old man's sick?' Paul asked.

'It's not his house, skinny,' Dumont growled. 'He's the caretaker. The owners left for their poncy villa in Saint Raphael weeks before the invasion.'

PT recognised that this house was in a different league to the farm cottages Dumont had taken them to before and his appetite for thieving overruled his need to stay out of trouble.

'OK.' PT smiled. 'I'm gonna show you amateurs a

simple trick for checking whether the house you want to rob is occupied.'

The boys watched as PT walked up to the front door and rang the large brass bell hanging above it. He gave it a second go after half a minute, then waved the others up the drive.

'What if they'd answered?' Marc asked.

'Just throw out some bull,' PT said, making sure Dumont was out of earshot as he stepped on to the front lawn. 'Ask if they want some gardening work done, ask for some random name and pretend that you're at the wrong house. When my dad cased a joint he'd always put on a suit and pretend to be an encyclopaedia salesman. People expect salesmen to be crafty and thought nothing of it, even if he'd been sneaking around the side of a house and peeking through windows.'

Dumont was sizing up a large flower pot. 'I could throw this through the front window, easy.'

PT backed away from the house. 'You said the old caretaker staggered into the village with a burst appendix. I doubt he went around locking all the doors and windows first.'

Two ground-floor windows were open along the side, but Marc hit the jackpot when he turned the back door handle.

'Nice one,' PT said, as he followed Marc into a large kitchen. 'Now we've *got* to be careful in a place like this because if the caretaker comes back he'll call the gendarmes. They might dust for fingerprints. We haven't got gloves, so pull the sleeve of your shirt over your hands or grab a piece of rag before you touch *anything*.'

Paul had never done anything like this before and couldn't help thinking that it was stupid because it would attract attention. But he had no leverage over the older boys and knew he'd look a hopeless wimp if he complained. He swiped a doily from the hallway table and wrapped it over his hand before leading into the living room.

Dumont broke the silence by knocking a pair of china horses off the mantelpiece and crunching them under his boot.

'Up yours, Mr LeConte.'

'Who's Mr LeConte?' Marc asked.

'The owner,' Dumont said. 'My dad hates his guts. He built this place with money he made ripping off my grandfather back in the day. I'm gonna do the biggest piss all over this joint.'

Marc started to laugh. 'You're like a tom cat! Why have you got to piss on everything?'

Dumont was too busy kicking over an occasional table and stamping down on its spindly legs to bother answering. Paul followed PT up the stairs.

'Are you sure we should be doing this?' Paul asked nervously.

'I smell money here,' PT replied, as he stopped by a table and picked up a small golden statuette of a mummy. 'Feel the weight of that,' he said as they passed it between cloth-covered hands.

'Blimey,' Paul said.

'Solid gold,' PT explained. 'Egyptian, probably three to five thousand years old. Untraceable and probably worth more than two thousand dollars at a New York auction house. So how about we let the fat idiot have his fun downstairs, and you and I can make a little money?'

Paul still wasn't comfortable, but he liked PT taking him into his confidence, especially after he'd brained him back in Bordeaux.

'And I tell you what else.' PT smiled. 'Dumont's *totally* ignored what I told him about fingerprints. If there's any trouble, we can drop him right in it.'

Paul was no fan of Dumont, but PT's callousness sent a chill down his back.

'I thought he was your mate,' Paul said.

PT shrugged. 'There are people I like and people I don't in this world, but no one's my mate. That's how I've survived on my own since the day the cops murdered my dad.'

It was a horrible attitude, but Paul understood how tough it must have been for PT to arrive in France at thirteen years old without knowing anyone. The experience would either break you or make you hard.

'Nice little library,' PT noted, as he disappeared into one of the bedrooms.

The balcony overlooking the front hallway contained eight levels of fitted shelving, each stuffed with books. Paul loved to read, but all his books had been left behind in Paris.

'Is it OK if I take some of these?' Paul shouted.

PT's answer was muffled because his head was inside a wardrobe. 'You'd be rather a bad burglar if you didn't.'

Downstairs Dumont knocked something over and screamed out in pain.

Marc emerged from the living room, laughing so hard that he had to hold his stomach. 'You should have seen it, Paul. Big marble column, right on the idiot's foot!'

'Shut up!' Dumont whined.

Paul scanned the rows of books. He didn't have a bag, so he was limited by what he could carry in his arms. He picked out three adventure novels, but grew more excited when he found a row of books on famous painters. The trouble was, they were all huge so he picked a single leather-cased volume of works by Picasso and used it as a tray, stacking it up with a couple of smaller art books before finishing off with a pile of novels.

By the time he'd made his pick, PT had searched all four bedrooms and emerged holding a bunched cloth filled with three good quality watches, seventy francs, two sets of diamond cufflinks and the mummy.

'Imagine how much money these people have,' PT grinned. 'I mean, this is just the stuff they left behind.'

Paul followed PT downstairs. Dumont was busy trashing plates in the kitchen, while Marc had found a bag of children's clothes under the stairs and grabbed himself a change of shirt and trousers and a hardly-worn pair of boots.

'These ones I'm walking around in are massive,' Marc explained, as he reached into the cupboard and threw a wicker basket at Paul.

'Oooh, I can get more now,' Paul said, but PT grabbed him as he headed back to the stairs.

'We've been here long enough,' PT said. 'Especially with fat boy making all that noise ... Dumont, we're outta here.'

Dumont laughed when he saw Paul with the basket of books. 'Books,' he snorted. 'You are *such* a girl!'

Marc shook his head. 'Just because you can't read, Dumont.'

'So what if I can't read?' Dumont yelled defensively. 'You get someone to read it out loud, don't you?'

Marc had meant it sarcastically and froze on the spot. 'You mean you *really* can't read?'

'I knew you were dumb,' PT laughed, 'but not that dumb.'

'Screw you,' Dumont shouted. 'I could still smash all of your faces in, any day of the week.'

Paul saw that Dumont was upset and looked up at him. 'It's not hard to read, I could show you.'

But all Paul got for his sympathy was a dig in the back. 'You think I care?' Dumont said. 'I swear, if your brother and cousin weren't here I'd take you and all your books outside and wring your neck like the skinny little chicken you are.'

'Hey,' PT shouted. 'Don't talk to Paul like that. He was being *nice*. We're the ones winding you up.'

'Whatever,' Dumont moaned, as he realised he was the only one leaving the house empty-handed. 'Wait up, guys. There's wine in the kitchen, why don't we steal some bottles and get loaded?'

Marc looked back from the patio outside the rear door. 'I thought you said wine upsets your stomach.'

Dumont was on the defensive after the revelation that he couldn't read. 'It's nothing,' he said. 'I got sick sometimes when I was little and my mum gave me watered-down wine with dinner, but I'm sixteen now.'

'Hurry up and get some wine then,' PT said, 'and a corkscrew. And Marc, wipe your fingerprints off the back door.'

CHAPTER EIGHTEEN

Paul got bored hanging out. The books were heavy and he didn't like the taste of wine, so he carried all the loot back home. Following PT's instructions, he hid everything in a tool store behind the cowshed, but he was excited about his books and sneaked the big Picasso volume back to the attic bedroom he shared with Rosie.

Paul had the roof hatch open so that the room streamed sunlight on to the pages. He slipped it hurriedly under his blankets as Rosie came up the ladder.

'Where'd you get that from?' she asked.

'Nowhere,' Paul said, which he immediately realised was the stupidest and guiltiest sounding answer he could have given.

Rosie snatched the book. 'Looks expensive,' she noted. 'So how come I never get invited when they go out on their wrecking sprees?'

'Because you're a girl, I guess.' Paul shrugged.

'Maxine said to come down, wash your hands and have dinner. Henderson's early; he got a ride in one of the staff cars.'

As Paul rubbed his hands, turning soap into grey foam, Henderson sat at the table while Maxine carved the rabbits. She was in a sour mood because of the boys.

'It's starting to get on my nerves,' Maxine explained. 'I mean, they're out all hours doing god knows what. Marc is supposed to be feeding and milking the cows, but last night he rushed out to do it last thing before bed. I set them chores in the mornings, but they do everything half-arsed.'

'I do *my* chores,' Paul said defensively as he shut off the tap and dried his hands on his shirt. 'I cleaned out and painted the two side rooms.'

'You're not so bad,' Maxine said, as she passed him a bowl of vegetable stew and a side plate piled with rabbit meat. 'I'm talking about PT and Marc.'

Henderson was in a good mood and didn't want Maxine to bring it down. 'They're just lads of a certain age doing what lads of a certain age do,' he said dismissively. 'Leave 'em be.'

Maxine thumped Henderson's stew bowl down so hard that its contents sploshed over the table. 'I don't mind helping, Charles. But those two treat me like a servant and the looks on their faces when I ask them to do the simplest thing . . .'

'Fine,' Henderson said, slightly irritably. 'When they get home I'll have a word about them showing you more respect and doing their chores properly. If that doesn't work out I'll give them both a thrashing.'

Maxine shook her head. 'Violence isn't the answer to *everything*, Charles.'

Henderson raised his hands. 'Fine – I won't thrash them,' he said. 'But words will only take you so far when you're dealing with boys that age, so don't go expecting miracles.'

By this time Paul, Rosie, Maxine and Henderson had all settled around the table and started on dinner.

'Nice rabbit,' Paul said, as he bit a long strip in half. 'Tasty herbs.'

'Thank you.' Maxine smiled. 'It's rosemary. It's growing like wildfire out back.'

Paul looked at Henderson. 'Did you see the leaflet they dropped down at the beach?'

'Yes,' Henderson replied, as he broke into a laugh. 'Oberst Ohlsen came back from the demonstration in an absolute state, then spent an hour getting his ear chewed off in the general's office. The leaflets were getting passed around at headquarters.'

'What was the reaction?' Rosie asked.

'Most people seemed to think it was damned funny,'

Henderson said. 'The only problem is, they're suspicious about the leaflet drop taking place while Goering was present. They're saying British intelligence might have a spy who told them he'd be there.'

Maxine looked concerned. 'Is that going to create a problem for you?'

'Not me specifically,' Henderson answered. 'The Nazis keep their security tight and even the Oberst didn't know Goering was going to be there until the general told him on the drive out this morning. But it will ratchet up the tension and make everyone that bit more suspicious from now on.'

'What about the intelligence gathering?' Rosie asked. 'Our transmission window isn't until eleven tonight, but I can start working on the encoding straight after dinner.'

'I got into the plan chest while everyone was out,' Henderson said, smiling. 'The invasion is set for September sixteenth. I had the map in my possession for a good ten minutes. We won't get all the information into tonight's transmission, we'll have to spread it over two or three nights. Obviously, we send the most important information first.'

'Have you ever seen any sign in headquarters that they're out trying to detect radio transmissions?' Maxine asked.

Henderson shook his head. 'No, but Abwehr –

military intelligence – and the Gestapo both work out of separate buildings to us. They might have crack squads out looking for spies, they might have nothing at all. There's no way of knowing. All we can do is keep our transmissions short and change locations once in a while.'

*

'We'll help you home,' Marc said, as Dumont leaned on a fence, gasping for breath. The teenager had just been sick and was trembling.

'Nah,' Dumont gasped. 'If my mum knows that I got sick drinking wine she'll go bananas.'

PT had drunk a whole bottle of wine and regretted it. After all the walking they'd done he was dehydrated and a thumping headache more than cancelled out any pleasant sensation of drunkenness.

'Why'd you drink wine if you know it makes you sick?' PT asked.

'I dunno,' Dumont said. 'I thought I might have grown out of it.'

It was just after seven. They were in a lane close to the village and PT had no appetite for the walk home. Marc had barely drunk anything. He was fed up with Dumont and only had an appetite for his dinner.

'Look,' Marc said pointedly, 'I'm hungry, I'm knackered and I've got cows to deal with back home. But I don't want to leave you here, Dumont. At least let us take you down to the village green where someone will help if you get worse.'

Dumont shook his head slowly. 'Leave me,' he moaned. 'Everyone in the village knows me. They'll get my dad out.'

PT spoke to Marc. 'We've offered to help and we're not his nurse maids. Let's go home and get fed.'

Marc shrugged awkwardly. 'But he's really sick, PT. What if he passes out or something? His mum will get really worried.'

Dumont leaned forwards and retched again, but nothing came out. 'Screw it, take me home,' he said reluctantly. 'I've brought most of it up now, I reckon. I'll tell my mum it's something I ate.'

PT stood beside Dumont and let him put a fat arm around his neck. 'Let's walk.'

As Dumont stumbled forwards, Marc supported him from the other side. 'Why'd you have to be so fat, Dumont?' he complained.

They made it over the drainage ditch at the edge of the field and started crunching up the gravel lane towards the village green. A truck was coming up behind and PT looked over his shoulder to check it out.

'Germans,' he said.

'Who else would have petrol?' Marc replied.

As the truck closed in, PT and Marc guided Dumont over the verge. The lane didn't take you any place that the coast road wouldn't get you to faster which made the truck a rare sight, but the boys didn't give any thought until it blasted past, showering them with dirt.

'Nazi pricks,' Marc coughed, as he flicked grey dust out of his hair.

Anger turned to alarm as the driver slammed on the brakes and the truck came to a crunching halt twenty metres ahead. The back flap slammed down and three young soldiers jumped out from beneath a canvas canopy with their rifles in hand. Marc recognised their leader, a broad-shouldered fellow with round glasses. He was always the loudest voice in the little crowd that spent its evenings outside the village bar.

Marc and PT both thought about running, but Dumont was a dead weight and they had no chance of outrunning German bullets.

'Piss in our car?' the big chap shouted in bad French, as he swung wildly with his rifle butt.

The blow hit Marc in the chest, knocking him backwards and sending Dumont crashing down on top of him.

'Piss in our car?' the German repeated.

His second swing smashed Dumont in the ribs. PT turned to run, but the other two Germans had built up speed and caught up within a couple of paces. One grabbed PT by the arms as his mate slugged him in the belly. Once PT had doubled over, they dragged him forwards, knocking him head first into a tree and then kicking his legs away so that he sprawled face first on to the knobbly roots around the trunk.

As the German in the round glasses ruthlessly laid into Dumont with heavy boots and rifle butt, the driver grabbed Marc off the ground and slapped his face hard before twisting his hand up behind his back.

'French piece of shit,' he shouted, as he swung Marc around and frogmarched him until he slammed into the side of the truck. 'I borrowed that car from our major. You know how long it took to scrub up?'

'I don't know what you're talking about,' Marc replied in German.

'Let me jog your memory,' the German said, before smacking Marc's head against the mudguard over the wheel. 'Major Ghunsonn's put us all on report because of you. Then he sent us up here to find the boys that pissed in his car.'

'There's lots of boys living around here,' Marc lied, a chill going down his back as he noticed that Dumont had gone quiet.

'You're the only ones we ever saw,' the driver growled. 'I saw one of you going around the side of the bar, but it wasn't you, was it? He was taller than you.'

'I swear I don't know,' Marc said, tears streaming down his face as the German tightened the grip on his arm so that it felt like his shoulder was about to rip out of its socket.

'There's a prison in Calais,' the German said nastily. 'Twenty men in a cell built for six and you'll be the smallest one in there. You won't last two days . . . But if you tell me who it was, I'll let you go.'

Marc tried to focus his mind, but all he wanted was for the pain to stop. 'Dumont did it,' he sniffed. 'The fat guy in the road.'

'Thought so,' the German said, as he let Marc go.

Marc gasped, but his relief only lasted until the German snapped a set of rigid metal cuffs over his wrists.

'Climb in the truck,' he ordered.

'You said I could go.'

'I lied.' The German smiled. 'Sabotage of German property is a serious matter. You're in very deep shit, young man.'

Marc had an awkward time boarding the truck with his hands bound together, but he'd fared better than the other two. PT got dragged from the trees, with his head hanging forwards and blood streaming down his face.

Dumont was worst of all, barely conscious with his clothes shredded and welts the shape of rifle parts all over his body. It took two Germans to lift him. They bent him forwards, so that he stood in the gravel with his head in the back of the truck. Marc watched as the driver grabbed a length of towing rope, then made a noose out of it before pulling it tight around Dumont's neck.

'End of the line for you, fatty,' the biggest German said.

'Please,' Dumont sobbed. 'Please don't kill me.'

Marc and PT exchanged a desperate glance as they lay on the floor of the truck.

'Just gotta find a nice strong branch to hang you from,' the German smiled, pulling hard on the noose, before grabbing Dumont's belt and hitching him up into the truck.

CHAPTER NINETEEN

'Their dinners will be stone cold again,' Maxine said angrily, as Paul helped her wash the dishes. 'And Luc Boyle said those cows need regular milking if we're going to get a decent yield out of them.'

'I said I'll speak to them,' Henderson answered, with a touch of annoyance creeping into his voice. 'Let me concentrate on encoding this message.'

He sat at the table with Rosie. A road map of northern France was spread out and notepaper sprawled around it.

If Henderson had been deliberately sent on a long-term spying operation, he would have been accompanied by a professional radio operator who could transmit and receive Morse code at between forty and sixty words per minute. Henderson and Rosie struggled to transmit any more than twenty words per minute. The maximum safe transmission time was ten minutes, restricting them to a two-hundred-word message each night.

While Henderson used the notes he'd made that lunchtime, carefully sorting all the facts in the order of importance, Rosie compressed them. The 106 characters of *I have viewed the official German invasion map at headquarters and you can regard the following information as authoritative* was slashed to the thirty-three characters of *VWD OFFICL INVSIN MAP AT HQ. RGD INFO AS VG.*

When Rosie wasn't sure if the compressed message was comprehensible, she'd get Paul or Maxine to read it back. If they didn't understand she'd rewrite it.

'I think we can get most of the pertinent information into two ten-minute messages,' Henderson said, as he chewed the end of his pencil.

Rosie looked up from the notebook she was using to encode the message. Henderson's key phrase was a short chapter from Dickens' *Little Dorrit* entitled 'Mr Merdles' Complaint'. Henderson knew the words by heart and over the last few weeks Rosie almost felt that she knew them herself.

'Put the trimmings out for the chickens and see if there's any eggs,' Maxine said, as she handed Paul a mixing bowl filled with potato peelings and carrot tops. 'You'd best get a move on if you want to listen to the news.'

Henderson glanced at his watch and saw that it was

almost eight. As Paul headed out into the evening light, Rosie went through to the living room to warm up the radio they'd brought up from the pink house in Bordeaux.

There was a cool breeze as Paul headed outside. He didn't want to stir Maxine up by complaining, but he was cross because the chickens were supposed to be PT's job. As he hurried across the front lawn, Lottie the goat caught the smell of vegetables and thrust her head into the bowl.

'Scoot,' Paul ordered, but the goat didn't take the hint so he tossed a few shavings off into the distance and gave her a shove.

The chickens knew food was coming and ran to the wire as Paul approached the cage, but he stopped because there were two cars coming up the road. None of the nearby farms was occupied and as this was the first traffic he'd seen since they'd moved in, he dropped the peelings and ran back to the house.

'Cars,' Paul gasped, as he broke into the kitchen. 'I think they're coming here.'

'Shit, shit, shit,' Henderson said, as he frantically folded the road map and stacked away the papers and the encoding grid. 'Rosie, get back in here.'

'I heard,' Rosie shouted, 'I'm just tuning the radio away from the BBC.'

Pas-de-Calais was a special military zone and listening

to an overseas radio station was on the long list of offences the German Army deemed punishable by death.

'They might search,' Henderson yelled frantically, as he stuffed the map and paperwork into his briefcase. 'Get these papers out of the house. Keep low so they don't spot you.'

As Rosie raced out the back door with Henderson's briefcase, Maxine walked on to the front lawn to welcome the two cars coming up the driveway. The first was a luxurious Citroën saloon, with Luc Boyle at the wheel and his wife Vivien in the passenger seat. There were two Germans in the Kübelwagen behind.

Luc pulled down his window as he came to a halt and Maxine saw that his wife was crying.

'Whatever happened?' Maxine asked, as Henderson stayed back in the house.

He'd made a contingency plan for a German raid and kept a loaded German service revolver under a paving slab out back. If the situation looked bad, he'd go out the back door, grab the weapon and sneak up on the two Germans.

'Something to do with your boys,' Vivien sobbed. 'They're in Calais with Dumont. We led the Germans out here because they didn't know the way.'

Henderson strode out when he recognised the passenger stepping out of the German car. He was military police and Henderson had translated in several meetings with him before being reassigned to Oberst Ohlsen.

'What's the matter, sir?' Henderson asked, in German.

The policeman pointed at the rear seats of the car. 'You and your wife, get in. You must come to Calais at once and speak with Major Ghunsonn.'

Paul watched from inside the house as his surrogate parents climbed into the open-topped Kübelwagen. Henderson was trying to hold a conversation with the military police officer, but judging by the body language he was in no mood to listen.

Lottie the goat bleated with disgust before scrambling off as the two cars used the front lawn to turn around. When the headlights disappeared from view, Paul slumped into a dining chair and felt sick with nerves.

A moment later the door creaked and Rosie came in. 'What was that all about?'

'Maybe they found the radio,' Paul suggested.

'I doubt it,' Rosie said. 'I mean, if they thought we were spies they would have taken everyone and turned the house upside down looking for clues.'

'Plus Luc and Vivien were there, and earlier . . .' Paul tailed off, but Rosie glowered at him.

'Earlier what?' Rosie snapped. 'Spit it out.'

'We robbed this house. Like, a really nice one with loads of fancy stuff in it. Maybe they found out.'

Rosie bristled with contempt. 'I know Marc and PT

are always up to no good with that fat moron Dumont, but why did you get involved this time?'

'I didn't really,' Paul explained. 'I only wanted to tag along and not be such a loner for once.'

'What a *complete* mess,' Rosie sighed. 'I mean, robbing a house. It's not like there's anything we badly need and it's attracting attention that we can do without.'

'So what do we do now?' Paul asked anxiously. 'What if Maxine and Henderson don't come back? What about all those notices the Germans put up everywhere about shooting people for doing any tiny little thing wrong?'

Paul backed up because Rosie had the look she always got when she was about to thump him.

'Boys!' Rosie shouted. 'You're total morons, all three of you.'

'So what do we do?' Paul asked.

'Henderson's got all that information to send. I've already started encoding the message.'

'You're still going to transmit?'

'Absolutely.' Rosie nodded. 'And if Henderson isn't back we'll sit up until two and listen to the return message too. I'll go out the back and grab Henderson's briefcase. You'll have to help me go through his notes and work out which information is most important.'

*

PT, Marc and Dumont sat against the wall of a bare hotel

room. Strip out the furniture, strengthen the doors and weld bars over the windows and just about any hotel makes a prison. There was a bucket on the floor as a toilet, which created a nauseating stink because Dumont had used it to throw up. A bare bulb illuminated walls and a floor spattered with blood and down the hallway a woman screamed horrifically as the military police worked her over.

Marc was in the best condition out of the three boys, but he almost wished that he was drifting in and out of consciousness like PT or paralysed with fear like Dumont, who still had the noose around his neck. As the woman's screams pierced the walls, Marc looked at a crusted pool of blood on the floor. Death had never felt closer.

He tried not to think, but it was too important not to. *Whose blood was it? Men or women's, kids as young as him? What had they done? Had they begged for mercy? Was it a bullet through the head or something slower or more painful? And how idiotic was it to earn yourself a spot in this hell hole because of Dumont's stupid idea?*

'Pass the bucket,' Dumont said.

Marc got to his feet. The bucket had been emptied but not cleaned out properly and there were bugs and streaks of shit stuck all over the outside, so he used his boot to sweep it across the floor. He couldn't bear to watch or smell Dumont throwing up again and the furthest away he could get was to stand up near the door and peek out through the spyhole.

The corridor outside hadn't changed from when it was a hotel, with moody lighting and carpeted floor.

'What can I know? What can I know?' a man screamed. 'Just kill me now.'

As Marc shuddered, Dumont groaned. A second later the door burst open, knocking Marc into the room. It was Major Ghunsonn, accompanied by the bespectacled brute who'd worked Dumont over in the lane.

'So,' the major smiled, speaking in German as he loomed over Dumont. 'This is the little cockroach that pissed in my car?' Then he switched to French so Dumont would understand. 'I think he's a spy. Don't you, grenadier?'

'Absolutely, sir.' The grenadier nodded.

'You know what we do to spies, cockroach?' the major said, as he made the shape of a gun with his fingers. '*Bang.*'

'Please,' Dumont sobbed, 'I'm sorry.'

The major ignored Dumont's plea and resumed talking in German. 'Grenadier, I want that fat bag of shit on the firing-squad list for tomorrow.'

'Yes, sir,' the grenadier said enthusiastically. 'What about the other two?'

'Tell the police to take them down to the holding cells for a couple of days. Make sure they get a few lumps knocked out of them and then send them home. We need to give these French peasants a clear message about what happens to people who mess with our equipment.'

Marc spoke in German, 'Major, sir,' he said meekly.

The twelve year old trembled as the two Germans swivelled towards him. 'Something to say?' the major asked.

'Dumont's parents are wealthy,' Marc explained. 'Perhaps they could pay for the damages or something.'

There was a sharp crack as the major knocked Marc to the floor with a hard slap.

'What about you?' the major growled. 'Are *your* parents wealthy? Maybe you could take Dumont's place. I'm a sworn officer of the Reich. How *dare* you suggest that I'd take a bribe.'

*

Three floors below, Vivien Boyle sat in an interview room, bawling, as a female translator explained that her son had confessed to urinating in a German officer's car and that Major Ghunsonn had ordered him to be put before a firing squad at noon the following day.

'He's a simple boy,' Vivien wailed. 'He wouldn't have known what he was doing.'

Maxine stood behind. 'What about my two?'

The translator patiently explained that Marc and PT would be released in a few days. As Luc Boyle hugged his desperate wife, Henderson backed out of the room and searched for a telephone.

'Aren't they entitled to a trial?' Luc asked.

'Criminal offences are dealt with by French police,' the translator explained. 'Offences against the German forces are dealt with in summary fashion. No lawyers, no courts.'

Henderson walked down a long hallway and found a public telephone near the reception desk in what had previously been the hotel lobby. He picked up the receiver and asked the operator to connect him to the army headquarters where he worked.

Army HQ was permanently manned, but there was only a skeleton staff at night. It took several minutes to get one of the operations staff to pick up the telephone and some smooth talking to get the switchboard operator to hand over the number of Oberst Ohlsen's quarters. Luckily the Oberst was in his hotel suite across town.

'Sir, I know this is a terrible liberty,' Henderson explained meekly, 'but my oldest son and two of my nephews got themselves involved in something rather stupid and have landed themselves in a cell at military police headquarters.'

'I see,' Ohlsen said suspiciously. 'What *exactly* is something stupid?'

'Something to do with urinating in a Kübelwagen. It's

wrong, I know, but boys often do such things.'

Ohlsen's tone became more jovial. 'Was that Major Ghunsonn's Kübelwagen, by any chance?'

'Probably,' Henderson said. 'I mean, how often do your Kübelwagens get urinated into?'

'Good point,' Ohlsen said cheerfully. 'Ghunsonn's a pompous prat. Never would have made any kind of rank if he hadn't married the daughter of a well-connected general. I'll put a call in to the duty commander.'

'Sir, that's *wonderful*,' Henderson said, gushing with genuine relief. 'I owe you a great deal and I assure you that I'll be thrashing those boys to within an inch of their lives when they get home.'

'Good,' Ohlsen said. 'I've got a call to make, so you'd better hang up. You stay by that phone and I'll let you know if there's a hitch.'

*

The translator exited the interview room, leaving Luc and Vivien crying. Maxine felt horrible, knowing that Marc and PT faced a much less serious fate, but it was still a shock when Vivien turned on her.

'My Dumont has never been in trouble before he met your two,' she snapped.

Maxine knew Vivien was hurting and ignored the jab. 'Let's try to stay calm, eh?'

'Oh, that's so easy for *you* to say,' Vivien screamed.

'You'll have your boys back in a few days, but my Dumont will be dead.'

'I'm so sorry,' Maxine said. 'I know this is horrible. I wish I could say something that would help.'

'It was your two who put Dumont up to it,' Vivien said. 'Like that first night when you arrived at my house. Straight away those two little devils of yours had him sneaking the wine and my Dumont was up being sick all night afterwards.'

Maxine was irked, but stayed calm. 'I don't think that's entirely fair.'

This innocuous remark pushed Vivien over the edge. She broke free of her husband's grasp and lunged for Maxine's neck.

'Prostitute!' Vivien screamed, as Maxine thumped back against the wall.

Vivien carried more weight, but Maxine was half her age. Maxine felt pity, but had to defend herself from the attack. She reached out and ripped her long nails down Vivien's cheek.

'Bitch!' Vivien shouted, as her husband tried to prise the women apart. 'Your brats killed my Dumie. As good as murdered him.'

'Calm down,' Luc said, as he pulled Vivien away from Maxine, but she instantly turned on her husband.

'So now you take her side, you old bastard?' Vivien wailed, as she thumped on Luc's chest.

Maxine realised her best option was to leave the room but as she grabbed the door, Henderson pushed it inwards, hitting Maxine in the face and knocking her back within hair-pulling distance of Vivien.

Henderson bundled into the fray as Vivien wound Maxine's long hair around her hand and pulled with all her might.

Maxine screamed so loud that nobody heard Henderson shouting, 'It's going to be OK, I've sorted it.'

*

Marc shuddered as the cell door came open and an Unteroffizier[11] walked into the room. He had bright red hair, but after three hours of beatings Marc found himself judging fist and boot size before anything else.

'Can you walk?' the Unteroffizier asked.

'I can,' Marc said, using German because the Unteroffizier's French was terrible. 'The other two won't get far. Where are we going, anyway?'

'Out,' the Unteroffizier said, as he moved across to help PT stand up. 'Your parents are waiting in the reception area, I believe.'

Marc was elated, but didn't let it show in case it was a trap.

---

[11]Unteroffizier – a mid-ranked German soldier, equivalent to a British or American corporal.

'I thought . . .' Marc began, but the German cut him dead.

'Release papers are posted.'

PT could just about walk, but the German had to call one of his colleagues and the pair dragged Dumont down the hallway to a lift. The Germans shoved him into the lift and when it reached the ground-floor lobby Luc and Henderson rushed over to pick him up.

At the same moment, Major Ghunsonn came out of an office and went berserk.

'Who are you?' he shouted. 'Who authorised the release papers? Where in the name of Christ is my custody officer?'

Once Dumont was on his feet his parents supported him. Henderson gave PT his arm and Maxine gave Marc a quick hug. But as they reached the former hotel's entrance, Major Ghunsonn sent two armed men to block their path.

'Somebody tell me what is going on,' Ghunsonn demanded, as a worried-looking officer presented three sets of release papers. 'Oberst Ohlsen! What has this got to do with that bald cretin?'

Ghunsonn stormed over to Henderson and pointed at Marc. 'Your boy said that you're a wealthy family. How much did you bribe Ohlsen?'

Henderson spoke in his politest German. 'That's a very serious accusation to make about a senior officer in a public place, Major. If you feel aggrieved, I'd suggest putting your accusation in writing to General Schultz.'

The major was turning bright red. He eyeballed Henderson for several seconds, before looking at the two guards blocking the exit. 'Get them out of my headquarters.'

Luc took a deep breath and looked at Ghunsonn. 'The valet has the keys to my car – can you arrange—'

Ghunsonn sensed a chance for revenge and waggled the release papers under Luc's nose. 'I see papers for three boys. I have *no* papers for a car, in fact I believe that the only car that I saw has been requisitioned for essential use by the occupying forces. Now get out of my headquarters before I have the whole lot of you locked up for loitering.'

Marc was delighted to breathe outdoor air as they moved down the front steps of the hotel.

Luc turned towards Henderson as he struggled down the steps with Dumont. 'You clearly have some influence. Can you do anything about my car?'

Henderson smiled dryly. 'I got your son out. I'm not pushing my luck by calling back and asking to save a car.'

Vivien had bloody claw marks down her face and gave Henderson an evil look as Marc looked up and down the deserted street. The streetlights were off and the windows blacked out to prevent air raids.

'So how do we get home?' Marc asked. 'PT and

Dumont can hardly walk, it's thirteen kilometres and we've got no papers to be out after curfew.'

'I'll think of something,' Henderson said wearily, as PT's weight dragged on his back. 'I always do, don't I?'

CHAPTER TWENTY

Henderson stepped into Oberst Ohlsen's office holding one of the best bottles from Luc Boyle's cellar.

'Compliments of me and the rest of the Boyle family,' Henderson said. 'And I'd personally like to show my gratitude by offering to buy you lunch.'

'You look bloody awful,' Ohlsen noted, as he tipped back his chair and studied the label on the bottle.

'I had to come here and practically beg the night staff to set me up with a set of curfew papers,' Henderson explained. 'My nephew Dumont took a real hammering, so my brother Luc and his wife stayed in Calais with friends. It was nearly two by the time I'd walked thirteen kilometres home with my boys.'

Henderson obviously didn't add that he'd had to stay up another hour to listen out for the return message from McAfferty. After walking back from the barn, he'd ended up getting into bed less than two hours before he had to get up for work.

'The wine is appreciated,' Ohlsen said. 'But I'll have to decline lunch in case people talk. Major Ghunsonn came to my quarters in a furious temper, accusing me of taking bribes. He only calmed down when I reminded him of his rank and threatened to court martial him for insubordination. Ghunsonn is well connected and the type who bears a grudge, so you *and* your boys had better steer clear of military police from now on.'

Henderson nodded. 'Marc and PT have been told that if they put one toe off my farm they'll be getting a thrashing like they've never had before.'

'Do you know, my wife complains if I thrash my boys too severely,' Ohlsen said, as he aimed a hand at the picture of two fit-looking lads. 'But boys need discipline. It worries me what they get up to when I'm all the way over here.'

'Never did me any harm,' Henderson agreed. 'My father kept a cane in an umbrella stand by the front door. He only had to look towards the hallway for all thoughts of mischief to go up in smoke.'

The Oberst laughed. 'One thing came up when I was speaking with Ghunsonn. He said that the youngest of your boys spoke in German and even had the cheek to try bribing him.'

'That'll be Marc,' Henderson said, nodding. 'I tried with all three of my kids, but he's the only one who showed an aptitude for languages.'

'And he can hold a decent conversation?'

'Reasonably well,' Henderson said, wary because he didn't know where this was leading. 'He isn't fluent, but he gets by well enough.'

'You can't imagine the earache I've been getting since that landing demonstration went wrong yesterday. Goering's told everyone in Berlin that our invasion plans are a shambles and the general's made it clear that my career prospects will take a sharp slide if things don't come right. Our single biggest problem remains a lack of decent translators and I couldn't help wondering about your boy.'

'He's only twelve,' Henderson said. 'I think he'd struggle with the kind of intense translation work that's expected of us. And the hours – I have a thirteen-kilometre bike ride to and from headquarters and some nights I don't finish work until gone seven.'

'I realise he's young,' Ohlsen said. 'But I had one specific task in mind. We have a naval architect named Kuefer. He's working on barge conversions, but he wastes a lot of time trying to communicate with the local shipbuilders. It's creating a bottleneck, but I don't have enough translation staff to give him someone full time. Your boy might fit the bill.'

Henderson instantly understood the intelligence potential of the position, but he didn't know how Marc would cope with the job.

'Perhaps you could give him a trial,' Henderson suggested. 'The thing is, I only have one bike. With the ban on us French purchasing petrol I can't use our car.'

'I can arrange papers and fuel tokens,' Ohlsen said. 'And Marc will be paid the going rate for translation. We don't have any other boys so I expect he'll be paid the women's rate.'

'A trial then,' Henderson said warmly. 'It'll keep the boy out of mischief, might even do him some good.'

*

Maxine ironed a set of clothes for Marc before subjecting him to a severe haircut and a barely warm bath. Henderson roused him at six the following morning and made him put on the smart boots he'd stolen two days earlier, before an instantly forgotten lesson in the art of knotting a tie.

Henderson had lugged a can of petrol home the previous night and after a short battle to get Maxine's Jaguar started he blasted across empty countryside with the roof down and the speedometer touching seventy miles an hour.

After a brief stop at a regular checkpoint on the edge of Calais, the Jaguar created a stir as Henderson parked in the cobbled courtyard behind army headquarters.

Two guards stepped out to look at it and a small fellow who turned out to be the naval architect, Kuefer, got out of a Mercedes limousine to stroke it.

'Beautiful,' he purred. 'They say if a design looks right it *is* right, and this looks very right indeed.'

The Jaguar SS100 was a beautiful car, famed for being the world's first production car capable of a hundred miles an hour. But at that moment Henderson would have happily swapped it for a battered Citroën. Jaguars were the tools of château owners and playboys (play*girls*, in Maxine's case), and the vehicle jarred horribly with his back story of being a poor farmer.

Henderson also worried that some greedy officer might try to commandeer her and Maxine had already told him that he'd not be sharing her bed if any harm came to her most prized possession.

'Be good, listen carefully and do what you're told,' Henderson said, as he kissed Marc on both cheeks. 'I think I'd better move the Jag out to a side street.'

Kommodore Kuefer had a slight build and a feminine air. Despite the warm weather, he wore a leather overcoat on top of his navy uniform. Marc groaned as he settled into the rear of the Mercedes beside him.

'You're much too young to be making sounds like that,' Kuefer laughed.

'I got on the wrong end of a rifle butt and a couple of German boots,' Marc explained, giving Henderson a quick wave as the car pulled away. 'Where are we going?'

'Dunkirk first,' Kuefer said. 'It's about forty kilometres east. Then lunch, then back to my office. Hopefully you'll have a good sense of what I do by day's end.'

Dunkirk had been the last pocket of northern France held by allied forces. More than three hundred thousand soldiers – mainly British – had escaped across the Channel over a two-week period, while a million and a half French, Dutch and Belgians were forced to surrender.

Two and a half weeks of intense shelling and aerial bombardment had left little but rubble. Barely a handful remained from a pre-war population of fifty thousand, but every open space, from cemeteries to stadiums, contained malnourished and lightly guarded prisoners.

'They're our labour pool,' Kuefer explained, as the back wheels juddered over a thigh-width crack in the road. 'A herd. They throw in a few bread rolls and it's like feeding time at the zoo. You have to hose off the filth and feed them for a couple of days before they're fit for anything.'

Marc studied Kuefer's face, trying to detect pity or contempt for the prisoners in his expression. All he saw was a familiar numbness. If you gave too much thought to suffering you'd become paralysed, and apparently that applied as much to a naval Kommodore as a twelve-year-old refugee.

'There are similar camps near Calais,' Marc noted. 'But smaller. It surprises me that more don't try to escape.'

'The strong-hearted ones escaped three months back,' Kuefer explained. 'They're quite weak now. They'll have to be released before the winter comes, otherwise they'll freeze to death.'

The Germans feared disease and had used prisoners to clear and burn a hundred thousand bodies, but no effort had been made to rebuild the ghost town, except around the docks. Dunkirk had a huge manmade harbour with corridors of docks and canals that led deep into the countryside.

Kuefer told his driver to pull up at the edge of a large dry dock.

'Get out,' Kuefer said. 'You'll soon get a good idea of what this is about.'

Kuefer led Marc across scorched grass, beyond which a fence shielded the edge of a concrete dock. It was more than fifty metres wide, twenty-five deep, and vast metal gates kept the water out at the far end. More than a dozen barges were lined up on the dock's floor.

'In peacetime this is a painting dock for the hulls of large vessels,' Kuefer explained.

Marc leaned over the fence and looked down the

concrete face to the puddles and silt on the floor of the dock. More than a hundred prisoners and skilled foremen worked there. Sparks flew from welding gear on one side while another crew used wooden levers to jack a small barge on to its side so that the flat bottom of its hull could be inspected.

'You've gotta watch yourself on those,' Kuefer warned, as he pointed at the rusting metal ladders spaced every twenty metres along the dock wall. 'Your boots pick up silt and oil off the dock floor, which ends up all over the rungs. Then it rains and it's as slippery as hell. We've lost three welders from falls in the last seven weeks.'

'How many men have you lost altogether?' Marc asked.

Kuefer shrugged. 'Nobody keeps count. I only know about the welders because there's a shortage. If we lose a labourer or a painter they just draft a new man from the camps. If we lose a good welder it slows everything down.'

'How many barges are needed for the invasion?' Marc asked.

'All we can get,' Kuefer said. 'We're taking every barge, motor launch and tug we can lay our hands on out of northern France, Holland, Belgium and even a few from Germany. Originally the army asked for a minimum of ten thousand barges, but we'll be lucky to get seven thousand – and a good third of those are in no state to reach the open sea. Come on, I'll take you to the drafting room.'

A two-minute drive brought the Mercedes to one of the small number of dockside buildings that still had four walls and most of a roof. Every window was boarded and electricity came from a pair of diesel generators mounted on flatbed trucks.

'Kommodore, good to see you,' a bearded Frenchman said, speaking in French. 'We have eleven barges – arrived from Belgium yesterday.'

Kuefer pointed at Marc. 'I have a translator now. He's young, but Oberst Ohlsen assures me that he's capable. Marc, meet Louis – my head draftsman and engineer. Before we start, I want to show Marc what we do. This is our starting point,' Kuefer continued, as he led Marc towards a large draftsman's board on which was a partially drawn outline of a coal barge. 'How many of these do we have?'

Marc took a moment to realise that he was supposed to translate. After asking Louis he replied to Kuefer in German. 'He says there are six identical barges. Five are in reasonable condition, the sixth has suffered a collision on the way here and only appears to be afloat by the will of god.'

Kuefer smiled. 'Identical barges are desirable because it means there's less designwork per vessel. Now, once the drawing of the ships is complete decisions have to be made.'

Kuefer headed across to a bank of wooden school

desks with doors laid across the tops.

'This is a completed drawing and is usually accompanied by a condition report by a ship's surveyor. Under normal circumstances an architect such as myself will survey the ship, study these plans for a few days, make some suggestions and supervise the draftsman in drawing up plans for refurbishment work.

'At present we don't have that luxury. With thousands of barges to convert, I need to make rapid decisions based upon instinct and experience so that repairs and modifications can be completed quickly.'

'And if you get it wrong the boat sinks?' Marc asked.

'Hopefully not.' Kuefer smiled. 'But with four naval architects converting thousands of barges in the space of a few months, there's always a chance that things will go wrong.

'Now,' Kuefer continued, as he leaned over the completed drawing. 'My task is to turn this barge, which looks like it was designed for towing lumber along a river, into something that's seaworthy, capable of rapid embarkation and disembarkation and of carrying heavy equipment such as tanks and artillery pieces.'

As Kuefer slid a set of drawing instruments from his leather coat, the bearded draftsman pulled tracing paper over the drawing and cut it from a roll before clamping it in place with bulldog clips.

'Decisions,' Kuefer said, as his pencil hovered over the

paper. 'So Marc, this is a nice sized barge, designed for lumber. It's wide and metal hulled, so it's basically seaworthy. It might catch the wind and capsize in a gale of force eight, but there's nothing you can do about that. The barge floor is wood and any tracked vehicle or even a truck is likely to splinter it. In an ideal world, we'd lay aluminium over the whole deck, but the aviation industry has dibs on the entire supply.

'That leaves me with two options – either a thin layer of tar . . . actually, how much tar is available at present?'

Marc opened his mouth to translate, but Louis understood and Marc only had to translate the answer.

'He said we have enough for wooden hull repairs and deck patching, but it'll be weeks before there's enough supply to lay over the floor of eleven barges.'

'As I expected,' Kuefer murmured. 'Which means we have to go with a concrete floor. Concrete weighs twice as much and takes a full week to set. But it's all we have.'

As Kuefer explained, his hands were a whirl – jotting marks, lines and comments on the tracing paper. He drew crosses where anchor points should be set in the concrete. These would hold chains to strap down vehicles or cargo, or else they'd be threaded with ropes for soldiers to hang on to.

'Finally the ramp,' Kuefer said dramatically, before giving Marc a smile. 'Ideally, every self-powered barge would have the front chopped off. We'd install a drop-down ramp that would enable tanks and troops to run on to a beach and start fighting. Unfortunately we have no chains or gears and we certainly don't have electric winches or the welders and electricians we'd need to make them work efficiently. So we have this.'

Kuefer used a ruler to draw a pair of metal ramps with a hinge at their centre. One end was welded to the floor of the boat, while the hinged parts swung out over the front of the barge, enabling vehicles or men to run down the ramps on to the landing beach.

'*Voilà!*' Kuefer said, as he signed off his drawing and smiled at Marc. 'One Belgian lumber barge, expertly converted into a state of the art landing ship.'

Louis spoke in Marc's ear and Marc translated for Kuefer.

'He says the army have been rejecting a lot of barges as unstable and that four centimetres of concrete across the whole deck might be too heavy. He suggests strips on either side where tracks and tyres would run, leaving the centre of the deck as wood.'

'Obviously,' Kuefer roared. 'That's what I meant. Why would you *ever* lay concrete across the whole deck?'

Marc got the impression that Kuefer hadn't meant that at all, but didn't like being told he was wrong by a mere draftsman.

'Tell him to show me the next one,' Kuefer said sourly.

'The only food around here is army swill and I want to be back in Calais in time to get a decent table for lunch at Heuringhem's.'

CHAPTER TWENTY-ONE

A week after starting work with Kuefer, Marc was fed up with his boss. When the Kommodore was in a good mood he'd take time explaining how things worked, reminisce about childhood and speak fondly of his previous role designing gun turrets for cruisers and battleships. But he was under huge pressure from Berlin to convert thousands of barges with limited material and an under-skilled workforce, so mostly he was crabby and miserable.

Kuefer worked late nights and weekends and his young translator was expected to be available at all times. Marc often fell asleep on the way home and he even spent one night on the sofa in Kuefer's hotel suite when his boss demanded a five a.m. start for a meeting in Paris.

Most days they travelled between dockyards,

supervising barge construction along a three-hundred-kilometre stretch of coastline running from Le Havre in the west and as far east as Ostende in Belgium.

The thing that most irked Marc was that Kuefer and his German driver, Schröder, would make arrangements for lunch in a decent restaurant, leaving him to his own devices. While the Germans had three courses with wine and cigars, Marc found himself wandering around a strange town with nothing but a sweaty sandwich from home, or left at some dockyard or in the draftsman's office to eat whatever was served to the prisoners.

Each port had a slightly different atmosphere. The huge dry docks at Dunkirk were as miserable as the watery broth served for lunch. At Le Havre nobody spoke to Marc in case he snitched to his boss; Calais was OK because Henderson wangled him a pass to eat with the Germans at headquarters; but Marc found himself in Boulogne on this drizzly Wednesday.

Twenty small boatyards were situated along a broad canal behind the harbour. A few had gated dry docks for big boats, but most work was done on sloping concrete embankments. Although Germans gave the orders and prisoners did all the unskilled work, the yards remained in the hands of family businesses that had run them for decades.

Most of the owners were making good money from the

conversions and treated their unpaid labour force in a decent fashion that extended to a proper lunch and safe working conditions.

Marc sat on a bollard close to the canal's edge. The lunch ladies seemed to like him and his plate was stacked with fresh rolls, roasted vegetables and a huge slice of pork. He ate with fingers that were grubby from a morning spent clambering around boatyards.

Although conditions were better in Boulogne than in the other ports, there was still a hierarchy amongst the prisoners which determined what work they did and who they sat with at lunch.

Skilled labour was at the top of the pile. The Germans had advertised for welders, electricians, riveters and carpenters to come into the area, and these free men earned good wages. Next came the largest group, regular French prisoners of war. These men worked alongside tradesmen, carrying lumber, making repairs and painting. They worked twelve-hour shifts, but they were all volunteers who preferred hard work to being bored and hungry in the prison camps.

At the bottom of the pile were Poles and North Africans. The Nazis hated all Poles, but Polish prisoners in these parts were particularly disliked because they were fanatics who'd volunteered to fight for Britain or France after their own army surrendered.

The French Army had recruited more than a million

fighters from North African colonies. According to Hitler's racist theories, people with dark skin were little better than animals. White French soldiers were treated in accordance with the Geneva Convention, but the Africans were regarded as subhuman and suffered great brutality. In some areas, surrendering African troops had been moved into holding pens and machine-gunned by the SS.

In the dockyards the Africans and Poles got the least pleasant jobs, from hauling the barges up and down the embankment, to scraping barnacles off hulls and steam cleaning engine parts inside the workshop.

After half an hour for lunch the dock foreman rang a bell and more than six hundred men went back to work at the various yards along the embankment. Marc had nothing to do until Kuefer got back from a restaurant in town so he helped the lunch ladies to stack up the enamel mugs and plates. His reward was a big slice of the fruit flan reserved for the foremen.

As Marc ate he sat at the top of the nearest embankment and watched as six Africans began to haul a small cargo barge up the embankment.

To begin with four men crossed a bridge to the opposite bank and caught ropes thrown from the back of the boat. They pulled the back out until the bow faced the embankment. As they rushed back over the bridge, their colleagues jumped aboard and looped a metal chain through the mooring holes in the bow. The thick chain was wound around a pulley with an attached breaking lever, and finally linked up to an electric winch inside a building atop the embankment.

The next phase of the operation was the trickiest. The boat's wooden hull would get shredded if it was dragged up the concrete, so two men rushed forwards and placed a wooden roller under the bow. As the boat was hauled up, more rollers were wedged under the hull.

Once a third of the vessel was out of the water, wooden props shaped like a pair of triangles were slid under the hull-rollers and then turned upwards to prevent the ship from toppling on to its side. The six Africans had done this dozens of times and Marc marvelled as their heavy physiques coordinated ropes, rollers and props while the electric winch moved the boat slowly up the embankment.

But as the rear of the ship emerged from the water, a metallic grinding sound ripped from the shed containing the main winch motor. Marc looked over his shoulder and heard rattling as the broken chain dragged over the concrete.

'We lost it!' the winch operator shouted desperately.

The operator pushed his whole weight against the brake lever, but the pulley wasn't designed to support the weight of the boat and the juddering chain torn off the brake shoe. Realising that the end of the chain might lash back as it cleared the pulley, he dived backwards as the boat began rolling back towards the dock.

Marc saw the tension in the broken chain as it whipped around the pulley and feared it might fly in his direction as it broke loose.

'Clear out!' the foreman shouted.

As Marc ditched his soggy flan and dived back behind the winching shed, the crew pulling the cargo ship up the embankment abandoned their positions, as did the crew working on the next barge less than five metres away.

Marc and everyone else expected the end of the chain to slide around the pulley and break free, but its jagged end wedged in the brake mechanism. The sliding boat juddered to a halt halfway back in the water.

It seemed the end of the chain would remain jammed in the cogs, and the yard foreman stepped out gingerly to inspect it.

The shipyards were always full of noise, but Marc could hear his heart beating as he stood on the dockside surrounded by sweating prisoners. As the foreman crouched in front of the winch there was a sharp crack.

The twisted end of the chain remained jammed, but the weight of the boat had torn the brake lever and the pulley out of the concrete floor. As the cargo boat began sliding back on its rollers the chain whiplashed across the embankment with the pulley attached.

It catapulted several metres off the ground and crashed through the hull of the neighbouring barge. The momentum of the chain was enough to topple the cargo boat and it hit the bottom of the canal, leaning on its side.

The dilapidated hull had splintered and began flooding with water. To make matters worse a backwash rolled up the embankment, flushing everything from paint cans to welding gear into the canal.

'Is anybody hurt?' a foreman shouted.

Everybody had cleared the area in time, but the winch was wrecked, the little cargo ship lay on its side blocking the canal and the boat next to it had a lump the size of a motorbike ripped out of its hull.

Marc looked on as the foreman and the yard's owner inspected the remains of the winching system, eventually reaching the conclusion that the Algerian named Houari who'd been operating the brake lever had let the clutch out too fast, causing the chain to snap.

Houari was a powerfully-built twenty year old and unofficial foreman for the African workers.

'We've pulled boats three times that size up the ramp,' Houari shouted furiously. 'My work is good. It's your equipment that's decrepit.'

Foremen from neighbouring shipyards had come across. Some offered to send men over to help pull up the barge blocking the canal, others came to complain that they'd lost paint and tools in the backwash. The six Germans who guarded the prisoners had also come across to see what was going on and this was the melee into which Kuefer returned from lunch.

'Where's my translator?' Kuefer shouted. 'Get over here and tell me what's going on.'

Marc pushed through the adults and saw his boss's eyes bulge at him.

'Tell me what they're saying.'

Marc explained that the foreman blamed Houari for letting the chain out too quickly, but that Houari denied this and said it was down to the overworked braking system on the electric winch.

'How do we fix it?' Kuefer asked.

The foreman replied and Marc translated. 'He says that he can't get a boat in or out of this yard until the winch is repaired. The barge that's blocking the canal will have to be pumped and pulled out by a tug which will have to be brought down from Calais.'

'The *hell* it will be,' Kuefer shouted. 'I want this canal cleared *today*. I want men swimming in that canal salvaging all the equipment we've lost. Get horses and ropes and as many prisoners as you need from the nearest camp, then drag that boat out of the water. And if they have to pull boats in and out of water by hand until the winch is repaired, that's what they'll do.'

Marc had learned to use a notepad to translate

Kuefer's longer rants, but he'd left it in the back of the car so he just had to hope that he translated the complex instructions accurately.

Houari approached Marc. 'Tell your boss that we can't send men into the canal. Drums of lead paint went into the water along with oil, tar and god knows what else. Any man who goes in that water will be blinded.'

Marc explained, but Kuefer exploded.

'Let him go blind,' Kuefer shouted, before pointing at Houari. 'Guards, get this black bastard and his incompetent friends diving in that canal, fishing out tools and equipment. If you get any complaints, shoot them.'

Marc thought he was going to get strangled when he translated the instructions for Houari, but the big Algerian shoved Marc aside.

'Screw your canal, screw your barges,' Houari shouted, as he pulled a screwdriver from his trousers and aimed at Kuefer's neck.

Houari missed, instead thrusting the end of the screwdriver up through the base of Kuefer's jaw and skewering his tongue. Marc backed away as the German guards grabbed Houari's arms and Kuefer's mouth flooded with blood.

'Bollocks to Hitler,' Houari shouted, as the guards slammed him against the concrete.

One German booted Houari in the face as another pulled his service revolver and shot him through the heart.

Part Five

20 August 1940 – 10 September 1940

Hermann Goering, Supreme Commander of the Luftwaffe named 13 August Aldertag, or Eagle Day. It was the beginning of a major aerial offensive designed to destroy the Royal Air Force and clear the skies ready for the full-scale invasion of Britain, one month later.

After two years of military success, the Germans were confident. August 15–17 saw the heaviest fighting of the aerial battle between the Luftwaffe and the RAF. Both sides lost planes, but instead of the expected victory, two German planes were shot down for every British loss.

On 20 August the British Prime Minister, Winston Churchill, gave a speech to the House of Commons:

'The gratitude of every home in our island goes out to the British airmen who are turning the tide of the world war. Never in the field of human conflict was so much owed by so many to so few.'

CHAPTER TWENTY-TWO

20 August, Natural History Museum, London, UK

The stroke of a minister's pen had turned Eileen McAfferty from an admin assistant in an obscure intelligence unit to one of the most senior women in the Royal Navy. She still felt like an impostor in her uniform, however, and couldn't help smiling to herself every time someone saluted her in the street.

'How are the shoes?' Eric Mews, Deputy Minister for Economic Warfare, asked brightly.

'Very comfortable.' McAfferty nodded as she sat at a long but empty meeting table.

'You know Air-Vice-Marshall Paxton, don't you?' Mews asked.

McAfferty nodded before the stocky RAF officer spoke.

'Settling in, old girl?'

'Typewriters and filing cabinets arrived for the new offices last week,' McAfferty answered. 'The only thing is, I keep getting letters from the Admiralty telling me that I need to attend a two-week etiquette and decorum course for female Navy officers. I don't know when I'll find the time.'

'After the war, probably,' Paxton laughed.

'How's Henderson holding up?' Mews asked.

'Well enough, I assume,' McAfferty said. 'Because of the short transmission windows and the risk of detection, our communications are strictly matter of fact.'

'Of course,' Mews said, as he reached for his pipe. 'His intelligence has been absolutely top notch. It ties in with everything else we're hearing and at this moment it feels like we're on top of the entire German invasion plan.'

'Henderson's tip-off on Eagle Day was a huge help to the RAF,' Paxton said. 'From our point of view it's a pity he's not down in Beauvais getting specific information on Luftwaffe strategy, but the information meant we knew the assault was coming our way and we hit the ground running.'

'But now it's time to act,' Mews said, as he lit his pipe. 'We've intercepted a huge quantity of German military traffic and the entire German command is in agreement on three things. First, Hitler is absolutely determined to launch an invasion of Britain on September sixteenth and second and third, the two critical factors in a successful German invasion are control of the skies over the Channel and the assembly of a barge fleet.'

McAfferty nodded. 'I'm sure the Air-Vice-Marshall knows more about the air battle than I do. Henderson is getting information about the barge fleet from a source who works as a translator for their chief naval architect. As far as we can tell, the Army would like more boats but believes it will have enough to get the job done by mid-September.'

'And that's something we have to change,' Mews said.

Paxton explained. 'By early September the Germans will have to start moving their barge fleet into the harbours along the coast, ready for the invasion.'

'Northern France is home to a dozen German fighter bases, so it's not the ideal spot for a bombing raid,' Mews added. 'A daytime mission would be suicidal and even night bombing won't be easy.'

'We have a three-hundred-and-fifty bomber raid planned for September ninth,' Paxton continued. 'That's a little over two weeks. What I need from Henderson is accurate information on where the barges are and navigational markers for the locations.'

McAfferty didn't understand. 'Markers?'

'Anything that will help our pilots pinpoint the bombing zones at night,' Paxton explained. 'A large ship or building, a distinct curve in the river. Anything that's likely to be visible to a bomber pilot flying through darkness at two hundred miles an hour. Good visual markers can raise the accuracy of a raid from ten per cent to sixty or even seventy per cent.'

'The success of this raid is now Henderson's number one priority,' Mews added, as McAfferty jotted down some notes.

Pas-de-Calais, northern France

The Germans now practised daily on the beach near the farm. The exercise that had failed so dramatically in front of Goering a month earlier was now performed up to five times a day, with four hundred troops and up to eight barges each time.

Barges and canal boats converted in the yards at Boulogne and Calais were held in the natural harbour on the far side of the pier and tested for speed and seaworthiness by a specially assigned crew.

Another part of the beach was used to give swimming tests in the choppy waters. Anyone who failed to swim twenty metres out to a marker buoy and back again was subjected to the attention of burly swimming instructors. Their teaching technique mainly consisted of screaming in faces before throwing men over the side of a boat and whacking them with wooden oars if they tried grabbing at the ropes along the side.

Paul was fascinated by the way an army reduces men to cogs. A man lost his legs when he fell in front of a tank, several died when an unseaworthy barge caught a high wave and non-swimmers collapsed on the shore, only to be dragged back out to sea, but despite all this, the Germans kept improving.

More men could swim, the barge pilots were mastering tides and tank crews became expert in driving up the access ramps. In good weather eight barges could be loaded, taken back around the pier and unloaded on the neighbouring section of beach in twenty minutes. Soldiers repeated four cycles of loading and unloading, by which time new barges and new troops had arrived to repeat the exercise.

Paul's love of drawing had been consumed by an appetite for money. All the regular officers and instructors on the beach were used to him now and he'd even been given an authentic black SS helmet. It was supposed to be for protection during the occasional air raids, but Paul liked it and kept it on his head unless it got really hot.

All Germans received part of their pay in French francs, but there were few shops and little to buy in them. Paul drew from photographs of wives, girlfriends, daughters and cats, and he even did the occasional caricature of a commanding officer. Taking photographs home didn't work because most soldiers only came to the beach once, so he'd evolved a new style of simple pencil drawings.

Each one took less than fifteen minutes and Paul discovered that the soldiers were happy to pay twenty-five francs (or the equivalent in jam or chocolate) if he drew on large pieces of draftsman's paper which Marc stole from the dockyards and sold to him for two francs a sheet.

This probably made it the most expensive paper in France, but Paul didn't mind because on a good day he could sell a dozen drawings and he earned more in one week than a French factory worker made in a month. When Paul wasn't busy drawing he fantasised about all the things he'd buy when there were goods in the shops again.

Depending upon the tide the Germans usually finished their training for the day somewhere between two and six o'clock. Today was one of the earlier days and, after he'd been paid for his last batch of drawings by three soggy Germans, he grabbed his wicker basket and headed back to the farm under a dull sky.

The farm had changed significantly over the previous month. It was harvest-time for many crops and the Germans were anxious to avoid a winter famine. Some landowners and their families had been allowed back into the area, while prisoners of war were now allowed out of the camps each day to work the land.

Henderson had used his many contacts at headquarters to secure the daytime release of an experienced farm manager and two labourers, and a permit to buy diesel for the truck. With Henderson, Marc and Paul earning money and Maxine selling eggs and vegetables at market in Calais they'd become quite prosperous.

The house had been fixed up and painted, they'd bought three extra cows from Luc Boyle and taken over harvesting several of Luc's neglected fields on neighbouring farms.

'Afternoon, Eugene,' Paul said cheerfully as he saw the youngest of the prison labourers resting up against a dilapidated outbuilding.

Eugene was a villainous looking eighteen year old from Lyon, who was usually in good spirits. 'Ahh, it's the little collaborator!' He smiled, as Paul walked towards him.

'Chocolate?' Paul asked, as Eugene looked into his basket. 'Take a couple for your friends back at the camp. I've got more than I can eat.'

Eugene nodded gratefully as he took three bars and ripped the foil from one before sticking the end in his mouth. 'How much did you make today?'

'Only a hundred and fifty francs,' Paul said. 'But I'm asking for food and stuff whenever I can get it. There's plenty of food on the farm now, but with no transport and all the farms in a state I reckon there'll be a shortage this winter. So I'm telling the Germans to bring me tinned food and coffee and stuff and in a few months I'll be able to sell them for a mint.'

'You're a proper little capitalist,' Eugene said, grinning.

'What's a capitalist?' Paul asked.

'A greedy pig like you who thinks about making money on the back of other people's hunger.'

'I just *gave* you three bars of chocolate,' Paul noted. 'If I was greedy, would I have done that?'

'I know,' Eugene said. 'I'm teasing. You've got a good heart, so I expect we'll spare you after the communist revolution.'

'Are you OK?' Paul asked. 'You look tired.'

'Shattered dreams,' Eugene said vaguely, as he rubbed sweat off his brow. 'I'm starting to wonder about getting home, you know? It's better working here than being cooped up in the camp, but my own family has a farm. At first everyone was saying we'll be home in a few weeks. Then it was *They'll have to send all us prisoners home before it gets cold*, but now they've started sending prisoners to Germany. Six hundred went off to help with the harvest in Germany last week. I got back to camp last night and found that two trainloads more had been shipped off to Schwarzheide to work in a chemical plant.'

'Crap,' Paul said. 'They wouldn't do that if they were about to release everyone.'

'That's what I'm thinking.' Eugene nodded dismally. 'I'm a slave, and I've got a nasty feeling that the Germans won't be setting me free any time soon.'

'That's rough,' Paul said. 'But things change, you know? I mean everything's got worse this year, but who's to say it won't turn around some time soon?'

'You're a capitalist *and* an optimist.' Eugene managed a smile. 'If my knee hadn't been injured at the time I would have escaped in the early days, before the Boche got their security patrols organised. It's harder now, but I still reckon I could reach the south if I put my mind to it.'

*

After five weeks in the military zone Henderson was starting to look haggard. He worked sixty hours a week at army headquarters under the constant threat that his spying would be uncovered. When he got home each night there were messages to encode and problems on the farm to deal with.

On a good night he'd get five hours' sleep before he had to get up, walk three kilometres through the darkness to the transmitter's latest hiding place and then decode McAfferty's message. He rarely got back to sleep when he returned home and he'd lie awake, watching Maxine's chest rise under the blanket. Then he'd worry about everything, from a meeting the following morning, to the kids, to bigger stuff like politics and the course of the war.

Sometimes Henderson felt trapped, but the message he'd received from McAfferty that morning had led him to a decision. Once the labourers returned to their prison camp for the night he called a family meeting around the kitchen table.

'It's time to plan our exit,' Henderson said, in a dramatic tone that made Maxine and the four kids look up at him.

Everyone thought the same thing, but Maxine actually said it. 'Why would British intelligence want you to leave when you're in an ideal position at headquarters?'

Henderson shrugged. '*I've* made this decision. I'm sure headquarters in London would like me to stay here working as Ohlsen's translator until inevitably I make some small mistake and arouse suspicions. But I didn't sign up for a suicide mission and I most certainly didn't sign you five up for a suicide mission. I'm going to tell McAfferty that we're leaving before September sixteenth.'

'What if they order you to stay?' Maxine asked.

'Then I'll be court marshalled for disobeying orders. More importantly, you'll all be safe.'

PT looked pleased. 'How do we escape?'

'It's more complicated than that,' Henderson said. 'Last night I received two important pieces of information from McAfferty. The first confirmed that the Free French[12] Government in London want to parachute two spies and some equipment into this area. I've agreed to meet their men when they land and to get hold of all the paperwork they'll need to reach Paris.

'Secondly, McAfferty says that the RAF is planning a major bombing raid along the coastline on September ninth. They want intelligence on the locations of the biggest concentrations of invasion barges, *but* I'm going to send McAfferty a counter proposal.

'If we can get those two Free French spies to bring us explosives and set them in the right locations around the dockyards, we can start fires. If they're big enough, they'll act like beacons and the RAF bombers should be able to hit all their targets much more accurately.'

'Sounds good, boss.' Marc smiled. 'And after pulling that off, the Boche would be on the warpath so we'd have to escape?'

'Exactly,' Henderson said. 'Although it won't be easy because we'll have to steal one of the invasion barges and get away at the same time that the RAF are trying to bomb them out of the water.'

PT sounded less than enthusiastic. 'I thought you said

---

[12] Free French – While the Germans recognised the puppet Vichy Government led by Marshal Pétain, the alternative Free French Government had set up in London and claimed to be the legitimate government of France.

that you *didn't* sign us up for a suicide mission.'

'It's just an idea,' Henderson emphasised. 'I'm not saying that I'm going ahead with this, but I'd like all of us to put our heads together and work out whether this is doable. A successful air raid on the barge fleet will make it impossible for the Germans to launch an invasion before winter sets in.'

Rosie spoke after a brief lull. 'The Germans would ramp up security as soon as anything happened, so you'd need to attack all the bombing sites at once, and then somehow all meet up to escape afterwards.'

'Would you escape from one point, or would groups of us cross the channel on separate boats?' Paul asked.

'Unless you did it all with timers or something,' Marc said.

Henderson shook his head. 'You *can* make timed detonators, but they're not accurate and there's always a risk of the bombs being discovered. To pull this off we'd need men on the scene, setting off timed explosions.'

'What about manpower?' Maxine asked. 'You're surely not expecting the kids to be involved?'

'It might be the only way,' Henderson said uneasily. 'It's a lot to ask of anyone, let alone a youngster, but the stakes are huge and there aren't many people I can trust. We'll probably be able to use the two Free French spies and we could try recruiting some of the prisoners.'

'Eugene's desperate to escape,' Paul suggested.

'Although I think he wants to go back to his family farm rather than across the Channel to Britain.'

'Isn't he a communist?' Rosie asked. 'He's always going on about the workers taking over.'

'I don't care what his politics are so long as he hates the Nazis,' Henderson said. 'I'll sound him out next time I see him.'

Marc smiled. 'You know I told you about that Algerian getting shot in Bordeaux just after I started working for Kuefer? If you want people who hate the Nazis, the black men down there are your guys.'

'But we have to trust them,' Maxine said. 'I mean, Eugene is someone we've known for a few weeks and I'd say we can trust him. But bringing in people you don't know just because they hate the Nazis is a huge risk.'

'I know them,' Marc said. 'After Houari was shot the Germans started treating all the black guys even worse. They don't even get the same food as the other workers now. I feel sorry for them. Half the French prisoners still think they're gonna get released any day, but the North Africans know the Germans will never let them go. I've played dice with them a few times and sneaked them jam and tinned peaches because they're half starved.'

Paul shot up indignantly from his chair. 'My jam and peaches?'

'I didn't see your name on 'em.' Marc smiled. 'Eugene says that all property is theft anyway.'

'Bollocks to that communist,' Paul shouted, as he pointed accusingly at Marc. 'You owe me for those peaches.'

'Language,' Maxine said, as she jumped up and slapped Paul's face. 'How *dare* you speak like that at my table.'

'Calm down,' Henderson said fiercely, as Paul sat back down and buried his stinging face in his arms. 'Approaching Eugene and offering him a chance to escape across the Channel with us is probably a good idea. I'll have a think about the North Africans and how we can approach them.'

Henderson looked across the table at Rosie. 'How long until tonight's transmission window?'

'About an hour,' she answered.

'OK,' Henderson said. 'Meeting over. Rosie, you get the notebook and start encoding for me. I've got a proposal and a long list of questions to send to McAfferty.'

CHAPTER TWENTY-THREE

7 September

Of all the people living on the farm, the relationship between Henderson and PT was the most awkward. It was one a.m. and the pair walked through a forested area in their darkest clothes. They each grasped one leather handle of the heavy bag stretched between them.

'Are you sure you really want to be part of this?' Henderson whispered breathlessly.

'I'm here, aren't I?' PT replied. 'I've done all you've asked.'

'It *has* to be your choice,' Henderson said. 'I've got spare identity papers, and I can get a travel permit from headquarters if you want to head back to Bordeaux.'

'I'm not scared.'

'I'm not accusing you of cowardice,' Henderson said.

'But you've spent most of the last two weeks making it pretty clear that you don't like my plan.'

PT sighed as Henderson crouched down to pull the bag through a gap in a hedge. After a lot of crunched branches and some scratched skin, the pair made it through to a dirt road.

'You gave me the option to split before we left Bordeaux,' PT said, as they started walking uphill. 'I'd much rather we crept on board a barge and snuck across the Channel without any crazy plans involving beacons, explosions or Free French spies, but you laid it out to me. I knew what was on the cards when I agreed to come north with you.'

'This air raid could cripple the entire German invasion plan,' Henderson explained, as they moved off the opposite side of the road into dense trees. 'You told us what the escaping Poles you met on board ships said about the way the Nazis treated them, so you *must* understand how important it is that I try to save my country.'

'You don't understand,' PT said dourly. 'I was *born* into all this adventurous stuff. When I was three years old, my dad used to squeeze me through open windows and tell me to open the front door so that he could get inside and burgle houses.

'I spent three months digging a tunnel under Wall Street. My dad told me we were going to pull off the biggest robbery in history. We'd have fancy cars and a massive house and everything we could ever want. But what happened? My dad, big brother and two cops ended up dead. I end up on the run halfway around the world, I haven't seen my little brother in two years and I didn't have a friend worth the name until Maxine invited me back to the pink house to stay with you lot.'

'So why'd you try to steal my gold and run away?' Henderson asked. 'You were getting along with Maxine and the kids. It never even entered my head that you'd do a runner at that point.'

'I guess once you've seen your family ripped apart, you're scared of getting close to people. You remind me of my dad in a lot of ways. When you first started going on about going north to spy on the invasion and hatching your plan to help destroy the barges, you had the exact mischievous expression that my dad used to get when he was thinking up a robbery.'

'I guess I've always been an adventurer,' Henderson admitted, as the trees ended and they broke into an open expanse of grazing land. 'I'd sooner live a short life that counts for something than a long one that counts for nothing.'

PT stopped walking. 'No offence, Mr Henderson, but after what happened to my family, my ambition is to buy a little farm or a shop, live a quiet life and die peacefully in my sleep aged about seventy-five. I'll work with you because I hate the Nazis and want to get out of France, but I've got no taste for crazy schemes.'

Henderson slapped PT gently between the shoulders. 'Thanks for being honest with me.'

'It's OK,' PT said, as the bag thudded down in the shaggy grass. 'But if Paul, Marc or Rosie end up getting hurt in all this, don't expect me to forgive you.'

'I don't like using those youngsters,' Henderson admitted. 'But you saw what happened when the Germans invaded here. How many kids like Paul, Rosie and Marc will die if three Panzer divisions start blasting their way towards London?'

PT didn't answer. Instead he pulled a small torch from his pocket and inspected a map sketched by Paul.

'This is our spot,' PT said. 'How are we for time?'

Henderson glanced at his watch. 'Eight minutes past one, which gives us seven minutes to set up.'

The pair crouched down. Henderson unzipped the bag and pulled out three identical units. Each one comprised a pair of car headlights mounted in the base of a wooden vegetable pallet. These were linked by twenty metres of electrical wire to a pair of car batteries. The whole apparatus was controlled by a single switch.

The master lighting unit remained by the batteries. PT and Henderson each took one of the slave units twenty metres across the field. When they were both back by the batteries, PT flipped the switch on and off quickly to ensure that all six lamps worked.

'Three minutes,' Henderson said, as he craned his neck up to look at the stars in the moonlit sky. 'At least the sky's clear.'

They listened intently for the sound of an aeroplane, but as Henderson's watch passed one-fifteen there was no sign. All they could do was turn the lights on and hope for the best.

'I'll handle the lights,' Henderson said. 'You go uphill and check on the other two.'

A lot of effort had gone into scouting a good landing zone for the two French spies. Henderson's main criteria had been open land with a high vantage point nearby. As the lights blazed behind him, PT found his way towards a rusted metal shed. Marc crouched in the tangle of weeds surrounding it, with binoculars swinging around his neck.

'Any sign?' PT asked.

'Couple of German trucks went along the main road way over back about twenty minutes ago,' Marc answered. 'No sign of our plane yet.'

'And Rosie?'

'She's looking around the other side of the hill. She'll let us know if she sees anything coming.'

PT was knackered after lugging the lights and batteries across five kilometres of fields. He greedily drank water from Marc's hip flask as the minutes dragged.

'Where the hell's this plane?' PT moaned to himself as he watched the stars.

'Sssssh!' Marc said, moving suddenly and aiming the binoculars up at the sky.

PT heard the rumble of propellers. Down in the field, Henderson heard the same and began repeating an agreed signal: three quick flashes of light, followed by the lights staying on for five seconds. This was designed to prevent the spies from being dropped if the Germans captured the lamps. The wrong sequence or continuous beams would make the pilot fly back to Britain without dropping the spies.

The droning grew louder over the next half minute, but Marc and PT still got a fright as the twin-engined Whitley bomber swooped overhead, rattling the trees and making the metal shed behind them shake.

Aircraft technology had improved rapidly in the build-up to the war and the Whitley's five-year-old design lacked speed and manoeuvrability. Flying without a fighter escort, the medium bomber would be easily picked off by German fighters. Its only defence was to hedge hop – the technique of flying extremely low in pitch darkness. This required a highly-skilled pilot but made the aircraft nearly impossible to detect either on radar or from the confines of a fighter cockpit several thousand metres above.

Henderson watched the bomb doors open as the

aircraft skimmed the hillside at more than a hundred and fifty miles an hour. A large pod dropped out of the bay and slammed down in the field a few seconds later.

After signalling four flashes to indicate a safe drop, Henderson switched out the lights, grabbed the large canvas bag and raced across to check the next field, where the pod had landed.

'That's our cue,' Marc said.

As PT ran back downhill to help Henderson, Marc and Rosie watched through binoculars as the Whitley applied full power and went into a steep climb. While it was safe to drop items like plastic explosives and guns into a field, more delicate items like radios, detonators and humans need parachutes, which require a much higher altitude to open safely.

After climbing to more than three hundred metres, the Whitley turned in a wide arc. Once the bomber was facing back towards him, PT flicked the lamps on. Rosie had moved around to the same side of the hill as Marc and the pair now acted as spotters, watching as the parachutes opened and then tracking their path to the ground.

'I'm following the one on the left,' Marc said, as he watched the moonlight reflecting off the top of a white 'chute through his binoculars.

'Right,' Rosie said, as she momentarily lost track of the second parachutist. She took the binoculars away from her eyes and saw that the wind was blowing her target severely off course. 'He's going way left of the field,' she said anxiously. 'It's all woods over that way, he'll get tangled.'

Rosie began sprinting downhill towards the trees, glancing up occasionally to track the parachute. Once Marc was certain that the first parachutist was going to land on target he chased after her.

As the pair neared the bottom of the hill, the bomber had passed behind and was making a rapid dive for its treetop-skimming ride home.

PT switched out the signalling lights for the last time as Marc and Rosie crashed through the undergrowth beneath the trees. It was pitch black and as neither of them had a torch their only option was to feel blindly until they heard a crash in branches less than twenty metres ahead, followed by a blood-curdling moan.

'That's not good,' Marc gasped, as he charged towards the noise.

The moonlight illuminated streams of white parachute silk hanging down between the branches, but there was no sound apart from mulch crackling underfoot.

'Hello?' Rosie called, cupping her hands around her mouth. 'Hello?'

Marc looked up and saw that the ropes attached to the parachute led high up into the trees. He couldn't see the parachutist, but there was the unmistakeable outline of a large backpack snagged in a fork between the branches.

'Mate?' Marc asked uncertainly, as he gave a gentle tug on the rope.

This produced some rustling, until the pack overbalanced and the whole thing came crashing down. Marc dived back so that it missed his head, but the pack was heavy enough to knock him down when it hit the lower part of his leg.

'Ooof!' Marc groaned, as tree roots jarred his back.

Rosie closed in, half expecting to see a man hooked into the arm straps. 'You OK?'

'I guess,' Marc said. 'But where the hell is he?'

As Marc shoved the pack off his legs and stood up, Rosie noticed torchlight coming through the trees behind them.

'We've spotted traffic,' PT reported when he'd made a few more steps. 'Looks like a Boche truck coming up the road. Might be routine, but they could have spotted the parachutes. Whatever it is, Henderson's run off with the other parachutist and the equipment from the pod. He wants us to escape around the back of the hill so that we don't cross the Germans' path.'

'We need to find our parachutist first,' Rosie said nervously.

PT only now realised that there was no sign of the spy. He shone his torch up into the branches and solved the mystery.

Rosie covered her eyes and turned away in horror. The parachutist had landed high in the branches and must have remained conscious for long enough to release his 'chute and equipment, but as he'd tried to climb down he'd slipped. His throat was impaled on the jutting remains of a snapped branch. His jawbone held him up like a coat hook and his feet swung freely.

'Gruesome,' Marc winced.

PT turned off the light, before looking back and realising that the German truck had passed them by. Its rear lights were now heading uphill.

'We need to tidy this up so that the Germans don't find him when it gets light,' PT said calmly. 'If they know spies have been dropped into the area they'll tighten security and that's the last thing we need right now.'

'How do you tidy that up?' Marc asked.

'I'll yank him down.'

'He's hooked up there,' Rosie said. 'You'll have to tear the bottom half of his face off!'

'If I have to, that's what I'll do,' PT said bluntly. 'We'll roll him in the parachute silk, strip off his gun and equipment, and stuff him inside that metal pig pen at the end of the field.'

*

The surviving parachutist was a tubby little man named Bernard Prost. He wore rectangular glasses and sat at the kitchen table trembling over a mug of coffee. Everyone was up except for Paul, who'd picked up a bad cold and was sleeping upstairs.

PT stood at the sink scrubbing blood out of his shirt, while Maxine sat out on the doorstep, comforting Marc and Rosie, who'd been upset by the shocking death and the trauma of hiding the disfigured body.

'It's a mess,' Bernard mumbled. 'We needed two people to successfully infiltrate the telephone—'

Henderson raised a hand and interrupted. 'Think about your training, man,' he said firmly. 'You don't tell me or anyone else about your mission. What if one of us was captured and interrogated? Now, where are your photographs?'

'In the small case,' Bernard said.

Henderson had no confidence in this rather nervous man. 'I know that the death of your partner is a shock,' he said, as he opened the suitcase. 'But that goes with the territory of being a spy. You have to be strong . . . oh, for god's sake. What the *hell* is this?'

Henderson pulled a bar of chocolate with English writing on the wrapper out of Bernard's case.

'I understand food is in short supply in many areas,' Bernard explained. 'Chocolate has a high energy content.'

'But it's *British* chocolate!' Henderson gasped, as he threw more things out of Bernard's case. 'The first checkpoint you reach, the Germans will open your case and arrest you on the spot. And this, look at this!'

Henderson held up a shirt with a Fifty Shilling Tailor label stitched into the collar. 'Didn't MI5 train you in anything? You'd better go through your things and remove anything that looks even slightly British.'

'I've never met anyone from MI5,' Bernard explained. 'I've not had any formal training. I believe the Brits are building a training facility for undercover agents, but it won't be ready for several months.'

'Hopeless,' Henderson said, tutting loudly as he turned over more items in the suitcase and found the identity photographs he needed to complete Bernard's fake paperwork.

Maxine stepped in from the doorway as Henderson trimmed the photograph to the proper size for a French identity card. She looked at Bernard and spoke.

'Would a woman be a suitable replacement for your missing partner?'

'I suppose,' Bernard said uncertainly.

'I've always fancied Paris,' Maxine said, smiling.

Henderson shook his head. 'Don't be ridiculous, Maxine. You're returning to Britain with me and the kids.'

'Do you think I'll get along with your wife?' Maxine replied sarcastically.

Henderson shrivelled in his chair. 'I've already explained that my wife has certain difficulties. It's not a normal marriage in any sense.'

'So you'll be filing for divorce?' Maxine snapped.

Bernard had a smug little grin on his face that made Henderson want to thump him.

'Maxine . . .' Henderson mumbled. 'I can't authorise you to do this.'

'*Authorise*,' Maxine scoffed. 'You're in no position to *authorise* me to do anything, Charles Henderson. It's settled. If we successfully complete the air-raid operation I'll head to Paris and work with Bernard.'

'But,' Henderson spluttered, turning uncharacteristically red.

Rosie came in from the doorstep and looked at Henderson. 'Sorry to interrupt your argument,' she said, 'but it's three-thirty a.m. We need to send a message to McAfferty to confirm what happened with the drop.'

Bernard rose up out of his chair. 'I'll help,' he said.

'That's not necessary,' Henderson replied, scowling at the tiny photograph now glued to Bernard's identity card.

'It's more secure,' Bernard said insistently. 'My transmission averages fifty-two words per minute.'

CHAPTER TWENTY-FOUR

9 September 05:57 The Farm

Rosie, Maxine and Bernard stood around the kitchen table in their night clothes. PT, Paul, Marc and Henderson were dressed and ready to leave in the truck.

'OK,' Henderson said. 'Our big day is finally here. Did we all sleep well?'

There were a few nervous laughs before Henderson cracked a smile. 'Me neither,' he said. 'You all know your jobs and you all know how important they are.

'PT, you're off to Dunkirk, via Calais. Marc is handling Boulogne. Paul and I will deal with Calais. Finally, Maxine and Bernard will be setting incendiary beacons at Dieppe and Le Havre respectively. I'm not one for great speeches, but I do want to say keep *calm* at all times and make absolutely sure you have all the equipment on your checklists before you leave the farm.

'I set my watch by BBC radio when I first woke up and the time is now five fifty-eight. All of you have pocket or wrist watches. Make sure they're properly wound and telling exactly the right time. The RAF raids on all five ports are set for eight-forty. We'll want beacons at all five ports burning three minutes before that, so that the bombers have a target for the final ten miles of their approach.

'Everyone except Maxine and Bernard is due back here before ten p.m. If you miss the boat, there are emergency supplies, navigational charts, maps and blank identity documents hidden on this farm and at two locations nearby. There are small vessels all along the coast and my best advice is that you wait for a calm sea and try crossing the Channel. Britain's pretty big, so navigation isn't a problem, but be careful you don't hit any mines as you come ashore.

'Now, Marc and I have to go to work. Paul and PT are riding with us so now's your moment if any of you want to say goodbye to Maxine.'

As Henderson headed outside to start the truck, the three boys took turns hugging Maxine. She soon had tears streaking down her face.

'You're all so brave,' Maxine sniffled. 'I couldn't be any prouder if you really were my sons.'

'Don't forget to drop my gear off when you pass through Boulogne,' Marc said.

Maxine nodded. 'Between two trees, after the duck farm, before the junction, and there's a stone slab with your initials scratched into it.'

'You can't miss it,' Marc confirmed.

Paul was the youngest and the most upset. He gave Maxine a second hug as Henderson walked out to start the truck. The vehicle was more than ten years old and usually needed a few turns with a hand crank before it got going in the morning.

'Thanks for all the great dinners, Maxine,' Paul said, trying to hide his tears behind a smile.

'Paul, you've been a joy to have around. Thank you, and I'll write to you in England as soon as I can.' Maxine was now crying again.

'We're up and running, boys,' Henderson yelled from the doorway.

After briefly wishing Rosie and Bernard good luck, the three boys jogged out and squatted on top of the equipment in the back of the battered old truck.

Maxine looked at Henderson. 'Are you still sulking, or do I get a goodbye kiss?'

The Sunday between the parachute drop and the day of the air raid had been planned as a time to relax and prepare, but Henderson had been unhappy with Maxine's decision to stay in France and the tension between them had soured the mood.

But Henderson managed a smile and pulled her close for an intense goodbye kiss. 'If I'd only met you before my wife,' he said.

But Maxine wasn't fooled. 'We had fun,' she said, smiling bravely. 'And now it's over, because you'll either go back home to your wife, or get yourself killed.'

Henderson quickly shook Bernard's hand before climbing behind the wheel of the truck. Maxine was right about him never leaving his wife, and in some ways her staying behind had saved him from an awkward break-up. But he liked Maxine a lot and felt miserable as he drove off the farm, watching in the side mirror as she disappeared through the cottage door and catching a final glimpse back at her Jaguar as the truck turned on to the road.

He'd grown used to driving the sports car and the hedgerows seemed to move in slow motion as the clattering truck drove down the empty lanes. The security post on the outskirts of Calais pulled Henderson over.

'Slumming it today,' the guard noted.

Henderson pointed into the back. 'My youngest's got a doctor's appointment, so the Jag wouldn't cut it.'

A five-minute ride took them into the cobbled square behind army headquarters. Henderson shook Marc's hand through the hatch behind his head.

'Be safe,' he said, feeling unnerved by the smallness of

Marc's hand. 'I'm asking a lot of you, boy. There's no shame in failing, just make sure you're on that boat by ten o'clock tonight.'

As always, Kommodore Kuefer and his driver, Schroder, stood by their big Mercedes, smoking cigarettes. The German architect had spent three days in hospital after being stabbed by Houari and bore a large pink scar on his chin.

'Sorry Marc's late,' Henderson said. 'This old truck isn't so swift.'

Unless it was raining Kuefer and Henderson always exchanged a few words in German. Henderson wanted to make sure that no last-minute alteration would ruin Marc's schedule.

'Boulogne today?' Henderson asked.

'Meeting here in Calais first, then down to Boulogne,' Kuefer confirmed. 'If ever you're down that way you have to eat at Gérard's, the food is *magnificent.*'

Kuefer blew a kiss to emphasise his point as Marc climbed into the car. The German hadn't met the other boys before. Henderson introduced Paul as his younger son and PT as his nephew and the two lads politely shook Kuefer's hand.

Marc stared at the back of Schroder's head as the Mercedes drove out of the cobbled square, uncomfortable with the thought that if everything went to plan the two Germans only had a few hours to live.

06:44 Calais

Henderson acted like a model employee and never missed an opportunity to please Oberst Ohlsen. He'd set a regular schedule each morning, spending ten or fifteen minutes flirting with the female admin staff and picking up the latest gossip. Then he'd go to the wireless room and collect any radio messages or telegrams that had arrived overnight, which meant that he often knew what was going on in Berlin before the Oberst himself.

When Ohlsen and his assistant arrived shortly after seven o'clock, Henderson would be waiting with fresh coffee, German newspapers and the urgent messages. Unless Ohlsen was exceptionally busy, Henderson would be invited to stay for coffee and the Oberst's general mood and off the cuff remarks often contained as much valuable intelligence as the official communications.

On this particular Monday, Henderson also sprinkled a vial of toxic crystals into the sugar bowl. He wasn't sure what it contained, only that it had been specially prepared by a London chemist and carried over by the dead parachutist.

'How was your day off?' Ohlsen asked cheerfully as he came into the office ahead of his assistant.

'Any day off is a good one,' Henderson replied, as he

took the Germans' coats and hooked them up outside. When he got back, Ohlsen's assistant was pouring coffee into the three cups.

'You don't take sugar, do you Boyle?' he asked.

'Four spoons for me,' Ohlsen said, as Henderson shook his head.

12:15 Boulogne

Marc yawned as the Mercedes pulled up across the street from Gérard's fish restaurant.

'You don't look so good, Marc,' Kuefer noted.

'Tired,' Marc said, as he looked behind for traffic before opening the car door out into the road.

'Things should calm down in a week or two when we run out of barges to convert,' Kuefer said. 'I can go back to designing gun turrets instead of converting rotten canal barges, and I've heard that the administration will be reopening schools once the harvest is in.'

'And I'll not have to drive up and down these damned coast roads,' Schroder added. 'I'll probably have the pleasure of fighting my way through the English countryside instead.'

Marc looked across the street and saw that Gérard's was already filling up with its usual lunchtime crowd of German officers and wealthy French. It rankled Marc that in all the time he'd worked with Kuefer he'd never once been invited inside.

'If you see Louis at the dockyard, tell him I'll be arriving at around two-thirty.'

'Right,' Marc said, as he started to walk.

Gérard's maître d' stepped out beneath the grubby cloth canopy over the doorway. 'Good to see you, Kommodore Kuefer. Your garden table is ready.'

Once his boss was out of sight Marc quickened his pace. If he was hungry he'd usually go straight to the dockyard to beat the queue of labourers to a hot lunch, but the dockyard stew only took a few minutes to eat so Marc had often used his boss's leisurely lunch breaks to explore, and he'd come to know Boulogne well.

After turning off the street, Marc broke into a run. Like all the ports in the Pas-de-Calais, Boulogne had a heavy German presence, but he was known as Kuefer's translator and nobody ever bothered him. After skimming past a pair of miserable looking soldiers he sprinted down an alleyway between two rows of houses, ducking beneath strands of washing and getting yelled at when he crashed into an old man hidden behind yellowed bed sheets.

At the end of the alleyway, he ran past filthy wire cages crammed with ducks, then jumped over a fence into the overgrown garden of a bombed-out house. There were two mature oaks and a tall hedgerow between himself and a convoy of German trucks blurring past on the main route east.

As instructed Maxine had left a canvas bag between the trees. Marc crouched down and unbuckled it to check what was inside: phosphorous bombs, plastic explosive, detonators, fuse cord, piano wire and two pistols. He noticed a sheet of pink paper jutting from the front pocket and smiled when he read it:

I saved you the last piece! Good Luck. M.

Marc pulled a soggy block of bread pudding out of the pocket. Maxine cooked a mixture of French and English dishes and bread pudding had become his favourite. He checked the pocket watch Henderson had given him and made sure he had time before tucking in greedily.

The last mouthfuls were tinged with sadness. Would he ever see Maxine or taste her bread pudding again?

When there was nothing left he licked the sugar off the greaseproof paper and realised that Maxine was the closest thing he'd ever had to a mother. Rather than throw her pink note away, he folded the paper three times and tucked it deep into his trouser pocket.

Marc struggled with the heavy bag and took a different alleyway back towards the docks. Rather than risk being searched on his way into the secure perimeter around the docks, he stopped by Kuefer's Mercedes, unlocked the trunk and buried the bag deep inside beneath rolled-up plans, umbrellas and leather coats.

The roads around the dockyards were sealed off by gates and sentry boxes, but the German on the gate was used to Marc coming and going and barely glanced at his paperwork.

'Where's your boss?' the guard asked miserably.

'Stuffing his face at Gérard's,' Marc said. Although his German still wasn't fluent, it had improved hugely over the weeks he'd spent working as Kuefer's translator.

'Officers,' the guard said, making the word sound like a curse and giving an *up yours* gesture as Marc ducked under the gate.

'Tell me about it,' Marc smiled.

The port had two large rectangular harbours which were separated by a natural peninsula. The sun was high and as he walked along the waterfront more than two hundred barges bobbed on the twinkling water, tied ten to fifteen abreast at each mooring.

They varied from huge coal barges more than a hundred metres long and now converted to carry tanks, down to narrow boats made for the still waters of the Dutch canal system. All had been given a thin coat of grey paint and had numbers stencilled on the side of their hulls.

At the far side where the harbour broke on to the open sea, Marc noticed that there were fewer barges than there had been the previous Thursday. This confirmed intelligence picked up by Henderson that the Germans were beginning to spread the barges across beaches in preparation for the invasion in exactly one week's time.

Behind the twin harbours lay a broad canal that was a kilometre long and lined with the small boatyards where the conversion work was still progressing. The prisoners took lunch in two shifts and Marc sidled up to two African men. They formed part of a larger group of dark-skinned prisoners who'd finished eating and were throwing dice against the upturned hull of a fishing boat that hadn't touched water in a decade.

'Khinde, Rufus,' Marc said, as he pulled a length of wire out of his trouser pocket and raised one eyebrow teasingly. 'You all set?'

Khinde was a fearsome looking man who always worked bare-chested. Rufus was a Moroccan. Pale skinned, slender, and whose accent had more in common with a wealthy Frenchman than a North African.

'You got the equipment, Peaches?' Rufus asked, as he and Khinde backed away from the boat and the dice game. Marc's nickname came from the tins of fruit he brought them.

'It'll come in the boot of the Mercedes,' Marc explained. 'Did you hear your message on the BBC?'

Marc had been friendly with Khinde and Rufus since the day the Germans murdered Houari, but tins of peaches weren't enough to convince them that a twelve-year-old boy offered a genuine chance of escape, so Henderson had arranged for the BBC to transmit a message in the list of announcements that were made after the evening news.

'It's not easy getting your ear to a radio in the prison camp,' Rufus smiled. 'But we managed: *Peaches sends best wishes to the friends of Houari.*'

'So you believe me now?' Marc asked.

'We believe,' Rufus said, as he pulled Marc into a heartfelt embrace.

Khinde spoke loudly. 'These Germans call us apes. They won't ever let a black man go. So better to die trying to escape, eh?'

A couple of the other African prisoners overheard. Rufus moved further back and gave Khinde a withering stare.

'Peaches *said* it was a small boat,' Rufus growled. 'We can't help the others.'

'We could take more men,' Khinde said. 'Let them escape, let them find another boat.'

'If there's no escape plan they'll be massacred,' Rufus said. 'The French hate us as much as the Germans. How far do you think they'll get?'

'The other men look up to you,' Khinde said. 'You're a leader.'

Marc knew he had to act, but he wasn't comfortable ordering grown men around. 'I need to know,' Marc said resolutely. 'You help me with the plan *exactly* like we discussed and you'll have a good chance to escape. Otherwise I'll walk away and you can slave for the Nazis until they either shoot or starve you. Decide *now*.'

Marc started walking towards the draftsmen's huts and was hugely relieved when the two Africans started to follow.

'I like Peaches when he's angry,' Rufus smiled, and Khinde laughed noisily.

Marc stopped at one of the wooden picnic benches where the French supervisors ate lunch. 'Kuefer wants a couple of men,' he explained. 'I'm taking these two.'

The supervisor looked baffled as he scraped a dirty hand through his hair. 'Why the hell does Kuefer want labourers?'

Marc shrugged. 'Ask him yourself. You think he discusses every detail with me?'

'Are you sure you want blacks?' the foreman asked. 'Or does he want someone who'll actually do some work?'

The other foremen all laughed and Marc pretended to be irritated. 'If you want to argue with Kuefer I'll send 'em back, but he's in a shit mood today, so I wouldn't recommend it.'

The foreman waved his hand towards the offices and smiled. 'And who am I to argue with the orders of our mighty occupiers?'

'Dickhead,' Marc mumbled to himself as he led Khinde and Rufus between two recently built huts where the drawings were made for the barge modifications.

Beyond this was a storage yard stacked with dozens of empty tar drums.

'Take one each,' Marc said.

At the far side of the yard was a fire-damaged warehouse that had served as the draftsmen's office until the construction of the weatherproof huts.

'Go in there and keep quiet,' Marc said, as he passed Rufus and Khinde strands of piano wire. 'You've got to be ready as soon as they come through the door.'

CHAPTER TWENTY-FIVE

13:12 Calais

Henderson spent most of the morning translating at a planning meeting between a German major and French railway bosses. The railway officials had mastered the art of appearing to cooperate while subtly raising objections and declaring that virtually everything the occupiers asked for was impossible.

He'd struggled not to laugh aloud when one railway controller abruptly told the Germans that the best way to bring fuel and other supplies required for the invasion would be to release the thousands of French railway engineers who were being held in prisoner-of-war camps and then wait six months while repairs were completed, or better still to have not bombed so many French railway lines and bridges in the first place.

When the railway meeting was over, Henderson walked across the square and headed up to Oberst Ohlsen's office with a bunch of papers tucked under his arm. He feigned surprise when one of the Oberst's French admin assistants stepped in front of him.

'They both looked green,' she explained. 'The Oberleutnant walked out, but Oberst Ohlsen ended up in an ambulance and the noises that were coming out of his bathroom . . . He may be a Boche, but I must admit I felt sorry for him.'

'What a shame,' Henderson said as he stepped towards the Oberst's office.

'It's locked,' the assistant said. 'The military police said it could have been a poisoning attempt by French rebels. Major Ghunsonn gave orders that the door was to be locked and nobody allowed to go anywhere near the office.'

'Damn,' Henderson said. 'I have these papers and they need to be signed and sealed today.'

The papers were junk, but the curse was well founded. Henderson needed to get inside Ohlsen's office. The crystals were supposed to give Ohlsen stomach cramps bad enough to make him go back to his quarters and rest, but it seemed the reaction had been too violent and now Major Ghunsonn suspected foul play.

'Oh well,' Henderson sighed. 'It'll have to wait, I suppose.'

He backed down a wood-panelled hallway and stepped into the executive dining room at the top of the main staircase. He was ready with an apology if there'd been a meeting inside, but all he found was a cleaner dusting the model ships.

'Afternoon,' Henderson said politely, but the miserable old girl didn't bother to respond.

After cutting through the old kitchen, Henderson leaned into the hallway, unsure whether Major Ghunsonn had left a guard on the door of the Oberst's office. Mercifully, the only step taken was to lock the door and slide the Oberleutnant's desk in front of it.

Henderson paused for a moment, calculating the risks: if he was caught he'd be tortured and shot, but the main plan to create the beacons wouldn't be affected and his whole team had fall-back escape and liaison plans. If he pulled this off, he could be on the other side of the English Channel before anyone found that a British spy had stolen the three dossiers containing every detail of the invasion plan.

After a final glance, Henderson patted his jacket for a reassuring touch of his silenced pistol. He then took the key and moved quickly towards the double doors of the Oberst's office.

13:31 Boulogne
Marc waited for the Mercedes by the main dockyard

entrance and signalled for Schroder to pull over. He crouched at the open window beside Kuefer.

'Just spoke to Louis,' Marc explained. 'They've had a power failure in one of the huts. They'll be working in the warehouse building until the generator comes back up.'

Kuefer always downed a bottle of wine with his lunch. He chilled out under the influence and Marc could have told him that his mother had died without getting any more than a dumb smile in return.

'Better hop in then,' Schroder said.

Marc hoped Kuefer didn't look across and see his hands shaking as the big Mercedes drove the three hundred metres down a badly cracked road. About a million things could go wrong: Rufus and Khinde could chicken out, Louis or one of the foremen could spot them entering the warehouse and come over to investigate, Schroder didn't drink as much as his boss and might suspect something . . .

'You been running?' Kuefer asked, as they got out of the car.

Marc's mouth was almost too dry to speak, but he had damp patches around his armpits and his shirt was stuck to his back.

'I ate lunch sitting in the sun,' he croaked, as he grabbed the handle of the warehouse door.

'There's nothing in here,' Kuefer said as he stepped

under the badly burned roof beams.

Schroder looked suspiciously at Marc as he followed him into the warehouse. 'What did Louis tell you exactly?'

Before Marc could answer, Khinde whipped the piano wire around the driver's throat and pulled tight.

Kuefer was small, but Rufus hesitated and the Kommodore ducked beneath the wire and reached for the gun holstered around his waist. Marc made himself wide and ploughed forwards, wrapping his arms around Kuefer's waist. Rufus grabbed the German's arm and snatched the gun as Kuefer clattered backwards into one of the metal tar drums.

'Don't shoot – half the dockyard will hear,' Marc warned.

Khinde let go and the German driver hit the floorboards with a thud. Rufus bludgeoned Kuefer with the base of the pistol before Khinde knocked him out with a blow from his huge fist.

'This one's for Houari,' Khinde said, looking half crazed as he crushed Kuefer's throat under his boot.

Marc leaned on one of the tar drums and caught his breath. He recoiled when he noticed the growing pool of blood around Kuefer's head.

Rufus put his hand on Marc's shoulder. 'You OK?'

Marc felt queasy, but managed to nod. 'Put the bodies in the tar barrels and turn them upside down. I'll go get the explosives from the back of the Mercedes.'

*

13:41 Calais

Henderson hung around inside Oberst Ohlsen's office until he was certain that most of the admin staff had gone to lunch. After hurriedly relocking the office door, he cut back through the kitchen and meeting room, struggling with a large box of files which contained the latest draft of the invasion map and three reams of important documents.

After the short walk back to his desk in the empty admin office, Henderson removed his two good fountain pens from his desk drawer and pocketed the tubs of Benzedrine pills which he relied upon when he was tired or stressed. Then he loaded the box on to a two-wheeled trolley and took them down to the ground floor in the lift.

The security guards thought nothing of Ohlsen's personal translator coming in and out with a document box and one guard even lifted the base of the trolley as he went down the steps.

After Marc and Henderson had been dropped off, PT and Paul had taken the truck a few hundred metres in a quiet side turning behind a laundry.

'You're late,' PT said to Henderson. 'I was starting to wonder.'

'Your old friend Major Ghunsonn took an interest. He locked Ohlsen's office, and this little trolley's a pig on the cobbles.'

As Henderson raised the documents up into the truck, Paul dragged a pair of identical boxes across the floor of the van. As he held one out for Henderson to grab it, his fingers slipped from the handle and the box thumped against the tailgate.

'*Careful!*' Henderson yelled, as his heart missed several beats. 'That's explosive in there.'

Paul looked sheepish as he jumped out of the truck, and Henderson gave him a friendly pat on the head.

'Don't worry,' Henderson said. 'Just keep calm. Now, I've got to get this lot back to headquarters. Have you boys got some food?'

PT nodded. 'Maxine made us sandwiches and stuff.'

'Good,' Henderson said. 'And you know where you're supposed to be meeting Eugene?'

'Quarter to three, in the Café de la Pomme,' PT said. 'Then we'll drive over to the stables and wait for a big bang.'

'That's it.' Henderson nodded. 'If I'm not there within ten minutes of the bomb going off, start without me. If the bomb hasn't gone off by six o'clock and you haven't seen me, drive back to the farm and help Rosie deal with the boat.'

'Gotcha,' PT said. 'Good luck.'

Henderson headed back towards army headquarters with the two document boxes balanced on his trolley. The same German guard helped him carry the trolley back up the stairs and Henderson walked along the ground-floor corridor towards an archive room, which sat directly beneath the offices of several senior German officers.

There were two Germans and a French admin assistant in the room, but the shelves went up to the ceiling and the boxes and files stacked on them provided anonymity. Henderson found a row of shelving that ended at a large window and looked out into the busy square. Flocks of pigeons raced between the pedestrians and picked at crumbs dropped by French girls eating packed lunch on the wrought-iron benches.

Henderson felt guilty, knowing the bomb would kill people inside the building and injure many more as shards of hot glass blasted across the square. It was one of thousands of bombs that would go off that day and far from the largest, but that didn't make it any easier to look out of the window and know that some of the pretty office girls and the young soldiers flirting with them were in the last hours of their lives.

After looking back to check that nobody was watching, Henderson took the cardboard lid off the first box and shifted a dozen sticks of gelignite explosive into the second. He then took a brass three-hour detonator tube from his jacket, crushed the end under his heel and dug it into one of the soft gelignite sticks.

The crushing released acid into a chamber inside the

detonator. This acid would slowly eat through a piece of metal and release a spring. The freed spring would create a spark, which would ignite a small gunpowder charge. This in turn would detonate the twenty-four sticks of gelignite.

Unlike a clockwork detonator, which is bulky and makes a ticking noise, the acid detonator was silent. However, whereas a good clockwork detonator can be set to explode within a five-minute window, acid detonators are only accurate to within thirty per cent. So the bomb was likely to go off in somewhere between two and four hours.

Henderson put the lids back on the two boxes and slid them on to a high shelf. Then he left army headquarters for the last time.

13:44 Boulogne

Marc felt weird, squatting on the warehouse floor, knowing that the two dead Germans and the rags they'd used to clean up their blood were squeezed into the tar drums beside him. He opened the canvas bag and pulled out a sketch drawn by Paul, before explaining to Khinde and Rufus.

'This drawing shows the port,' Marc explained. 'One big harbour, one even bigger harbour and the canal system behind it. Right where the canal meets the harbours is the coal yard and, most importantly, these two large tanks for boats that run on diesel. If we can blow those tanks, we can get an explosion going that lights up the sky. The only problem is that fuel burns fast, so we need these.'

Marc pulled a grenade-sized package out of the bag and handed it to Rufus.

'Phosphorous bombs,' Marc explained. 'These explode into fragments that burn white hot for up to half an hour and set light to anything they come into contact with.'

Marc pulled something that looked like a block of marzipan out of the bag. 'This is plastic explosive. Powerful, sticky, and you can mould it to any shape you like. What we have to do is get up into the fuel yard and drop a bunch of these phosphorous bombs into the fuel tank. At around eight-thirty tonight we go back to the fuel tanks and stick a lump of this plastic to the side of each canister, we light a two-minute fuse, then run like hell, and drive away in Kuefer's Mercedes.'

'They'll miss us before then,' Khinde said. 'The Germans will search.'

Marc shook his head. 'Kuefer's moody, nobody wants to upset him. If I say Kuefer's taken you two on some special assignment nobody is going to care enough to ask any more questions.'

'What about getting through the perimeter security?' Rufus asked.

'Everyone knows Kuefer's car. Nobody ever stops us.'

'Sounds like you've thought of everything.' Khinde smiled.

Marc shook his head. 'Not me. Henderson came down here the Sunday before last and scouted the whole place. All I'm doing is following his instructions.'

'So what now?' Khinde asked.

'I've got Kuefer's camera and a fifty-metre rule so that you guys can pretend to take measurements.'

Marc hooked the Leica camera around his neck, grabbed the bag and walked several hundred metres, passing the huge open-sided coal shed. A small crew worked in the shed repairing a narrow-gauge steam train that distributed coal around the docks, but nobody took any notice as Marc stepped up to the diesel tanks and began taking photographs, while Khinde and Rufus held opposite ends of the measuring tape.

Marc was climbing up a ladder on to the top of the tank when he saw Louis, the head draftsman and engineer, heading towards them.

'Where's your boss?' Louis asked angrily. 'I saw his car, but I've been waiting for him in the office like a goddamn turkey for forty minutes.'

'I've got no idea,' Marc said. 'Something weird's going on. I met him up by the gate, but he drove off in another car with some black uniforms inside.'

'The SS?' Louis said warily. 'What do they want with Kuefer?'

Marc shrugged and acted irritated. 'Why do you people think *I* know everything? The boss tells me to get two labourers, then come out here and measure these tanks, then wait for him to come back. He says it might be a few hours.'

'The Germans only installed those tanks a few weeks back,' Louis said. 'I wonder what they're playing at now.'

Marc pointed at Rufus and Khinde. 'And these two guys are worried that they'll be missed down at the yard. Can you make sure everyone knows they're working for Kuefer?'

'Sure,' Louis said. 'If Kuefer comes back, tell him I need to see him. I've got three docks sitting still, waiting for his approval on revised drawings. And I don't know why he's got you taking measurements and pictures. The Germans must have full sets of engineering drawings somewhere.'

'I've told you all I know,' Marc said. 'I don't like it either. I've got cows to milk no matter how late I get home.'

'German arseholes,' Louis said, as he turned to walk away. 'Shouldn't be using a kid your age anyway.'

'Smooth talker,' Rufus said, smiling at Marc as Louis disappeared around the side of the coal shed.

Marc reached the top of the ladder and swung back an inspection hatch. The diesel fumes made his eyes sting as he looked inside. Khinde passed up the canvas bag and a few seconds later the first phosphorous bomb sploshed down into the tank.

CHAPTER TWENTY-SIX

14:48 The Farm

There were two labourers working somewhere out in the fields, but to all intents Rosie was alone. She'd spent the morning making sure everything was packed. After preparing lunch for Eugene and the other two prisoners who worked on the farm she'd gutted three chickens Eugene had killed before he left for Calais on a bike and put them in the oven together with a leg of pork.

As three o'clock approached she crossed the road and the overgrown field of a neighbouring farm, eventually reaching a cottage with a small shed at the end of the garden. She checked the battery meter on the transmitter before flicking the power switch and watching the familiar orange glow of the valves behind the perforated metal grille.

Every Morse operator has slightly different preferences and as Henderson had used the key last, Rosie adjusted a pair of knobs to set the keying height and the power of the spring. The set was still warming up so she tapped out I FEEL SORRY FOR GUTTED CHICKENS, to make sure she had everything right before plugging in the Morse key and her headphones.

On the stroke of three Rosie double checked the frequency dial and began to transmit a coded message saying that everything was fine. Usually, McAfferty would only transmit a short phrase to say that she'd received the message, but today she transmitted more and Rosie jotted down the letters. When the transmission ended, she took out a pencil and decoded the message.

TELL SERAPHIM ALL IS GOOD. 337 BIRDS SET FOR RAID. WEATHER CLEAR. YOU'LL BE HOME IN TIME FOR BREAKFAST. LOOKING FORWARD TO SEEING YOU, MCAFFERTY OUT.

16:21 Calais

It was a warm afternoon and the stuffy meeting room was giving Henderson a headache. He stood at the head of a table beside an SS officer translating a long rant from the chairman of the Calais Chamber of Commerce.

'. . . furthermore, we feel that it is impossible to work in an environment where the Germans do business with a gun to our head. The army sets ridiculously low prices for our goods and labour and if we refuse to sign contracts on their terms either our businesses are confiscated, or the goods are requisitioned. The French economy will be nothing but ashes if affairs continue in this way.'

The SS officer stood up and spoke angrily. 'The Reich is at war and French business must serve the war economy, in addition to this—'

Before the German uttered another word, the glass rattled and it felt like the air was being sucked out of the entire room. In the next instant the window frames flew inwards. A huge roaring sound filled the air, the floor shook and broken glass sprayed across the tabletop, embedding itself deep into the far wall.

Henderson shielded his face as his body was thrown back against the fireplace behind him. At first a few stones and a chunk of masonry blew across the table, then the entire room was engulfed in dust.

The Frenchmen around the table cursed, but had only suffered cuts. Outside in the cobbled square were screams and a loud crash as a blinded truck driver swerved into an oncoming horse and cart. There seemed no chance that the meeting could continue, but Henderson feared that the SS officer might require him for some investigative task, so he bolted out into the corridor.

The rooms on one side of the long hallway had taken the full blast of the explosion in the headquarters building across the square. People working in the offices at the back were only affected by noise and vibrations. They gawped in shock as colleagues poured into the hallways, dusty, coughing and with glass shards embedded in their flesh.

An emergency siren blared as Henderson bounded down a set of fire stairs. He made it out into the square and the dust had cleared enough for him to see some of the damage his gelignite sticks had caused to headquarters. A huge section of the façade had been ripped away, whilst inside the second and third floors had concertinaed down into the first, making a further collapse likely.

Blood drizzled from a cut over Henderson's right eye, but he couldn't stop to investigate because he needed to meet the boys at a stables, five minutes' walk away, that was used as a supply depot.

The ports along France's northern coasts were prime bombing targets so the Germans split their supplies between fourteen depots. The stable block was lightly guarded because it usually stored nothing more deadly than office supplies and a few spare boxes of ammunition. However, Henderson had forged Oberst Ohlsen's signature and used his position inside the German bureaucracy to arrange for boxes of detonators and half a truckload of high explosives to be transferred from an armoury further out of town.

Henderson walked past his truck and gave the slightest of nods to Paul and PT as they peeked between the canvas flaps at the back.

The guard on the gate leading into the stables knew Henderson and was anxious for news. 'What's going on up there? I didn't see any bombers.'

'Some kind of explosion, gas leak maybe. Luckily I was in a meeting across the square, but there's a lot of injured and the French haven't got much, so I ran around to pick up all your medical supplies.'

'Good thinking,' the guard said. 'Vogt's inside, he knows where to find everything.'

The Germans kept their horses elsewhere, but the place still had a whiff of manure as Henderson walked around to a small office and found Vogt, a First World War veteran with a wooden stump at the end of his right leg.

'Boxes delivered from the barracks yesterday,' Henderson said urgently. 'Ohlsen needs them.'

'The explosives?' Vogt said incredulously. 'I had them put over in the end stable, well away from *me* and everything else. But I can't release weapons to anyone but German army personnel, you should know that.'

Henderson knew this would be a problem and resolved it by pulling his pistol. Two gasps from the silenced weapon made a textbook execution: one bullet through the heart and one through the head. Henderson strode briskly across the courtyard and banged on the entry gate. As the guard opened up, Henderson punched him hard in the face and yanked him inside. The German reached for his machine gun, but Henderson beat him to the trigger and shot him through the head.

After looking up and down the street to make sure nobody was coming, Henderson yelled across the road to his truck. Eugene had started the engine the instant he saw the guard disappear and Henderson had to drag the dead guard away by his ankles before the truck's front wheels ran him over.

Henderson closed the gate as Eugene, PT and Paul jumped out.

'Paul, come with me,' Henderson ordered. 'You boys pick your vehicles from the paddock.'

Henderson's closeness with Oberst Ohlsen had enabled him to keep Maxine's Jaguar and the ancient truck, but most Frenchmen faced a different reality. The German Army had requisitioned hundreds of vehicles, sometimes with the promise of compensation and sometimes by outright theft. Two dozen of these were kept in a paddock at the side of the building.

While Henderson stripped the machine guns from the dead guards and helped Paul to load some of the explosives and detonators into the back of his truck, Eugene and PT shopped for an extra truck and a motorbike.

Any which had been painted with German markings were out. Eugene identified a newish Renault truck and jumped in to check the fuel gauge as PT found an elderly but solid looking motorcycle with a big leather seat.

'Keys in the ignition,' Eugene said, as the pair lifted the motorbike and some fuel cans into the back of the Renault truck.

As Henderson helped PT and Eugene load the rest of the German explosives into the Renault, Paul leaned into the back of Henderson's truck and wrote the vehicle registration numbers on to a set of stolen travel permits with Eugene's name on them.

'Don't fold the paper until the ink dries,' Paul said, as he gave PT the documents, then helped him transfer phosphorous bombs and some other equipment from Henderson's truck into the Renault.

Five minutes after entering, Henderson, Eugene and the three boys ended up standing on the cobbles in between the two loaded trucks.

'I believe that's everything,' Henderson said, before looking at Eugene. 'Are you OK with your background story and the route to Dunkirk?'

'No problems,' Eugene said. 'Me and PT will be ready to meet you back at the harbour near the farm. You've got enough of your own stuff to worry about.'

Henderson looked at Paul. 'Get the chain and the notice, then go open up.'

Henderson climbed behind the wheel of his truck, while PT and Eugene got into the cab of its much more impressive looking companion. Once both engines were running, Paul opened the gate and gave PT a wave as they turned right and charged up the cobbles. Henderson turned left and stopped at the kerb.

Paul quickly closed the gate, then locked it with a hefty padlock and chain before sticking up a cardboard notice and running off to jump in the back of Henderson's truck. The notice was written in German and read, *Gone to lunch, back in 35 minutes.*

16:57 *Cliffs, near the Farm*

Rosie had tied back her hair, put on her best dress and even a dab of lipstick. She strolled along the clifftops, staring out to sea like she hadn't a care in the world. The tide was way out and a few German soldiers walked along the beach, collecting up the last of the equipment that had been used in the day's training exercises.

The white cliff tapered down when it reached the pier. Rosie found herself standing close to a German guard post. She looked at the four powered barges and a matching pair of medium sized tugboats painted in military grey before stepping on to the wooden boards of the pier.

A smoking German stepped away from the guard hut. His tone was firm, but not unfriendly.

'Sorry, my dear,' he said, using fairly decent French he'd learned while trying to pick up girls. 'Can't come any further.'

Rosie had never spoken to the soldier before, but she'd seen him walking up and down the beach. 'Oh,' she said listlessly, before cracking a lipstick-red smile. 'I wasn't thinking. I'm not at all with it today.'

The soldier took a long puff on his cigarette. He was small but stocky, with prickly black hair sticking out around the sides of his helmet. Rosie guessed he was twenty-one at most.

'What you all dressed up for?' he asked.

'Dunno.' Rosie shrugged. 'Just felt like it. There's *nothing* to do here except work on the farm. No school, no money, not even petrol to go anywhere.'

'I've got a sister your age,' the German laughed. 'She's the same. When she was ten she tried to run away. Told my mum she was going to Berlin to become a dancer. She got as far as the train station and my dad dragged her home and thrashed her. Me and my little brothers thought it was so funny, because usually only us boys copped it.'

'Can I have a puff?' Rosie asked.

The German looked at her like he knew he shouldn't, but gave her the cigarette anyway. Rosie took the biggest puff she dared and was surprised by the heat of the smoke in her lungs.

'Haven't seen your artist brother for a few days,' the guard noted as he took the cigarette back.

'He's had a bad cold,' Rosie explained. 'Gone into Calais today to see a doctor. So, are you out here on your own all night?'

The guard pointed towards the hut. 'There's three of us. One of us is supposed to be out here on lookout, but it's *so* dead. Mostly we sit inside and play cards or listen to the radio.'

'Sounds boring,' Rosie said, with a dramatic sigh.

'Life's boring,' the guard laughed. 'But I tell you something. I'd rather be guarding some nowhere harbour like this than about a million other jobs you can get in the army.'

'So how long do you have to stay on duty?'

'It varies,' the guard explained. 'It's supposed to be twelve-hour shifts, but they're low on manpower, so they put it up to fourteen or even sixteen hours.'

'So what time do you get off?'

'You're a bit young for a date if that's what you're driving at. You should be careful – some of the guys in my barracks are animals. They'd get you drunk and try all kinds of dirty stuff.'

Rosie flushed red with embarrassment. 'I didn't mean *that*,' she gasped. 'Just . . . I dunno, making conversation, and I wondered how long you had to go.'

'I'm off at eleven,' the guard said.

'Right,' Rosie said. 'And does anyone bring you hot food or anything?'

'Nothing as exciting as that, girl. We bring stuff out in tins, like corned beef. You get sick of it.'

'Revolting,' Rosie said, smiling. 'And boring.'

The German laughed. 'You know, maybe you and my kid sister are on to something. When you get down to it, life *is* pretty boring.'

'Well,' Rosie said, smiling as she pointed her thumb backwards over her shoulder. 'I'd better get home before my mum yells at me for not helping with the dinner. Nice meeting you – er . . .?"

'Manfried.' The German smiled.

'I'm Rosie,' Rosie said. 'Maybe I'll talk to you again some time.'

CHAPTER TWENTY-SEVEN

17:10 The Farm

When Rosie got back to the cottage the kitchen was stifling and filled with the smell of the rosemary she'd rubbed on to the slow cooking pork. The fire under the oven seemed low, but as she grabbed the tongs to add coal she was startled by footsteps coming from the hallway that led towards the bedrooms.

'Dumont,' Rosie said, startled. 'What are you doing here?'

'Cases and bags all packed up,' Dumont said suspiciously. 'Where are you going?'

The back door was never locked, so stepping into the kitchen and yelling to see if anyone was about would be OK, but Dumont had clearly been nosing around inside the bedrooms. Rosie was furious and had to think quickly.

'We're not going anywhere,' she answered unconvincingly. 'We've been getting a lot of mice, so we didn't want things to get chewed up. What were *you* doing back there, anyway?'

'I came looking for the boys. Thought they might want to hang out for a couple of hours.'

Paul, Marc and PT had been banned from going anywhere near the village since Marc and PT's arrest, but PT still occasionally went hunting with Dumont.

'Marc's working,' Rosie said, as she dropped a small shovelful of coal into the kitchen range. 'PT's gone into town to take Paul to a doctor.'

Dumont raised his eyebrows. 'Your brother's so weedy. I never get sick.'

Rosie had never liked the way Dumont picked on Paul. 'I suppose no self-respecting germ would go near you,' she said curtly.

'Cheeky,' Dumont said, as he stepped up close to Rosie. 'You know, you look pretty with all that lipstick. What you need is a good strong boyfriend, like me.'

Dumont made Rosie uneasy at the best of times and he was close enough that his body odour was overpowering the herbs.

'Go home and take a bath,' she said, crinkling her nose and stepping back. 'You smell worse than a pig.'

Dumont didn't like this. He hissed as he grabbed

Rosie's arms and shoved her back against the worktop beside the sink.

'Get off,' Rosie screamed, as Dumont pressed his body against her and forced a kiss on the lips.

'Make me,' Dumont teased, as he tasted the lipstick smeared over his top lip with the tip of his tongue.

Dumont grabbed Rosie's thigh with one meaty hand and dug his thumb in hard. She was determined not to give him satisfaction by showing how much it hurt as she glanced around, looking for a weapon.

'You're all on your own,' Dumont teased, as he put his other hand on Rosie's bum. 'What you gonna do to stop me?'

Rosie's classmates in Paris often teased her about her bulky shoulders and unladylike arms, but they were a distinct advantage as Dumont tried another vile kiss.

'You're so powerful,' Rosie said meekly, smiling as if she'd changed her mind and wanted him.

Dumont grew excited and clutched Rosie's bum tighter, but as he started to kiss her again Rosie grabbed his ear and tugged with all her might.

'*Bitch!*' Dumont shouted as he took half a step back. Rosie was weaker than Dumont and only had a few seconds to stick the advantage. She lunged forwards and sunk her teeth into Dumont's nose.

'Happy now?' Rosie screamed, pulling herself free as Dumont clutched his face.

She thought about running out the door and screaming for one of the two labourers, but she didn't know where they were and couldn't risk being caught by Dumont, so she moved towards the oven, grabbed the coal scoop and dug out flaming lumps of coal.

Dumont had regained enough composure to lunge forwards, but Rosie swung around. Her leg seared with pain as it caught the knob on the oven door, but she threw the burning coals at Dumont's chest and his shirt caught light as he backed away.

'I'll kill you,' Dumont screamed, frantically bashing his flaming shirt as he crashed backwards into the kitchen table.

Rosie grabbed an iron frying skillet that hung above the stove and gave Dumont a two-handed smash on the kneecap. Still on fire, he fell to the floor and rolled on to his chest to smother the flames. Rosie stepped astride his body and knocked him out by smashing the heavy skillet against the back of his head.

'Dirty pig,' she screamed, dropping the skillet as smoke continued to rise from Dumont's smouldering shirt.

Dumont was unconscious, but instead of relief Rosie's stomach churned. She collapsed against the kitchen dresser and doubled over sobbing. For a few moments she gave in to the horror of what Dumont had tried to do, but as she looked down at his unconscious body she was determined not to let her emotions affect their carefully laid plan.

17:24 Calais

While Eugene and PT drove to Dunkirk in the freshly stolen truck, Paul and Henderson parked up and headed for a hotel near the port in Calais. The bombed headquarters were less than a kilometre away and you could still hear ambulance sirens and see smoke from small fires billowing into the sky.

'A terrible business,' the elderly woman on the reception desk said. 'The man who cleans my windows was up that way. He tells me they're pulling one body after another out of the rubble. Mostly Boche, but a lot of French too.'

'I didn't see any bombers either,' Henderson noted, trying to sound innocent as he wrote *Charles Boyle* and the farm address into the hotel register while the receptionist swapped his banknotes for a room key.

'Is that on the top floor, Dad?' Paul asked eagerly.

'He likes to watch the big boats come and go,' Henderson explained to the woman.

The receptionist smiled. 'It's right up top, with a lovely view over the harbour. Now, our air-raid shelter is across the street and, obviously, with our location we get our share of those. Our restaurant is permanently closed because our chef went south, but there are a few nice cafés along the canal.'

'Thank you so much.' Henderson smiled as he took the room key off the countertop and began walking up a flight of narrow stairs with a heavy suitcase in his arms.

Paul opened the door and breathed musty air as he stared at two rusting single beds and a cracked washbasin on the wall with a chamber pot standing beneath it. As Henderson closed the door and threw the suitcase on the bed by the balcony, Paul opened up the doors and stepped outside.

In comparison to the large harbours at Boulogne, Calais was a warren of natural inlets and manmade canals, with docks spiking off in different directions. The invasion barges were spread about, making it more difficult for the RAF to destroy large numbers in one go, but on the upside, the port sprawled through the heart of the town. The homes and businesses all around made it impossible to build a truly secure perimeter around the docks.

'You see why I picked this hotel?' Henderson said quietly, as he stood on the balcony beside Paul. 'The main port entrance and open sea less than fifty metres away, docks going off to either side and these old buildings will burn like tinderboxes.'

'I wonder if that lady owns the hotel,' Paul said, a touch sadly, as he headed back into the room.

Henderson opened the lid of the suitcase, exposing

two dozen sticks of gelignite and more than fifty golf-ball-sized phosphorous flare bombs.

'You've got to look at the bigger picture,' Henderson said, as he pulled a tin of detonators out of his jacket pocket. 'Do you think I'm proud that I set a bomb that's probably killed fifty or sixty people inside army headquarters? Some people will probably die when these buildings burn. More will *certainly* die when the bombers arrive.'

Paul nodded as he sat on the bed and peered into the suitcase.

'I'm setting everything up for you now,' Henderson said. 'You're using a four-minute detonator. Light the end of the cord, run downstairs, up the street and unlock the bike. Are you certain you know the route back to the farm in the dark?'

'It's easy enough,' Paul said. 'Left at the top of the road, then the turn-off for the coast road; you'll all be waiting at the harbour.'

'Excellent,' Henderson said.

Paul gave Henderson a serious look. 'Do you ever think about dead people? Like my dad, or the people who drowned on the *Cardiff Bay*? I always do. I get nightmares sometimes too.'

'I don't think you'd be human if you didn't get upset,' Henderson said. 'I guess the difference between me and you is that I chose a life of adventure, and you had adventure thrust upon you. Your father was one of my closest friends. I know he'd be incredibly proud of what you and your sister are doing for your country.'

Paul smiled a little as Henderson took a large bar of Belgian chocolate out of his jacket. 'A nutritious dinner for you,' he said, smiling. 'Now I've got to drive back to the farm and help Rosie to sort out a boat for the ride home.'

18:28 Boulogne

When you're scared the worst thing that can happen is that you have to sit alone with nothing but the voices in your head for company. Lunchtime had been Marc's only opportunity to separate from Kuefer and meet up with Khinde and Rufus, but that left six agonising hours between planting the phosphorous bombs inside the fuel tanks and the air raid.

The two prisoners had hidden in the complex of burned out wharves behind the harbours, but Marc had to keep up the pretence that he was mystified by Kuefer's disappearance, and that meant sticking close to the Mercedes. He'd chatted to the ladies who made lunches and scrounged some extra food, he'd occasionally wandered into the office and asked if anyone had seen his boss, but mostly he'd sat in the back of the Mercedes and made himself feel sick, worrying about all the things that could go wrong.

The prisoners rarely worked any later than seven and Marc had his eyes shut and was half asleep when knuckles rapped on the car window. He jumped when he saw a German guard with a machine gun over his shoulder.

'Where are your black buddies?' the guard asked, as Marc pulled down the window. 'Last truck's heading back to the prison camp. Is Kuefer gonna drop them back, because we're gonna cop hell if two prisoners go missing.'

Marc tried to sound a lot calmer than he felt. 'I don't know anything. Kuefer came and took them away, then went off with the SS officers again.'

Henderson had suggested adding phantom SS units into Marc's story and it had worked well. The SS were elite units attached to the Nazi party rather than the military. They had absolute powers and scared ordinary German soldiers as much as they scared French civilians. The merest mention of SS involvement ensured that there would be no investigation into whatever Kuefer was supposedly up to.

'Dammit,' the German said. 'I bet whatever happens, it's me that cops the blame.'

'Sorry.' Marc shrugged. 'I'm just stuck here waiting for my boss. I need to get back to my dad's farm, but I've got no idea how long I'll be stuck out here.'

CHAPTER TWENTY-EIGHT

19:00 The Farm

Henderson arrived home in the truck as Rosie was slicing the joint of pork. People would be coming and going at different times, so rather than cook a conventional meal she planned to use the chicken and pork to fill baguettes which people could grab whenever they arrived.

'Meat smells good,' Henderson said brightly, as he came in and bent forwards to give Rosie a peck on the cheek.

'Don't,' she said firmly, as she backed away.

Henderson was surprised, but he didn't think much of it until he saw how upset she looked.

'Dumont tried to force himself on me,' Rosie admitted, with a shudder.

'Damn,' Henderson roared, as he pounded on the table. 'Did he run off? If I lay my hands on that little son of a—'

'He's tied up in your bedroom,' Rosie said. 'He saw all the cases packed. I couldn't let him get away and I didn't know what else to do.'

Henderson strode through to the bedroom he'd shared with Maxine and was startled by the state Rosie had left Dumont in. He lay on the floor, conscious but bloody-nosed, with deep burns across his chest. His ankles were tied and his wrists bound behind his back.

'Please,' Dumont begged, as he crawled back towards the wall. 'You've got to let me go, she's crazy!'

Henderson kicked Dumont hard in the stomach before pulling out his gun and sticking the muzzle against Dumont's head.

'There's only one good reason why I'm not gonna blow your brains out right now,' Henderson yelled. 'And that's because in my book, people who try to molest young girls deserve to die slowly.'

Henderson stood up and shouted back towards the kitchen. 'Rosie, my petal, bring in the meat cleaver.'

'Please,' Dumont grovelled. 'She's a lying bitch, I *swear*. She came on to me.'

Henderson booted Dumont in the stomach again. 'Don't you *dare* call her a bitch,' he shouted.

Dumont sobbed as Rosie came into the room,

conspicuously not holding a cleaver. She suspected the suggestion was a scare tactic, but with Henderson you could never be sure.

'Just say the word, sweetheart,' Henderson said. 'If you want him dead, he's dead.'

Rosie put her hands over her face and shook her head. 'There's enough death in the world right now,' she said. 'Take him out somewhere and make sure that I never have to see him again.'

Henderson crouched down and loomed over Dumont. 'On your feet,' he growled. 'You're damned lucky Rosie's a better person than I am.'

19:07 Dunkirk

Marc had warned Eugene and PT about the desolation around Dunkirk, but nothing prepared either of them for mounds of debris and swarms of rats scuttling out on to the road in front of them.

The port complex was more than ten times the size of Calais, centred on vast twin harbours, the largest of which was more than two kilometres wide. The eastern harbour was more modest, but both fed into a huge network of canals and docks.

In Boulogne and Calais it was a question of lighting a beacon that would provide a focus for bombing the entire dockyard. Although more than five hundred tugs and barges had been refurbished and docked around

Dunkirk, having them spread along more than twenty kilometres of canals and docks made precise targeting impossible.

But Marc had identified two high value targets in the canal leading from the eastern harbour. The first was the huge dry dock where most barge conversions were done. The second was a nearby canal where the Germans had built a refuelling station and kept more than twenty fast patrol boats, carefully disguised amidst the remains of the Dunkirk fishing fleet.

The Royal Navy had the English Channel blockaded at both ends, preventing the German Navy from bringing in any large surface ships. This meant that defence of the invasion fleet would rely upon submarines and these lightly armoured patrol boats. A successful bombing of the patrol-boat base at Dunkirk would destroy a quarter of the German fleet in one swoop.

PT and Eugene's starting point was a dockside camp, comprising twenty large wooden barrack huts which housed both skilled French workers and much of the local German garrison.

The Germans paid good wages in this area and even though the barge conversion programme was nearing its end, skilled Frenchmen were still coming in to undertake rebuilding works around the docks.

'Recruitment office is closed till morning,' a German guard explained as the Renault truck stood at a security gate. He gave Eugene's travel permits the briefest of inspections before continuing, 'You can bunk in one of the French huts if you can find a bed. You'll get a meal in the bar. What's inside the truck?'

Eugene shrugged. 'Just my little brother and a bunch of tools. Search it if you want.'

The back of the truck was full of explosives, but Marc said the Germans never searched vehicles entering the barracks, only the nearby docks.

Eugene rolled through the checkpoint and drove a couple of hundred metres to the only place in town that had any life coming out of it.

PT led Eugene inside and found the narrow space crammed with Germans, who all went spookily quiet. One man even pulled a pistol.

'French in hut eight, up the other end,' a man sitting near the door explained.

They backed out nervously and found the bar where the French workmen socialised. The Germans ensured that there was plenty of food and booze for these valuable workers, who crammed the bar and spilled outside, sitting on chunks of dockside rubble and lining up to piss into a nearby canal.

The only women inside stood by a piano – one playing badly, one singing badly but compensating for it by being beautiful and topless. It took Eugene an age to reach the bar, where he bought two bottles of German beer and enquired after a man named Wimund.

'Somewhere down the far end,' the sweat-streaked barman answered, as Eugene paid.

Marc had described Wimund as a stocky man with a balding grey head who always wore a blue overall, but that could have been any of thirty workmen. Eugene grew anxious and considered switching to a less effective fall-back plan, after they'd spent more than fifteen minutes squeezing between bodies and asking questions.

They were about to give up when PT got touched on the shoulder.

'You the boy that's looking for me?' Wimund asked.

Eugene smiled warmly. 'You know my little cousin, Marc?'

Wimund had downed plenty of booze. His eyes seemed a little lost and his expression was blank. 'Can't place him, but there's a lot of men around these docks.'

'Not many twelve year olds though,' Eugene said. 'Little blond guy, works as Kuefer's translator?'

'Ahh, the boy.' Wimund nodded, wagging his finger knowingly. 'Nice little chap. Tips me off when his boss is on the warpath.'

'We just arrived from Calais,' Eugene yelled, as PT moved in close so that he could follow the conversation over all the singing and banter. 'We're both carpenters. Marc said you're the man to talk to if you want a decent job.'

As Eugene said this, he produced a bottle of top quality brandy from a canvas bag.

'For a small consideration, of course,' PT added.

Wimund glanced about anxiously to see who was standing nearby. 'Don't let people be seeing that out in the open,' he said. 'Your boy Marc's done me a few favours. Tomorrow you get your papers sorted and work wherever the Germans assign you. Then come see me after work and I'll sort you out, no charge.'

Eugene broke into a big smile. 'That's *very* decent of you, sir. I'll be sure to buy you a drink at the least.'

'And I'll be glad to accept it,' Wimund said, nodding again.

'I'm stepping out for a piss,' PT said, 'excuse me.'

Eugene said thanks to Wimund as he turned around. 'Better not lose my brother,' Eugene said. 'He's only sixteen.'

It took another couple of minutes for the two teenagers to make it through heat and smoke into fresh outdoor air.

'You get them?' Eugene asked.

PT pulled a set of keys from his trousers and jangled them. 'I couldn't see them bulging,' he explained. 'Had to feel my way down three pockets, but it's reassuring to know that I've still got the magic fingers, just like my dad taught me.'

*

Henderson was loading the last of the suitcases into the truck when Dumont's dad Luc Boyle came up the dirt driveway on a bicycle. Henderson hurriedly pulled the cloth flaps over the back of his truck so that the farmer couldn't see inside.

'Evening,' Henderson said cheerfully, as Luc stepped off the bike. 'What can I do you for?'

'Have you seen my son around?' Luc asked.

'Can't say I have,' Henderson lied. 'My boys have been in town all day. Marc's working, and PT took Paul to the doctor in Calais.'

Luc combed tense fingers through his hair as he stepped off the bike. 'Wife's giving me hell,' he complained. 'Can't find Dumont and after what happened before with those Germans in the village she's going frantic.'

Henderson shrugged. 'Sorry I can't help.'

'That *bloody* kid,' Luc cursed. 'My other two boys are prisoners, you know? Good lads, bright as you'd wish, but Dumont's always struggled. I don't think there's a mean bone in his body, but he's just not bright enough to stay out of trouble.'

Henderson didn't agree that Dumont was harmless after what he'd tried doing to Rosie, but he couldn't let on. 'He's always seemed nice enough to me. How are Lucien and Holly doing, by the way?'

'Not too bad,' Luc said. 'They miss their mum. Holly goes on and on about her all the time and it breaks my heart. Where's the Jag by the way?'

'Maxine's got it,' Henderson explained. 'You know, I'm still working on getting you a fuel permit and like I said you're always welcome to use the truck if needs be.'

'Appreciated.' Luc smiled. 'I'm going to ride back towards the village to see if anyone's seen Dumont. If he's not back soon I'll have to speak to the police.'

Henderson glanced at his watch. They wouldn't be leaving for up to two and a quarter hours and the last thing he wanted was police, locals and possibly even the Germans getting involved in a search.

'I do know where Dumont is,' Henderson said, as he ripped out his gun. 'I'll take you up to the cowshed. The labourers will untie you in the morning after we've gone.'

20:20 Dunkirk

Having invaded three large European nations in the space of two years and Nazi doctrine dictating that women should stay home and raise families, the German Army relied upon random searches and checkpoints – not because they were particularly effective, but because there was a shortage of men.

Guarding the kilometres of docks and wharves at Dunkirk would have tied up half a battalion, and Eugene and PT were relieved to arrive by the mesh gates around the dry dock and find the security post unmanned.

'Twenty minutes till the planes arrive,' PT noted, before jumping out into near darkness to unlock the main gate with Wimund's keys. They were behind schedule and it didn't help that PT had to try half a dozen keys before the padlock sprang open.

PT jumped back in the truck and Eugene drove cautiously along the wall of the dry dock with his headlamps switched off. The steel dock gates were nearly a metre thick at the base, and in the black void below lay more than sixty barges, tugs and patrol boats.

The Royal Navy had operated a fleet from Dunkirk in the run-up to the war and had sent Henderson detailed instructions. By opening the gates of a huge dry dock too quickly, the resulting wall of water will destroy the small boats sitting at the bottom. An engineer who'd worked in the docks even provided sketches of the control room, which had been dropped the previous Saturday along with Bernard and the plastic explosives.

While PT headed into a wooden shed to pull some hydraulic levers that opened two huge inlet channels built around the side of the dock gates, Eugene leaned against the truck, using binoculars to study the patrol-boat base less than a hundred metres away.

The Germans had used a mixture of netting, trawlers and fishing equipment spread over decks to disguise these precious high-speed boats from British reconnaissance planes, but from ground level the disguise was feeble.

While barge conversion work shut down at night because the artificial light needed to continue would make it an easy target for bombing, the German patrol fleet operated twenty-four hours a day.

More than twenty patrol boats lay beneath grey tarps that looked like bare concrete from two thousand metres up, but three fast launches were moored abreast at the dockside. Diesel plumes rose from their funnels, while a fourth was being refuelled at a pier. On the dockside, crew members in navy uniform hopped between boats, while others stood around looking bored and smoking.

Inside the control room by the dock gates, PT was alarmed by the crash of water as it rushed into the dry basin. He'd been told that the dock walls and heavy gates would make the sound virtually inaudible from the naval base a hundred metres away, but he was far from convinced as he pressed a coin-sized lump of plastic explosive against the base of the control levers and inserted a ten-minute acid fuse.

This would only produce a tiny explosion, but with luck it would wreck the control levers and make life difficult for any German engineers who tried to stop the deluge.

Eugene was back inside the truck with the engine running by the time PT ran out. 'Why's it so noisy?'

Eugene asked anxiously. 'The patrol crews don't seem to have noticed yet, but they're gonna.'

'I just did what I was told,' PT said defensively. 'I say screw going over the bridge with the main bomb, let's reverse back from here and hope the bombers finish the patrol boats.'

But Eugene looked determined and put the truck into first gear rather than reverse. 'We came this far,' he said. 'I'm not backing out now.'

CHAPTER TWENTY-NINE

20:28 The Farm

The sun had all but disappeared and the yard in front of the cottage was black. The old truck needed a hand crank to get going and Henderson yelled after Rosie as the engine spluttered to life.

'Come on, sweetheart. It's a good job it's less than two kilometres to the harbour. We're running on fumes. I should have topped up in town this morning, but I had about a thousand other things on my mind.'

Rosie had milked the cows for the last time, now she threw food into the chicken pens and felt a little sad as Lottie the goat followed her across the grass, expecting a handful of scraps.

'Out,' Rosie said firmly, as the goat chased her into the kitchen. But they wouldn't be back. Rosie remembered that there were some vegetables in the rack so, for the first time, the goat didn't find herself shoved out of the kitchen doorway on to the lawn.

As Lottie buried her face in carrots, Rosie grabbed a basket piled high with sandwiches and a metal jug filled with fresh milk.

'Sorry about the hold-up,' Rosie gasped, as she sat next to Henderson inside the truck with the basket on her lap. 'I wanted to make sure the animals would be all right until the labourers get here in the morning.'

She set the jug on the floor and squeezed it tight between her ankles.

'All set? Nothing forgotten?' Henderson asked.

'We've still got a while,' Rosie said. 'If it was important we could walk back in no time.'

Henderson pulled away and drove off the farm for the second time that day.

'Do you think I made enough sandwiches?' Rosie asked. 'We had eggs left over, so I hard boiled some to eat on the boat and left the rest for the prisoners.'

Henderson laughed as he turned on the road. 'I think you could feed half of Paris with that lot.'

20:31 Boulogne

Marc felt good as he stepped out of the Mercedes. After six hours waiting it was a relief to get underway. He looked around for any sign of Germans before throwing the canvas bag over his shoulder and starting to jog towards the fuel tanks.

His pulse quickened when he realised that the heavily insulated car had disguised the sound of approaching aircraft. And it wasn't a rogue German fighter, it sounded like the armada of bombers was running ahead of schedule.

'You hear them?' Khinde asked, startling Marc as he bobbed up behind a diesel tank.

'We've got to shift,' Marc said. 'We're gonna be in the middle of a shit storm if we're still standing here in five minutes' time.'

He took the bag off his shoulder and passed out six butter-pat-sized blocks of plastic explosive. 'Two on each tank, pull the pins out of the detonators and we'll have two minutes until they blow.'

As Khinde and Rufus stuck the sticky lumps of plastic explosive to the tanks, Marc began running the two hundred metres back to the Mercedes. The two grown men were faster and Marc was several metres behind as he got into the driver's seat and started the engine.

More than sixty bombers roared overhead, and an air-raid siren started up as Marc squeezed the accelerator pedal. Rufus and Khinde couldn't drive, so Maxine had given him a crash course behind the wheel of her Jaguar, but the Mercedes felt huge in comparison and even with Schroder's leather coat folded up under his bum Marc could barely see over the wheel as he approached the gate.

The guard was supposed to stop everyone coming in or out, but after thousands of kilometres' driving with Schroder, Marc knew that big Mercedes driven by German officers were rarely troubled.

As the wooden gate rose in front of them, Marc jammed the brake as he realised he was going way too fast for the sharp turn on to the road. He made eye contact and got a strange look when the guard saw how young he was, but before he could react the first of the three diesel tanks exploded and the German dived for cover.

'That one's for Houari!' Khinde shouted, thumping ecstatically on the padded roof as the big car accelerated away from the port.

A thirty-metre tower of flame seared up into the darkness, but the real spectacle took a few seconds longer. The exploding fuel had tossed two dozen phosphorous bombs across the heart of the docks. They burned with an intense blue light that lit up the entire dockyard, as white-hot fragments began burning through the tin roof of the neighbouring coal-yard.

20:33 Calais

Paul stood over the rusting bed. He popped the last square of Belgian chocolate in his mouth, then double checked that he had the key for the bike lock in his pocket before igniting the three-minute length of detonator cord curled inside the lid of the suitcase.

'Watch it!' a man shouted, as Paul burst out of the room and raced past him on the stairs.

'There's planes coming,' Paul shouted back. 'Get outta here.'

But the man thought he was just some crazy kid and by the time Paul hit the street he felt guilty. He'd left two dozen sticks of gelignite and twenty phosphorous bombs in the hotel room, which would create a blast double the size of the one that ripped apart the army headquarters.

The man would die, as would the nice woman who worked on reception and pretty much everyone else unlucky enough to be inside the hotel or one of the buildings on either side.

Paul's bike was a horrible contraption which Henderson had bought in a junk shop. It had solid tyres and a frame that had buckled and been knocked back into shape. Despite this it had attracted the attention of a couple of local kids.

It was the last thing Paul needed. They sized him up as he approached breathlessly.

'You've got no right,' the bigger of the two kids stated. 'This is our territory. You gotta pay tax to park your bike here.'

Paul's heart was thumping. The bomb would go off in under a minute and the bike was his only way back to the farm. Even the larger of the kids was probably two years younger than Paul, but he was only a few centimetres shorter and he looked strong.

'I'll get my dad on to you,' Paul shouted, as he pointed back at the hotel.

Both kids smiled. 'Go get him then, skinny.'

'Can't fight your own battles,' the younger one added. 'What a wimp!'

Paul realised he'd made a useless threat: the kids weren't scared because they'd disappear down an alleyway as soon as any adult showed up.

Although Paul had mostly recovered from his cold he still had muck on his chest, and running down the stairs had set some of it free. He took a deep breath and coughed a huge string of phlegm into his mouth. The warm blob felt disgusting, but as he was about to spit into the kerb he realised that other people would find it even more gross and flobbed it into the palm of his hand.

'I'm gonna rub this in your hair,' Paul warned, sweeping his snotty hand from side to side.

'Germs!' the little kid shouted, as both lads backed away enough for Paul to bend down and get his key in the bike lock.

Paul flicked the snot off his hand as he straddled the bike and started pedalling up the narrow lane. He just made it around the corner into the next street as the bomb went off. The huge blast shook the ground and ripped the handlebars out of his hand.

He tried to straighten up, but he looked up and saw that he was heading into the path of an oncoming car.

20:33 Dunkirk

Naval Leutnant Baure was seventeen years old and had spent the last three hours doing repairs inside the baking hot engineroom of a torpedo boat. The vessel had sprung a leak out at sea. A bank of six cylinders had seized up and the Kapitan was threatening to discipline Baure because he'd performed the final maintenance check before leaving port and had apparently failed to notice a critical drop in oil pressure.

The charge could ruin a career that had barely even started and Baure felt angry and miserable as he sauntered behind the wharfside building inside which numerous officers were doubtless cursing his name.

He squatted down on a bollard and pulled a cigarette from a metal case. As he flipped the lid off his lighter he saw a truck coming over a bridge out the corner of his eye. He noted to himself that he'd never seen trucks moving in the docks after dark, but shrugged, thinking it was no concern of his.

As Baure took his first puff he noticed that there was an unusually strong current in the canal alongside him. Then the truck stopped at the top of a mild slope which led down to the wharfside building behind him and he started to get curious as two men got out and dragged a motorbike out of the back.

'Guys!' Baure shouted, as he ran around the front of the building. But his name was mud after the engine failure and he only attracted contempt from his crewmates. 'I think something's going on by the bridge.'

'What have you ballsed up now, tit head?' someone asked.

'Truck came over the bridge and stopped dead,' Baure explained urgently. 'Two guys pulled a motorbike out of the back. I don't know what's going on but I don't like it.'

The men didn't know what to make of this, but within five seconds another man jumped ashore nearby and made an announcement. 'Water's running into the dry dock. Someone's opened the gate.'

It didn't take a genius to put the two bits of information together and realise that the docks were being sabotaged. A stocky officer shot to his feet and started shouting orders.

'You, you, you – inside. Grab some weapons. Get up there and see what's going on. Move!'

Less than a hundred metres away, Eugene leaned on the motorbike and gave it a kick start. PT pulled off the handbrake inside the truck and jumped out of the cab.

'Three minutes,' PT shouted, as Eugene threw him a crash helmet. 'Let's roll this thing.'

As the motorbike engine throbbed, PT and Eugene lined up behind the tailgate of the truck and put their backs in. The slope was gentle, but with the handbrake off the truck soon began rolling down the wharf, just as they noticed torch-beams and German voices, followed by figures running out the back of the building towards them.

'Shit!' Eugene yelled as he straddled the motorbike. 'Get on, get on!'

Two gunshots sounded as PT climbed aboard and locked his arms around Eugene's waist. More shots rang as the motorbike blasted across the bridge, then swerved left and right to run along the side of the dry dock.

The holes in the dock gates were now fully open and the torrent of water had sent the small boats crashing against the sides of the dock like rubber ducks clattering around a bathtub. The navy officers were on foot and had no chance of catching the motorbike, but a bullet clipped the truck as it continued rolling towards the patrol boats.

The instant the bullet hit the gelignite an area fifty metres around the truck erupted into a vast fireball, vaporising several dozen naval officers and the wharfside building as men further back dived into the water beneath the flames.

The explosions in Calais and Boulogne were beacons, designed to start fires and light the way for incoming bombers. The three hundred sticks of gelignite spread over the floor of the truck *would* help British pilots to find their target, but their primary aim was to destroy as many German patrol boats as possible.

'Jesus,' PT screamed. 'Where'd our two minutes go?'

Even from two hundred and fifty metres the heat from the fireball seared PT's back as he watched curling flames reflected in the back of Eugene's crash helmet.

But fire was the least of their problems. The early blast had sent a huge shockwave through the canal system. A wave more than three metres high seared over the wall of the dry dock. When it landed two small barges washed up over the end of the dock as the boats inside smashed deafeningly against the walls.

PT looked back a second before water spewed up over the side of the dock and hit the bike. No rider could have kept upright as the force of water lifted the wheels off the ground and sent the two teenagers skimming helplessly towards a metal-sided hut.

PT covered his face as his back slammed the metal. A huge wooden mast speared through the building less than twenty centimetres above his head.

'Eugene,' he shouted, using the impaled mast to lever himself up as the water drained back into the dock.

Eugene had almost been flushed back inside the dock

and had ended up clutching one of the giant bollards, perilously close to the edge. PT ran towards him, fearing he'd been knocked out, but Eugene was only winded and was standing by the time a smaller, reflex wave washed over their ankles.

'You OK?' Eugene asked, as he pulled off his sodden crash helmet.

'Fine.' PT nodded, looking back for any sign of someone coming after them. 'But the bike's wrecked. How the hell are we gonna get back to the farm?'

CHAPTER THIRTY

20:42 The Harbour

Henderson parked the truck fifty metres from the pier that formed one side of the small harbour, then set off along the dusky coast road with Rosie.

'Remind me what Manfried told you,' Henderson said, as explosions and flashes of light pulsed over Calais directly behind them.

'Three guards,' Rosie said. 'Two in the hut, one on patrol, but he said sometimes they all play cards inside because it's so quiet. The shift change is at eleven and they eat what they bring with them. Nobody comes to deliver food or anything.'

'Works for me.' Henderson nodded as he paused behind a white boulder, opened the cartridge of his silenced pistol and replaced the four bullets he'd shot at the stables in Calais earlier on.

'He's a decent guy,' Rosie said, as Henderson started walking again. 'Manfried, I mean.'

'He'll die fast, before he even knows it,' Henderson grunted.

'Isn't there another way?' Rosie asked. 'Couldn't we tie them up or something?'

'A plan's a plan once it's underway.'

Rosie hated the calculating way that Henderson plotted death.

'Manfried's only about eighteen and he seemed really nice,' Rosie said desperately, but only succeeded in irritating Henderson.

'This is a war, honey,' he said patronisingly. 'I have one silenced pistol, there's three of them and they have machine guns. What do you think this Manfried was doing during the battle for France? You think none of those soldiers shot any Frenchmen, or burned any villages?'

Rosie didn't like the answer, but supposed Henderson was right. They stopped behind a low ridge overlooking the harbour. A chink of light escaping the guard hut illuminated a pair of crude fishing rods that the guards had hooked on the pier.

'Two tugs,' Rosie noted, as she pointed across the harbour.

'Tugs are ideal,' Henderson whispered. 'Designed for

towing, so they're nippy when there's nothing tied behind them. Crossing to England should take around three hours. It'd be more like six or seven in a powered barge or canal boat.'

'Great,' Rosie said, though Henderson could tell she was still thinking about Manfried as he pulled a .38 revolver out of his jacket.

'You don't have to do this, Rosie, but I'm taking on three men and I'd feel a lot better with someone covering my back.'

Rosie looked solemn as she took the unsilenced revolver. What if she ended up having to kill Manfried?

'It's double action, no safety lock,' Henderson warned. 'It'll fire cocked or uncocked, but the trigger pull is very light when it's cocked.'

Rosie nodded as Henderson clambered over the ridge. He kept low as he crept through reeds behind the corrugated metal guard hut. When he reached the back, Henderson found a cable which led up to a radio aerial on the roof. It was vital that the guards didn't send out an alert, so he snipped it with wire cutters.

As Henderson poked his head around the side of the hut, the front door slammed and a German stepped outside.

'Four aces, you cheating bugger,' he shouted bitterly, as he stepped up to the edge of the pier and unzipped his trousers to piss over the edge.

'You're a rotten loser,' Manfried replied from inside.

The third man laughed inside the hut. Rosie shook as a deep rumble and a pulse of light made the loudest bang of the night.

'Oooh, big one,' the pissing German shouted to his comrades. 'Sounds like an ammo dump or something. Those heavy British bombers are nasty buggers. Say your prayers when you see them coming.'

Henderson had his gun aimed at the German, but the bullet would knock him into the sea and his comrades would hear the splash and come running out. So he waited two intense minutes, as the German peed, then walked over and checked the fishing rods.

'Another dumb idea of yours, Manfried,' he shouted. 'Corned beef again tonight.'

As the lanky German turned back across the pier towards the hut, Henderson shot him from the side. The range was less than three metres, but somehow Henderson conspired to miss and the German yelled out.

Henderson pulled the trigger twice more, hitting the German in the back and hip. Manfried and the third man burst outside as Henderson retreated around the side of the hut.

'He's over there,' the bleeding German groaned, as the other two cocked their machine guns.

Manfried spun around. More in hope than

expectation he sprayed half a magazine of ammunition into reeds and sand as Henderson dived behind and backed into Rosie.

'Can't believe I missed,' Henderson gasped furiously. 'Go around the other side, shoot anything that moves.'

Henderson heard Manfried creeping around the side of the guard hut.

'Can't see them,' Manfried shouted. 'Get back in the hut, call for help.'

As Manfried moved deeper into the reeds, Henderson shot two silenced bullets. The first hit the soldier in the gut, the second passed through his skull.

'Manfried?' the third German shouted from within the hut. He didn't fancy getting trapped inside and backed out.

Rosie realised that if he had any brains, the soldier would head away from where Manfried had been shot. Henderson was over that side, so only she could stop him getting away.

She dived out from behind the building and fired at a running shadow. The first blast missed, but the second hit his body and sent him careering across the pier into a wooden post on the water's edge. Horrified and shaking, she took two steps forward and aimed down.

The soldier's eyes begged and his hands came up in front of his face. Rosie knew she had to squeeze the trigger, but the soldier was barely out of his teens and looked so desperate that she wanted to hug rather than kill him.

Two dull thumps came from a silenced muzzle behind her. Rosie shuddered as the young German splashed into the water. As she staggered away in shock, Henderson rushed to the edge of the pier and pumped a third bullet into the floating soldier.

'I couldn't,' Rosie gasped, looking towards Henderson as she lowered her gun. 'I'm sorry.'

After a quick glimpse to make sure the German was dead, Henderson walked back and smiled slightly as he placed a hand on Rosie's wrist.

'Don't apologise,' he said. 'You did great.'

20:44 Dunkirk

Of the three hundred and thirty-seven bombers targeting the northern coast of France that night, eighty-eight would target Dunkirk, each carrying between three and a half and five tonnes of bombs. Eugene's ears started to ring when the first bomb went off, and twenty more landed within seconds. Then the next pair of bombers made their run, then the next.

Some dropped bombs, others sprayed mug-sized incendiaries that burst into flames upon impact. There was fire and heat on all sides, as the two dripping teenagers looked for an escape route.

The bombs were far from accurate. Eugene and PT

found a damaged section of the chain-link fence and cleared the dockyard, but remained at risk on artillery-shelled streets that had seen some of the heaviest fighting during the last phase of the British evacuation.

'What now?' PT shouted, as the pair slumped against a wall.

'Head for the barracks, maybe,' Eugene suggested. 'Steal a car, or another motorbike. It's only a couple of kilometres.'

'Yeah, but which direction?' PT screamed.

As a huge blast erupted less than five hundred metres away, a burning Halifax tore overhead as bricks rained down.

'We're in hell,' Eugene shouted. 'We died already and didn't notice.'

The Halifax was getting lower, and its flaming right wing was breaking away.

'That'll teach you to bomb me, you bastard,' PT shouted, punching the air.

'They're on our side,' Eugene said, as he stood up to start walking again. 'Come on, we can't stay here.'

'If they're bombing me, they're the bloody enemy,' PT said, as the pair moved off.

The blasts and smoke had disorientated them and with the streets covered in rubble it was impossible to gauge direction. The bomber's wing tore away and the unstable fuselage flipped end over end before thudding into the remains of Dunkirk's largest cinema, several hundred metres ahead of them.

Before the next turning the road itself had collapsed, exposing cellars filled with shattered wine bottles. By the time PT and Eugene had negotiated their way around they'd reached one of the small number of roads that the Germans had cleared to allow traffic to and from the docks. A black car sped towards them as the ground trembled again.

The dust and heat had dried PT's mouth and he was fighting a cough as the car slowed and came to a halt fifty metres shy of the crashed aircraft. A pair of Germans stepped out and aimed torches into the rubble.

'They're SS,' Eugene said. 'Probably hunting downed airmen.'

'Surrender,' the Germans shouted, as they moved unenthusiastically over chinking bricks.

But it didn't take much more than a glance to work out that nobody could have survived the crash and the black-uniformed pair swung their torches around and headed back for the car.

'Excuse me,' Eugene shouted, as he jogged towards them.

PT was shocked by Eugene's boldness, but realised the Germans were their only chance of getting out of the bombing zone quickly.

'We're from the docks,' Eugene explained. 'Can you

give us a ride out of here? We're desperate.'

The two SS men didn't understand much French, but their expressions made it clear that they weren't in the mood to pick up passengers.

'Walk, you lazy French scum,' one officer shouted, as he pointed along the clear road.

Eugene and PT's youth and peasant clothing meant that the Germans dismissed them as dockworkers, or some of the crazed locals who continued to live in the bombed-out town centre. They certainly didn't regard the boys as a threat and seemed far more concerned with brushing the dust off their black uniforms.

'Kill them,' Eugene mouthed to PT as he pulled his gun.

PT pulled his gun too, and it was only as he pulled the trigger that he remembered that both guns had been underwater. He got the horrible feeling that it was about to jam or explode in his hand. But it didn't.

Eugene had been a top-ranked marksman in the French army and he'd shot both Germans clean through the heart as PT's shot skimmed the falling bodies and ricocheted off rubble.

'That'll teach them to be so vain.' Eugene smiled. 'Bloody fascists.'

21:23 The Harbour

After pushing the three dead Germans into the sea,

Henderson drove the truck to the edge of the pier and hauled three sacks of coal up towards a tug called *Madeline IV*. He then climbed aboard and felt a pang of nostalgia for his days in the regular navy as he went below deck to stoke up the boiler.

Rosie sat on a stool at the base of the pier with a German machine gun resting on her lap. She reached out to grab it when she saw a figure moving on the cliffs.

'Only me,' Paul said, as he came scrambling down the clifftop with one arm held up rather limply. 'Shampoo,' he added, as he remembered the password.

'My god,' Rosie said, when she saw the grazes all down his arm and across his face. 'The state of you! What happened?'

'I don't exactly remember,' Paul said. 'The explosion knocked me off the bike. Then I was sitting on the pavement with all these people around me. I've got a bump on the back of my head, and the bike was smashed to pieces where it went under a car.'

'Smashed!' Rosie gasped. 'So how'd you get here so quick?'

'The German officer who ran me over. I was all confused and said I had no way to get home, so he put me in the car and gave me a ride to the farm. He dropped me off down on the main road. I started walking towards the house, then doubled back and came here once he was out of sight.'

'You're so lucky.' Rosie smiled as she shone a torch at her brother's cheek and felt around the back of his head. 'You've got quite an egg back there, but the grazes are nothing to write home about.'

'The whole front of the bike was mangled,' Paul said. 'The woman who picked me out of the road said the front tyre barely missed my leg.'

'And now we've got a boat ride to look forward to,' Rosie said warily.

The sinking of the *Cardiff Bay* was still fresh in both of their minds.

'Don't jinx it,' Paul said. 'Besides, we can't get sunk twice in a row. What are the odds of that?'

'Henderson said he wants whoever gets here first to start carrying everything in the truck up the pier to the tug, but you should sit down if you don't feel up to it and I've made sandwiches if you're hungry.'

Paul shook his head. 'I'm a bit queasy, but I can take some of the lighter stuff up to the boat.'

The truck was parked less than five metres away and the back flap was already down from where Henderson had grabbed the coal sacks. Paul looked inside and saw his case, along with everyone else's and the documents Henderson had stolen from headquarters. But he quickly realised something was missing.

'Rosie, where's my tins?' he asked.

Rosie laughed. 'Paul, I packed your clothes, your

drawing stuff and all the money you've made, but we're not lugging dozens of tins of food across to England. I left them on the kitchen countertop with a note telling the prisoners to take them.'

'Bloody hell!' Paul moaned. 'You said you were going to pack them for me.'

'Don't be an idiot!' Rosie said. 'Why don't we take Lottie and the chickens while we're at it?'

'I'm going back to the cottage,' Paul said bitterly.

'How are you gonna carry them? And besides, you just got whacked on the head – you should probably rest.'

Paul glowered at his sister. 'I got here early. I can easily get to the house and back before Marc and PT arrive.'

'Henderson won't like it if you break his plan.'

But Paul was determined. 'I can't carry all the tins of fruit, but I'm getting the two big tins with my strawberry jam and the dark chocolate sauce.'

'You're *such* an idiot,' Rosie said angrily, as her brother started walking back up the cliff. But she didn't go after him because she had the machine gun and Henderson had ordered her to guard the dock.

CHAPTER THIRTY-ONE

21:27 The Harbour

Rosie was still annoyed at her little brother when she saw the big Mercedes drive down the approach road towards the harbour. She was sure it was the car that had dropped Marc off at the farm a few times, but she backed cautiously into the reeds beside the guard hut and kept the machine gun ready until she saw the two African men coming out of the back.

'Khinde and Rufus,' Marc said, as Rosie shook each of them by the hand. 'This is my sister Rosie.'

'A beautiful name,' Khinde said. Rosie was overawed by his massive physique and a hand that enveloped half her arm.

'I think we can stop pretending to be brother and sister now,' Rosie pointed out. 'Did you get here all right?'

'Wasn't bad,' Marc said, nodding. 'Sailed through the checkpoint in Boulogne without getting stopped and the one on the coast road wasn't manned. I think they must have legged it when the bombing started. The only problem was a cratered road near Marquise. I had to turn back and divert through this crummy village. Windy little roads, pitch black, and it took *for ever* to find the main road again.'

'Making it's what matters.' Rosie smiled. 'Henderson's gonna set a timed fuse to blow the harbour after we leave. If you start wiring up the charges, Khinde and Rufus can carry the stuff up from the truck.'

21:32 *The Farm*

Paul had taken the walk between the beach and the cottage hundreds of times and knew the way even in pitch dark. His cuts stung and his head hurt, but his mind was focused on his anger at Rosie for not packing the tins in the truck – she knew how many drawings of Germans he'd had to do to get them. But he was also slightly scared. He thought Henderson might shout at him for breaking with the plan and leaving the harbour, but he reckoned it would be OK as long as he got back before everyone else arrived.

Paul was shocked when he headed out of the trees and saw the blazing headlights of a police car lighting up the front lawn. Vivien Boyle stood by the car, alongside a gendarme who bore a strong family resemblance. Paul remembered one of Dumont's many boasts: that his uncle was a local policeman who'd let him off after several burglaries.

'They've packed up and gone,' Vivien explained tearfully, as she walked up to the side of the cottage. 'Dumont hasn't been seen since lunchtime, so I sent Luc up to see if he was here. I waited an hour, then I walked up here and found the whole place empty. Just as I was leaving I saw Luc's bike abandoned on the driveway.'

Having been in Calais all day, Paul had no idea that Luc and Dumont were tied up in the cowshed. The gendarme adopted a slightly superior tone, as Paul backed into the bushes and listened intently.

'I didn't like it when that lot turned up,' the officer said. 'The whole set-up seemed odd. I saw that Maxine in the village. She was no farmer's wife to my eyes, with her boutique clothes and a Jaguar.'

'I know,' Vivien said. 'But they acted decently enough, and when this Charles fellow called, out of the blue, offering to bring Lucien and Holly home, what choice did we have?'

The officer leaned into his car and grabbed a torch. 'I'll take a quick look around. If we don't find anything we'll drive into the village and form a search party.'

'The family must have been here earlier,' Vivien explained. 'The chickens had fresh food and the cow's udders are empty. There's also a note on the counter telling the labourers to take whatever tins they want and to see what they could find in the cowshed.'

'Did you go up there?' the policeman asked.

Vivien shrugged. 'Why would I? It's probably just butter or cheese.'

'You never know,' the gendarme said. 'Let's start up there.'

Paul knew that whatever had happened to Luc and Dumont, the last thing the rest of them needed was a search party. He had to go back and warn Henderson, but he was less than twenty metres from his prized tins, so as Vivien and her brother set off on the hundred-metre walk towards the cowshed, Paul darted out of the bushes and kept low as he raced across the lawn and into the kitchen.

It was pitch black and Paul flew up into the air in fright as Lottie bleated noisily and crashed into the kitchen table before running outside.

'Damned goat,' Paul whispered to himself.

He felt blindly around the worktop until he found one of the large tins of jam and the distinctive barrel-shaped tin containing dark chocolate sauce. With one large can under each arm, Paul raced out of the door and headed back for the bushes as he heard Vivien scream out.

'Dumie, my poor baby! Oh my god, are those teeth marks on your nose?'

Paul was mystified and decided to wait. There seemed no point going back to warn Henderson without a clearer idea of what had happened to Dumont and Luc Boyle.

'They're blowing up the harbour and then leaving on a tug,' Luc shouted furiously, as he staggered out of the barn, glistening with cow shit. 'I don't know why they're doing it, but as Charles dragged me out here, the girl Rosie asked him a question about how many charges they'd need to blow up the harbour.'

'The harbour hasn't blown up,' Vivien said. 'We'd have heard it from the village.'

Paul was still baffled as to how Luc and Dumont had got involved, but Rosie and Henderson clearly knew and his priority was now to run back and warn them.

'I'll drive into the village and warn the soldiers who drink at the bar,' the gendarme roared. '*Nobody* treats members of my family like this!'

21:46 *The Village*

Eugene knew that the forty-kilometre drive between Dunkirk and the farm a few kilometres west of Calais took roughly an hour. In theory this gave them twenty spare minutes, even with the delay caused by the loss of the motorbike – but with a soundtrack of explosions as hundreds of bombers pounded the coastline and the real possibility that roads would be blocked off or damaged he drove as fast as darkness, acrid smoke and regulation covered headlamps allowed.

Their worst moment came at a snap checkpoint where they'd abandoned SS helmets and presented the travel permits Henderson had given them for the truck. Fortunately, the bored looking guard didn't notice the discrepancy in registration numbers.

PT glanced at his watch as they entered the village and sped past Luc Boyle's three-storey house. 'Twenty to ten. We'll make it easy.'

As they drove past the village square, PT noticed a police car parked on the village green and a gendarme gesticulating wildly.

'Looks like Luc Boyle and Dumont are with him,' PT said, as he noticed German soldiers running from the tables outside the bar and jumping into a pair of open-topped Kübelwagens.

'Who's Luc Boyle?' Eugene asked.

'Big-shot local farmer,' PT said. 'Slow down, I want to see this.'

Eugene squeezed the brake pedal, but they were doing sixty and their little Peugeot saloon didn't have the world's greatest brakes.

'What do you make of that?' PT asked.

'I'm concentrating on the road,' Eugene said irritably. 'I'm not making much of anything beyond whether or not I smash into a ditch and throw the pair of us through the windscreen.'

PT grew even more suspicious as he looked behind and saw the headlamps of the two Kübelwagens less than a hundred metres behind them.

21:51 The Harbour

Paul was back and he'd given warning that Dumont had been found. The last of three hundred and thirty-seven British bombers had dropped its load twenty minutes earlier, and as Henderson stood on the rear deck of the tug he could see fires burning in Calais and all along the coast in both directions.

'I see headlights,' Marc shouted, from the opposite end of the pier.

Rosie stood in the wheelhouse as Henderson grabbed a machine gun. 'Are we going to wait for Eugene and PT on the motorbike?'

'We'll stick it out for another nine minutes if we can,' Henderson shouted. 'You be ready at the helm. Paul, keep your head down on deck, but be ready to cast off and light the fuses as soon as you get the shout.'

There was only one road down to the harbour. Khinde and Rufus squatted in the reeds ready to stage an ambush. Marc lay on the clifftop fifty metres away, watching through binoculars.

'It's three cars full of Germans,' he shouted.

Henderson had to decide whether to cast off or stand his ground until Eugene and PT arrived. But he knew the gendarme had only had time to drive to the village and fetch the German regulars out of the bar. They were young, lightly armed and probably drunk, so Henderson fancied his chances.

21:52 *The Harbour*
'They're shooting at *us*,' Eugene yelled, diving to one side as bullets pelted the front of the car. 'Get your head out the window. They're expecting us to arrive on a motorbike.'

'It's us,' PT screamed. 'Shampoo, shampoo! The Germans are behind us!'

Streams of bullets whizzed past PT's head and Eugene had no option but to turn off the narrow harbour road. The two Kübelwagens running behind had stopped at the first sign of gunfire and soldiers were jumping out and running on to the beach, or taking firing positions behind their vehicles.

More bullets crashed into the bodywork as Eugene's Peugeot pitched upwards on to a sandbank and clattered through reed beds before breaking on to open beach. The tide was in and they came to a halt with the front wheels and steaming radiator in the sea.

'Shampoo!' Eugene yelled, raising his hands in surrender as he stepped out into the wash and ran towards the pier. PT followed, but lowered his hands as the Germans running along the beach started shooting from behind.

Henderson told Khinde to stay in position and stop the two Kübelwagens, while he moved back towards the pier to see what was occurring on the beach.

'Paul, cast off!' he bellowed.

Henderson was surprised by the sight of Germans shooting at two dark figures on the beach. Marc was running down from the clifftop, and had a better view than Henderson.

'It's PT,' Marc shouted, as he raced to within five metres of Henderson. 'Stop bloody shooting at them!'

'Shit, shit, shit,' Henderson roared, before turning to shout at Khinde and Rufus. 'Run for the boat. Marc, you get up there too. I'll cover.'

But Marc saw Eugene and PT struggling up the slippery rocks at the base of the pier. He locked one arm around a wooden post and gave PT a hand up, but as PT stepped on to the pier he took a shot in the arm.

'Bastards,' PT howled, as Marc used all his strength to hold on to his friend.

As Eugene pulled himself up on to the pier, Khinde and Rufus raced over the planks towards *Madeline IV.* Henderson reached into his pocket and grabbed two hand grenades, hoping they'd hold back the advancing Germans. After pulling the pins, he threw one long distance towards the road and aimed the second carefully through the open door of the Peugeot.

By the time the grenades landed, the leading Germans were less than ten metres from Henderson. He set off down the pier, jogging sideways and spraying the last few bullets in his machine gun. Khinde covered him from the rear of the tug as the first grenade blew all the glass out of the Peugeot.

'Fuse it, Paul, cast off. Rosie, start moving,' Henderson shouted.

The harbour, the remaining tug and the barges had all been rigged up to a two-minute length of detonator cord. PT was in a lot of pain and Eugene had to throw him aboard. Paul grabbed a lighter and ignited the fuse as Rosie opened up the throttles so that the boat began crawling away from the pier.

Henderson had told Rosie to do this, but she was wary. She'd never driven a boat before and was scared of leaving him behind.

'Stand clear,' Henderson shouted, dropping his empty machine gun before leaping athletically into the rear of the boat as it crept alongside the pier.

PT was laid out on the deck and Henderson tripped over his legs and sprawled across the floor as PT howled with pain. Rosie put the boat to full throttle as three Germans raced up the pier, shooting machine guns at the back of the vessel.

They were too far away for accuracy, but stray shots hit the rear deck and splintered the wooden bridge up near Rosie. She heard a metallic clang and felt liquid spewing down her legs as the boat cleared the end of the pier.

'Someone get up here,' Rosie wailed desperately. 'I've been shot.'

Back on the pier, the gendarme was warning the Germans that the pier was possibly rigged with explosives. But none of them spoke good French and with their machine guns blazing hopelessly at the disappearing rump of *Madeline IV*, they either didn't understand or didn't hear.

'Oh god,' Rosie yelled, as Henderson – head still throbbing from his encounter with the deck – climbed up the three wooden steps into the wheelhouse and felt his foot slide through something sticky. 'Take the wheel. I'm shot.'

The sea was calm and the boat was heading in a straight line, so Henderson was more concerned with Rosie than the boat.

'Calm down,' Henderson ordered. 'Where are you shot?'

'I don't know! This is exactly how my dad died. The wound was behind his shirt and we didn't know until it was too late.'

'Well, does it hurt?' Henderson shouted. 'Tell me where it hurts. Eugene, get up here and take the wheel for a minute!'

'I'm not sure, but there's blood everywhere!' Rosie squealed.

Henderson touched Rosie's leg and immediately knew the liquid was too thick to be blood. He raised his finger to his lips.

'Tasty,' he smiled.

'What!' Rosie squealed. 'Are you nuts?'

'It's your brother's,' Henderson said, as he looked around the floor and spotted the barrel-shaped can with the bullet lodged in it. 'German, dark chocolate sauce.'

'Paul,' Rosie yelled. 'I'm gonna wring his skinny little neck!'

Then the pier three hundred metres behind them exploded.

'Everyone brace,' Henderson shouted, as a huge wave caused by the explosion rushed towards the little boat.

CHAPTER THIRTY-TWO

10 September, 01:54 Sandgate, near Folkestone, Britain
The bullet had torn through PT's right bicep, but a tight bandage stemmed the bleeding and he sipped at a bottle of rum from the tug's medical cupboard to numb the pain. He was doing OK, and even shared some of the banter in the cramped crew quarters below deck.

The crossing could have been a nightmare, but there was no sign of enemy activity and the sea was calm. German submarines used hydrophones, which could detect even the smallest boats on a quiet sea, so Henderson kept the noise to a minimum by running *Madeline IV* at a moderate seven-knot pace.

Ten kilometres from Britain they encountered a search and rescue launch that had spent several fruitless hours looking for downed bomber crews. All British vessels had been warned to look out for a small grey tug, and the final stretch of their journey was spent under the protection of a vessel twice their length and with 45mm cannons mounted reassuringly front and rear.

Rosie and Henderson felt nostalgia for their homeland as they pulled in at a tiny fishing harbour. Paul only had vague memories of Britain, while Marc, Khinde, Rufus and Eugene felt apprehensive about the welcome they'd receive in a strange country whose language they didn't understand.

There wasn't much moonlight, but enough to make out the endless coils of barbed wire and tank traps stretched across the beach, along with the outlines of terraced houses behind the quay.

As soon as the tug was safely lashed to the harbour wall, the captain of the search and rescue vessel saluted from deck and sped off towards his base in Folkestone a few kilometres down the coast.

Two elderly home guardsmen helped secure the end of a boarding ramp. Henderson was the first ashore and was delighted to see Eileen McAfferty walking towards him, as quickly as bad feet would allow.

'Look at you in uniform!' Henderson shouted. 'Someone get me a camera!' It felt wonderful to be able to speak his own language with his own accent. 'And I do believe I'm going to have to start calling you *sir*, judging by all those stripes.'

'Bloody well done!' McAfferty said, as she reached out for a handshake.

But Henderson ignored the hand and kissed McAfferty on both cheeks before bringing her into a tight hug.

'Where's the boy who got shot?' McAfferty asked. 'We got the signal from search and rescue. There's an ambulance crew waiting.'

As PT was helped off the boat two ambulance men stood with a stretcher, but he made it to the ambulance with nothing but a bit of support from Eugene.

'We've got sandwiches and hot tea under the bandstand back there,' McAfferty said in French, as she pointed towards a hexagonal structure in a courtyard behind the quay. 'You must all be *gasping* for a cup of tea.'

Khinde and Rufus looked baffled as the home guardsmen looked them up and down.

'You'll need a shirt here, mate. You'll freeze your nipples off in winter!'

'Have you heard from Maxine and Bernard?' Henderson asked.

'Bernard transmitted a brief message about an hour ago,' McAfferty explained. 'Both their beacons ignited to the satisfaction of bomber command. They're going to meet up and take the first train to Paris in the morning.'

'And you must be Rosie!' McAfferty said brightly, as

Henderson shook hands with the home guardsmen. 'We finally meet face to face after all that Morse code!'

Rosie had pictured McAfferty as a glamorous Maxine type, and managed to be both startled and tearful as she was pulled into the ample bust of the Scotswoman.

'Is everything good with you, love?' McAfferty asked.

'It's so nice to finally meet you in the flesh,' Rosie said, grinning. 'And I'm *absolutely* fine, thanks for asking. It's a massive relief to be home – I couldn't be happier.'

Paul stood just behind, and he whispered in Marc's ear, 'As long as you don't mention my dark chocolate sauce to her, that is.'

The 9 September raid on France's northern ports was the largest bombing raid the world had seen up to that point. The successful ignition of phosphorous beacons at Le Havre, Dieppe, Boulogne, Calais and Dunkirk enabled the three hundred and thirty-seven bombers to attack under cover of darkness, while achieving bombing accuracy similar to a much riskier daylight attack.

The raid is thought to have destroyed more than a quarter of the German barge fleet, almost half of the available tugs and more than half of the Germans' fleet of high-speed patrol boats. This level of destruction, combined with the Luftwaffe's continued failure to take control of the air space over the Channel, forced Hitler into a new strategy.

On 11 September, the German Navy and the Luftwaffe jointly proposed that they could defeat Britain by starving and terrorising its population. The Luftwaffe would switch its focus from annihilating the RAF to the destruction of British cities. The German Navy would concentrate its submarine fleet on the destruction of British merchant ships supplying food and weapons.

On 16 September, Hitler formally agreed to abandon the invasion of Britain.

1 October, 1940

Dear Charles,

Following your memorandum on the value of underage operatives in occupied France and our discussions in London last week, we have, somewhat reluctantly, agreed to your proposal to train an espionage unit comprised entirely of boys aged between eleven and seventeen years.

I am uncomfortable with a use of boys that borders on exploitation, but these are desperate times and both the Prime Minister and I were compelled by your argument that these young men could give us a significant edge in the struggle that lies ahead of us.

The funds and necessary equipment for your new unit will be made available through your commanding officer, Eileen McAfferty. The designation of the new unit shall be Espionage Research Unit B.

Yours sincerely,

Eric Mews (Deputy Minister for Economic Warfare)

HENDERSON'S BOYS: SECRET ARMY

As 1941 dawned, Nazi Germany dominated Western Europe. Britain was under siege. Bombers blitzed cities from the air, while U-boats preyed on merchant ships bringing vital supplies across the Atlantic.

The previous year, British Prime Minister Winston Churchill gave the order to 'set Europe ablaze' by creating the Special Operations Executive (SOE). The job of this secret army was to gather intelligence and plan sabotage operations inside Nazi-occupied Europe.

SOE set up secret training campuses throughout the country. The most controversial of these was situated at the edge of an artillery firing range, deep in the heart of the English countryside. It was home to Espionage Research Unit B, under the operational command of Charles Henderson.

Turn the page to read an exclusive preview from *Secret Army*, coming soon from Robert Muchamore and Hodder Children's Books.

SECRET ARMY

'Stand by yer beds!' Evan Williams shouted. 'Lights out in *seven* minutes.'

He was a small Welshman with one big eyebrow. Twenty-four boys lived in his dorm. They hurried barefoot over the cold lino, putting toothbrushes in foot lockers and draping towels over radiators before standing at the end of their metal-framed beds ready for inspection.

Each bed was immaculately made. Belongings had to be packed neatly inside a foot locker, with boots or plimsolls cleaned and resting on top in a ten-past-ten position.

'Attention!'

Each boy snapped into a rigid position. Ankles together, eyes forward, shoulders back. Williams would have liked the boys to wear matching pyjamas, but clothing was short and newer arrivals wore whatever they'd brought with them.

'Not bad,' Williams said grudgingly as he passed the first pair of facing beds. At the next he reached under the mattress and dug two fingers between the rusted bed frame and mattress.

'In the name of our *lord!*' Williams gasped. His giant eyebrow fired upwards as he jabbed a rusty finger under the nose of a thirteen-year-old with curly brown hair and deep-set eyes.

Troy LeConte knew he was being fitted up: the beds were old and you could reach under any of them if you wanted rust stuck on your finger. It was Williams' way of showing that he could get you, even if you stuck to all of his petty rules.

'Well, LeConte?' Williams demanded. 'Cat got your tongue? What is this?'

Troy didn't know the English word for rust, but reckoned a quick answer beat none at all. 'It's your finger, sir,' he said, with a heavy French accent.

This raised cautious laughter from the other boys and Williams looked irritated.

'I know it's my finger, you stupid frog,' he roared. 'I'm asking you what's *on* my finger.'

Troy went cross-eyed as Williams dabbed his chunky finger against the bridge of his nose.

'I don't know the word,' Troy explained.

'You little retard!' Williams shouted, as he grabbed the neck hole of Troy's string vest, yanked the lad forwards and cuffed him around the head. 'Cold shower, five a.m.,' he barked, before letting go and moving up to the next bed.

Troy rubbed his head before standing crisply back to attention. He hated Williams, but had seen plenty of lads come off worse during inspection. He turned his head as far as he dared, watching the relief on each boy's face when Williams passed them by.

'Mason LeConte,' Williams said, when he was almost at the opposite end of the room, 'Well, well, it seems stupidity runs in the family.'

Troy's brother Mason was only eight, but that didn't stop Williams from twisting his ear and yanking it up until he dangled on tiptoes.

'The blankets are crooked, you *stupid* boy,' Williams shouted, as Mason gave a howl that turned his older brother's stomach.

Troy felt guilty as Williams ripped off his little brother's sheets and blanket. Mason was the youngest in the dorm and Troy usually helped him before inspection, but he'd been sent upstairs to fetch candles by the night matron and had barely had time to make his own bed.

'I've never seen such a shambles,' Williams roared,

as he took the metal lid from Mason's foot locker and threw its contents across the floor. 'Are you feeble-minded, boy?'

'No, sir,' the boy sobbed, as Williams upended Mason's metal locker, then shook him violently by the shoulders.

'This shoe-cleaning kit is filthy. *Nothing* is folded properly. Why is there mud on the sole of your plimsoll?'

After each sentence Williams jammed two fingers under Mason's ribs, sending his body into a spasm.

'Report to my office first thing,' Williams yelled. 'And cold showers for a week.'

'No!' Mason wailed, as he tried to wriggle away. 'Leave me alone.'

Troy knew he'd come off badly if he interfered, but what kind of person stood and watched their little brother get bullied?

'Unacceptable!' Troy shouted, using the only appropriate English word he could think of as he stepped away from his bed and strode purposefully down the narrow room towards Williams. A couple of boys whispered cautions, and one even stepped into his path.

'He'll murder you,' the boy warned.

'Keep your head down, mate,' another begged, but Troy marched on.

Troy imagined an heroic gesture: knocking Williams

out with a punch to the jaw or slicing his head off with a sword. But reality found a thirteen-year-old dressed in baggy shorts and vest facing a grown man with fiery eyes and hobnail boots.

'It seems I have a visitor,' Williams said, cracking a demented smile as he shoved Mason back over the end of his bed. 'What can we do for you?'

Troy was quaking, but couldn't walk meekly back to his bed with all the other lads looking on.

'He's eight years old,' Troy said. 'Why not help, instead of hurting him?'

'Or you'll do what, big man?' Williams taunted. 'This is my dormitory. I make the rules.'

Troy had fought a few times in his thirteen years. He'd won more than he'd lost, but the punch he threw now wasn't his best. It glanced off the fleshy part of Williams' arm with barely enough force to rustle his shirt.

'You dare raise a hand to me!' Williams roared, as Troy found himself being thrown forwards over the end of Mason's bed, with Williams wrenching his arm tight behind his back and his brother's legs trapped beneath him. 'George, Tom, deal with him.'

George and Tom were stocky lads of fifteen. They acted as snitches and enforcers for Williams, who let them bully and extort the younger lads in return.

'Put them both down,' Williams ordered, before

pointing at Troy. 'And make *his* trip an uncomfortable one.'

Troy didn't know what being *put down* meant, but there were sadistic grins on George and Tom's faces as they grabbed his arms and bundled him outside. After dragging Troy ten metres down a freezing corridor, they turned into an unlit cloakroom and shoved him in a corner with a coat hook digging into his back.

'Fists up, you French weed.' George grinned, as he made a boxing stance. The fifteen-year-old was bigger than his pyjamas and his muscular torso showed where his top was too small to button over his chest.

Troy raised his hands, but George was too strong. His first punch batted Troy's defences aside. The second was an uppercut that smacked his lower jaw and made his teeth clatter.

'I've got plenty more where that came from.' George laughed, as he grabbed Troy around the neck, bent him over and brought his knee up into his guts.

Troy groaned and belched as his throat filled with burning stomach acid. George backed away after a couple more punches, only for Tom to drag Troy out of the corner and hook his ankle, sending him sprawling across the floor.

'Stings, don't it, froggy?' Tom smiled.

Troy groaned as he rolled on to his back, then sat up, clutching his stomach and coughing.

'We can do what we like to you now,' George added. 'Fancy raising your hands to Williams! You just signed your own death warrant.'

Troy was defenceless, lying in the dark with two heavyweights looming. He hurt in a dozen places and blood drizzled from his nose. Out in the corridor he heard wailing and saw Mason's legs as Williams dragged him past the doorway.

George hitched Troy off the gritty lino, intending to knock him down again, but Williams called from the far end of the corridor.

'Get Troy out here. I want to be in my room before *Book at Bedtime* comes on.'

A metal bolt thunked. With one hand grasping Mason's neck, Williams booted a door open and bitter outdoor air rushed into the corridor. Troy finally understood what being *put down* meant as he was dragged barefoot on to the icy courtyard behind the building.

'I'm not going down there,' Mason sobbed as Williams lifted the hinged wooden flap that covered the entrance to the coal cellar. '*Please* don't make me.'

'It's the only way you'll learn,' Williams shouted. 'Now, sit on the edge and jump or I'll throw you down.'

The coal was piled high at one corner of the cellar. Mason made the short drop on to the highest part of the mound and scrambled down over churning coal to an area of bare floor in the far corner.

'Watch out for the rats,' Tom teased. 'They'll gnaw your toes if you fall asleep.'

George was ready to shove Troy down into the cellar. 'Hold up,' Williams ordered. 'Let's have a look at him.'

Tom clamped a muscular arm around Troy's waist. Williams moved up close and smiled, as Mason's sobbing echoed out of the cellar below them.

'I never did like Frenchies,' Williams said, before slapping Troy hard across his right eye. 'Throw him down.'

Troy's head swirled from the blow as Tom let him go. George kicked Troy behind the knees, buckling his legs and sending him face first into the mound of coal. The wooden cellar door banged shut over his head, and Williams fixed a joist over the flaps to lock it.

'Sleep tight, boys,' Williams said nastily.

'But don't forget the rats,' George added.

Mason stood with his back against an unplastered wall. It was pitch dark, his feet were in icy water and he shuddered, imagining bugs and spiders crawling all around him.

'Troy?' he said quietly, before erupting into a coughing fit as coal dust tickled the back of his throat.

Mason waited for the voices above to disappear before feeling his way back up the mound of freezing coal lumps. He sniffled as he rested a hand on Troy's back, between his shoulder blades.

'Troy?' he said, tapping his hand warily. 'What's the matter, Troy? Are you dead?'

HENDERSON'S BOYS: THE ESCAPE

The very first CHERUB adventure is about to begin . . .

Summer, 1940.

Hitler's army is advancing towards Paris, and millions of French civilians are on the run.

Amidst the chaos, two British children are being hunted by German agents.

British spy Charles Henderson tries to reach them first, but he can only do it with the help of a twelve-year-old French orphan.

The British secret service is about to discover that kids working undercover will help to win the war.

CHERUB: The Recruit

CHERUB: The Recruit tells James Adams' story from the day his mother dies. Read about his transformation from a couch potato into a skilled CHERUB agent.

Meet Lauren, Jake, Kerry and the rest of the cherubs for the first time, and learn how James foiled the biggest terrorist massacre in British history.

CHERUB: Class A

Keith Moore is Europe's biggest cocaine dealer. The police have been trying to get enough evidence to nail him for more than twenty years.

Now, four CHERUB agents are joining the hunt. Can a group of kids successfully infiltrate Keith Moore's organisation, when dozens of attempts by undercover police officers have failed?

James Adams has to start at the bottom, making deliveries for small-time drug dealers and getting to know the dangerous underworld they inhabit. He needs to make a big splash if he's going to win the confidence of the man at the top.

CHERUB: Maximum Security

Over the years, CHERUB has put plenty of criminals behind bars. Now, for the first time ever, they've got to break one out . . .

Under American law, kids convicted of serious crimes can be tried and sentenced as adults. Two hundred and eighty of these child criminals live in the sunbaked desert prison known as Arizona Max.

In one of the most daring CHERUB missions ever, James Adams has to go undercover inside Arizona Max, befriend an inmate and then bust him out.

CHERUB: The Killing

When a small-time crook suddenly has big money on his hands, it's only natural that the police want to know where it came from.

James' latest CHERUB mission looks routine: make friends with the bad guy's children, infiltrate his home and dig up some leads for the cops to investigate.

But the plot James begins to unravel isn't what anyone expected. And it seems like the only person who might know the truth is a reclusive eighteen-year-old boy.

There's just one problem. The boy fell from a rooftop and died more than a year earlier.

CHERUB: Divine Madness

When a team of CHERUB agents uncover a link between eco-terrorist group Help Earth and a wealthy religious cult known as The Survivors, James Adams is sent to Australia on an infiltration mission.

It's his toughest job so far. The Survivors' outback headquarters are completely isolated. It's a thousand kilometres to the nearest town and the cult's brainwashing techniques mean James is under massive pressure to conform.

This time he's not just fishing terrorists. He's got to battle to keep control of his own mind.

CHERUB: Man vs Beast

Every day thousands of animals die in laboratory experiments. Some say these experiments provide essential scientific knowledge, while others will do anything to prevent them.

CHERUB agents James and Lauren Adams are stuck in the middle.

CHERUB: The Fall

When an MI5 operation goes disastrously wrong, James needs all of his skills to get out of Russia alive.

Meanwhile, Lauren is on her first solo mission, trying to uncover a brutal human trafficking operation.

And when James does get home, he finds that his nightmare is just beginning . . .

CHERUB: Mad Dogs

The British underworld is controlled by gangs. When two of them start a turf war, violence explodes on to the streets.

The police need information fast and James Adams is the only person who can get it. Returning to the scene of an earlier mission, he has to team up with old friends and face an ex-girlfriend he thought he'd never see again . . .

CHERUB: The General

The world's largest urban warfare training compound stands in the desert near Las Vegas. Forty British commandos are being hunted by an entire American battalion.

But their commander has an ace up his sleeve: he plans to smuggle in ten CHERUB agents, and fight the best war game ever.

CHERUB: Brigands M.C.

Every CHERUB agent comes from somewhere. Dante Scott still has nightmares about the death of his family, brutally killed by a biker gang.

When Dante joins James Adams on a mission to infiltrate the Brigands Motorcycle Club, he's ready to use everything he's learned to get revenge on the people who killed his family . . .

Look out for *CHERUB Brigands* M.C., coming soon from Robert Muchamore and Hodder Children's Books.